21 QUESTIONS

Visit us at www.boldstrokesbooks.com

By the Author

Date with Destiny

Charm City

21 Questions

Writing as Yolanda Wallace:

In Medias Res

Rum Spring

Lucky Loser

Month of Sundays

Murphy's Law

The War Within

Love's Bounty

Break Point

24/7

21 QUESTIONS

by

Mason Dixon

2016

21 QUESTIONS

ISBN 13: 978-1-62639-724-8

THIS TRADE PAPERBACK ORIGINAL IS PUBLISHED BY
BOLD STROKES BOOKS, INC.
P.O. BOX 249
VALLEY FALLS, NY 12185

FIRST EDITION: NOVEMBER 2016

CREDITS
EDITOR: CINDY CRESAP
PRODUCTION DESIGN: SUSAN RAMUNDO
COVER DESIGN BY SHERI (GRAPHICARTIST2020@HOTMAIL.COM)

Acknowledgments

Writing this book was a challenge. At times, it felt like an extended therapy session. Choosing the titular questions was the first test. I wanted them to be interesting, obviously, but thought provoking as well. And, most of all, I wanted the answers to reflect the characters' thoughts and beliefs rather than mine. That, of course, was easier said than done, but it resulted in several in-depth conversations between my partner and me that allowed us to view our relationship—and each other—in a different light. Now our bond is stronger than ever.

I want to thank Radclyffe, Sandy Lowe, Cindy Cresap, and the rest of the BSB team for making the publishing process so much fun. Go, team!

I want to thank my partner for putting up with me for fifteen years and counting. My favorite question from you was answered with "I do."

And last but not least, thank you to the readers for your support, encouragement, and feedback. You inspire me to try to make each book better than the last.

Dedication

To my boo.
You are the answer to all my questions.

CHAPTER ONE

Kenya Davis parked her BMW in the valet area outside Azure, one of the most popular nightclubs in South Beach. As she watched a steady stream of well-dressed lesbians head inside, she tried to convince herself to shut off her car's engine and head inside the bar instead of returning to her condo and helping herself to a pint of pistachio gelato while she binge-watched the eight episodes of *Scandal* she'd saved on her DVR. Watching Kerry Washington look flawless in an endless string of designer fashions while the series' writers heaped on one unbelievable plot twist after another had to be better than subjecting herself to the humiliation waiting for her on the other side of Azure's trademark blue doors.

Had it really come to this? Was she so desperate for companionship she had to resort to speed dating in order to improve her chances of finding true love?

She was settled in her career—blessed with job security and a six-figure salary that might not make her rich but left her feeling comfortable in the present and optimistic about the future. Her love life, however, didn't inspire similar sunny thoughts. She hadn't been in a relationship for so long she didn't know if she still had what it took to sustain one. Did the fault lie with her or the women with whom she had chosen to share her life?

She took a long look at herself in the rearview mirror, subjecting herself to the kind of careful assessment she gave potential employees when they sat nervously across from her for an interview, their portfolios bouncing on their knocking knees. She didn't look as frightened as some prospects she had evaluated over the years, but she definitely looked scared.

"What are you afraid of?" she asked her reflection. "It's less than two hours of your time. What else do you have to do on a Friday night?" She thought about the eight episodes of *Scandal* and the pint of gelato calling her name. "Olivia Pope isn't real. Tonight, you have a chance to meet someone who is."

And more importantly, conquer her fear that she was far better at selecting the perfect employee than she was at finding the perfect mate.

With an effort, she opened her car door and climbed out of the driver's seat. Then she traded her keys for a valet parking ticket. After the attendant drove off with her primary means of escape, she threw her shoulders back and tried to project an air of confidence she didn't actually feel.

She habitually made two lists after she got out of the shower each morning, a to-do list and a wait list. The to-do list included tasks she wanted to accomplish before the end of the day. The wait list was composed of items that weren't nearly as pressing. Things that could be put off for another day. For too long, finding love had been on the second list. Perhaps it was time to give it higher priority.

The bouncer, a handsome butch with the body of a mixed martial arts fighter and the tattoos to match, nodded in Kenya's direction and opened the door for her. "Welcome to Azure. Enjoy your evening."

Like most nightclubs and restaurants in eternally hip South Beach, Azure didn't start filling until after nine p.m. Since it was only a little before eight, Kenya expected the place to be mostly empty. Instead, it was packed with so many lesbians she didn't know where to turn.

She needed a wingman. Someone to help her navigate the choppy waters of a dating pool that seemed to get deeper and younger every year. But Bridget Weaver, her closest lesbian friend, was lolling on a beach in Hawaii with her fiancée for another week, and her work wife, Celia Torres, was more apt to be available to help solve Kenya's crises that happened between nine a.m. and five p.m. than those that occurred after the work day was done, when Celia's attention turned from office politics to her one-year-old twins' dirty diapers.

Forced to fend for herself, Kenya opted for a liberal dose of liquid courage. Several other women must have had the same idea because the crowd at the bar was at least three deep. Kenya found a spot in line and waited to place her order.

Four servers dressed in skinny jeans and Azure-branded tank tops stood behind the marble-topped bar. All were young, hot, and flashy. They tossed sterling silver cocktail shakers like expert jugglers as they mixed drinks for the dozens of women standing in line. None of the bartenders seemed to be a day over thirty. Neither did the patrons, who took turns slipping their favorite bartenders their phone numbers.

Kenya had never been a fan of one-night stands, and she was too set in her ways to become a convert now. Not for the first time, she wondered if she should just turn around and leave. She was looking for someone who already had her act together, not someone who was still trying to figure things out. She didn't want a fling. She wanted forever. But could she find it in a place like this, where some relationships lasted only as long as the dance music track blasting from the state-of-the-art sound system?

Despite her misgivings about the setting, she felt her attention drawn to the bartender on the end, the one with shoulder-length dreads, caramel-colored eyes, mocha skin, and a dazzling smile. Kenya liked her energy. There was a stillness about her that stood in stark contrast to her caffeinated coworkers. Mineral water, as opposed to Red Bull. Equally refreshing but without the sugar crash that was sure to follow a few hours later.

"What can I get you?" the bartender asked when Kenya finally made her way to the front of the line. Kenya started to reply, but the bartender held up a hand before she could respond. "Wait. Let me guess." The bartender looked her up and down, her gaze slowly traveling from Kenya's face to her feet and back again. Kenya felt every inch of the journey, her nipples hardening under the intense scrutiny. "An old-fashioned with bourbon instead of rye. Am I right?"

Kenya arched an eyebrow in surprise. "How did you know?" she asked as the bartender began muddling a sugar cube, a dash of bitters, and a tablespoon of water in a highball glass. "Most people peg me as a cosmo drinker."

The bartender shook her head. "Cosmos are for girls who have watched too many reruns of *Sex and the City*. You're a woman who knows the value of hard work and likes to be rewarded for it. You do everything one hundred percent. You don't hold back. When you love someone, they know it. And when you don't, they know that, too." She poured two fingers of bourbon into the glass, added a twist of lemon peel, then threw in slices of lemon and orange, and topped the whole thing off with a maraschino cherry. She stirred the concoction with a swizzle stick and pushed it toward Kenya. "How did I do?"

Kenya took a sip and nearly moaned in ecstasy. "Perfect."

"The drink or my assessment?" the bartender asked with a wink.

"Both." In fact, Kenya wondered how a stranger could know her so well. Guessing her favorite drink was a nice parlor trick, but listing her personality traits so precisely took real skill. Kenya admired her powers of perception, along with her obvious physical attributes. She had the body of a track athlete—lean, but powerfully built with the carriage of a sprinter and the long legs to match. For an instant, Kenya imagined having those long, powerful legs wrapped around her as she settled between them. Then she banished the images from her mind. She came here tonight to play a game, not play the fool. Yet that seemed to be exactly what she was setting herself up to do. *Not again*, she promised herself. *Never again.*

"How much do I owe you?"

"Eight dollars."

Kenya pulled a ten from her purse. "Keep the change."

"Thanks." Kenya turned to leave so the bartender could wait on the next customer in line, but the bartender called her back. "Not so fast. Are you here to watch the speed dating or participate in it?"

"Participate," Kenya said, wondering if she looked as desperate as she was starting to feel.

"I would say, 'Good luck,' but a woman who has it going on as much as you seem to probably doesn't need it."

"Thank you." Kenya tipped her glass in the bartender's direction. "For the drink and the compliment."

"My pleasure. The mini-dates only last ten minutes. Unless your game is tight, that doesn't give you much time to get to know someone. Do you want to practice on me until the fun starts?"

The bartender ran a towel across the bar top to mop up the spilled remains of someone's drink. Her movements were quick but effortless. Was she that smooth in bed, too? She placed her hands on the bar. Her fingers were long and tapered like a musician's. Kenya barely suppressed a shudder as she imagined those fingers playing her body like a musical instrument, hitting all the right notes in a very different kind of symphony. Looking for a way out of the conversation before she got in too deep, she glanced at the growing line behind her.

"Thank you for the offer, but there are a lot of thirsty women waiting to take my place."

"Then it's a good thing I can mix drinks and hold a conversation at the same time. When I really get going, I can walk and chew gum, too," the bartender said with a smile as charming as her self-deprecating statement. "So are you interested, or would you prefer to save your moves for someone who counts?"

Kenya laughed despite herself. "If I had moves, I wouldn't be here tonight."

"Why don't you let me be the judge of that?" the bartender asked after she fielded an order for a mojito and a rum and Coke—and fended off a request for a date. "What's your name?"

"Kenya." She had decided to remain on a first-name basis with everyone she came across tonight unless she met someone who convinced her to be more forthcoming. Unless she met The One. Fat chance of that happening since she didn't believe in love at first sight. Infatuation, yes. Lust, definitely. But love? Like fine wine, that took time to develop. And when she finally found it, she hoped it would taste just as sweet.

"Pleased to meet you, Kenya. I'm Simone. Before you ask, my roots are Jamaican, not French, but my mother's favorite singer was Nina Simone."

"Mine preferred James Brown."

Simone nodded in appreciation. "The hardest-working and most-sampled man in show business. I don't think there's a single hip-hop song from the eighties and nineties that doesn't have a James Brown hook in it somewhere," she said with the authority of a music historian. Despite Simone's calm demeanor, Kenya could practically feel the passion seeping through her pores. "What kind of music do you like? I'm better at determining favorite drinks than preferred music styles, but if I had to hazard a guess, I'd say you were a cool jazz aficionado."

Kenya started to say yes just to humor Simone since she was going out of her way to help her relax, but she decided to be honest rather than polite.

"Actually, I prefer Motown to jazz. Whenever I need an emotional pick-me-up, I crank up my MP3 player, grab a hairbrush, and pretend I'm Diana Ross fronting the Supremes. When I have a bad day at work, I channel Aretha Franklin and demand my R-E-S-P-E-C-T. And when it's time to set the mood, I bust out the Marvin Gaye. But I thought I was supposed to be the one asking you the questions, not the other way around."

Simone grinned as she poured the ingredients for a pomegranate martini into a cocktail shaker. Her taut biceps flexed as she manually blended the drink. "Fire away."

Kenya ran through a list of questions in her head. Talking points she had picked up on the Internet to help break the ice when she sat across from ten complete strangers for ten minutes at a time. As she mentally browsed through the collection of potential opening lines, she tried to find one that wouldn't make her seem presumptuous or shallow.

"What's your favorite guilty pleasure?" she finally asked.

"Conch fritters and cheesy science fiction movies. Preferably at the same time. What about you?"

"Fast cars and loose women."

Simone's jaw dropped in an almost comical expression of surprise. "Really?"

"No, but it makes me sound much more interesting than I really am."

Simone held her hand on the top of the blender to keep the lid from flying off as she prepared a frozen strawberry daiquiri. "You're a tough nut to crack, aren't you?"

Kenya shrugged. "I guess I'm more used to asking questions than answering them." Tonight, however she would have to be able to reveal more than she withheld. But was she willing—or able—to do it?

"In that case," Simone said, "just tell me one thing."

"What do you want to know?"

"When can I see you again?"

Kenya hesitated. Simone had many things going for her, but she and Kenya obviously moved in different circles. Simone could never be anything other than a one-night stand, a luxury Kenya hadn't afforded herself since college and one she wasn't willing to indulge in now. Not if it meant risking her reputation as well as her heart. "I'm flattered, but—"

"You're not interested."

She might be if Simone were in a different line of work. Bartending was a job, not a career. It was all about enjoying the moment, not planning for the future. Kenya wasn't looking for a playmate or a drinking buddy. She was looking for a partner. Someone who needed emotional rather than financial support.

"I'd still like to take you out sometime," Simone said. "No strings. No pressure. Just two people taking some time to get to know each other better. Are you free for dinner tomorrow night?"

"That remains to be seen." If the evening turned out to be as successful as the organizers had promised, she might be busy for the foreseeable future, if not the rest of her life. "Thanks for the drink."

Kenya could feel Simone's eyes on her as she walked away. She put an extra switch in her hips to make sure Simone enjoyed the show. Simone's attention had given her the confidence boost she needed to make it through the rest of the evening, but she wondered if the ten mini-dates she was about to have would be half as exciting as the one she had just turned down.

❖

Simone Bailey watched the most intriguing woman she had ever met walk out of her life just as quickly as she had walked into it. And she had no choice but to let her go. The crowd in front of the bar was growing by the minute and there was no relief in sight.

"Struck out, huh?"

Amanda Chun, one of the three other bartenders sharing Simone's shift, barely waited until Kenya was out of earshot before she tried to break Simone's balls. Simone and Amanda competed for everything from who could snag the most tips during a shift to who could down the most vodka shots at one sitting, so Simone wasn't the least bit surprised Amanda tried to rub her spectacular failure in her face as quickly as she could.

"She doesn't know what she's missing," Simone said, trying to downplay her disappointment. She sneaked another peek across the room. Kenya was well put together. From her navy skirt and pink silk blouse to her low heels and bobbed black hair. Simone sensed something lay hidden under the professional exterior, however, and she wanted to feel the heat beneath the cool surface.

"I doubt she's missing much." Amanda gave Simone a friendly punch on the shoulder, being careful to avoid the metal bottle opener strapped to Simone's arm so she wouldn't bruise her knuckles while she dented Simone's ego. "Don't look now, but the boss is taking up your slack."

Simone turned to see Mackenzie Richardson slap on a name tag and take a seat opposite Kenya like she was just another schlub looking for love instead of a millionaire entrepreneur who could get any woman she wanted—and often did. Mackenzie owned Azure, as well as Azul, the high-end restaurant across the street, along with Azul's counterparts in New York, Chicago, Los Angeles, and San Francisco.

What was Mackenzie doing participating in tonight's event? She hadn't signed up beforehand, and her presence would skew the numbers unless someone else joined the party to even things out. Besides that, Simone knew for a fact Mackenzie didn't lack for bedmates. She had served drinks to way too many women crying in their champagne cocktails over how easily they had been replaced. Was Kenya about to join the crowd?

"Sorry, girl," Amanda said, "but there's no way you can compete. You party too much, you drink too much, and you spend every penny you make as soon as you get your hands on it. A woman like that isn't looking for a good time. She's looking for forever." She poured a shot of vodka and slapped it on the counter. "Guess which one you could give her."

Azure's management had decreed that employees weren't allowed to drink during a shift unless a customer was footing the bill. Some rules, however, were made to be broken, especially in a situation like this.

Simone tried to think of a snappy comeback as she downed the shot, but she couldn't come up with one. Mackenzie had style, sophistication, and more money than God. Everything a woman like Kenya would want. Logic said she didn't have a chance, especially after Kenya had shut her down on her first attempt to bring them together, but she wasn't willing to concede defeat.

"I'm going to make her mine, Amanda. Just wait and see."

Amanda snorted as she added hot sauce to a Bloody Mary. "How do you plan to do that?"

Simone thought about how hard it had been to drag information out of Kenya and how much fun she'd had making the attempt. She had read an article once about a psychologist who created a list of questions designed to make sure two people fell in love by the time they answered them all. She didn't know if the results were guaranteed, but it couldn't hurt to put the list to the test.

"I plan to do it one question at a time."

CHAPTER TWO

K enya couldn't believe her eyes. Mackenzie Richardson, the most eligible bachelorette in south Florida, was looking at her like she was a perfectly cooked prime rib and Mackenzie hadn't eaten in a week.

"Welcome to Azure. I'm Mackenzie Richardson. Are you having a good time?"

Mackenzie's slight Italian accent made every word she uttered sound like it ended in a vowel, even when it wasn't meant to. Kenya wanted to hear more. Much more.

"Yes, thank you."

"I'm new at this speed dating thing," Mackenzie said with a modest smile, "and it's probably against the rules for me to be sitting here with you like this without a timer counting down every second, but I wanted a chance to talk to you before the event begins. You're Kenya Davis, aren't you?"

"I am." Kenya was taken aback. She had seen Mackenzie's picture splashed on the pages of the Society and Business sections of the *Miami Herald* more times than she could count, but as far as she knew, she and the jet-setting thirty-eight-year-old entrepreneur had never crossed paths. Because that would have been an encounter she wasn't likely to forget. "How did you know?"

Mackenzie's smile broadened, her straight white teeth providing a brilliant contrast to her olive-hued skin. "I make it a point to know the names of most beautiful women I hope to meet. In your case, I saw you at a charity event last fall, but the room was so crowded I never got a chance to make my way over to you and introduce myself. Then you disappeared before the main event began."

Kenya wracked her brain to try to pinpoint the event to which Mackenzie was referring. The only thing that came to mind was a fundraiser for a local homeless shelter that housed mostly LGBTQIAA teens. The headline event that night had been a charity date auction, but she hadn't wanted to take part in or witness an auction featuring people as the objects being purchased. Despite the lighthearted mood and the philanthropic intent, the scene had turned her off, reminding her too much of the humiliation her ancestors had endured centuries ago when they were paraded across similar stages wearing chains instead of tuxedoes.

"I'm sorry I missed you that evening," she said, "but I had a prior engagement." Namely with a Sanaa Lathan romantic comedy and a bowl of caramel popcorn.

"I hope you don't have anything on your agenda tonight. If you're free, perhaps we can make up for lost time."

Kenya tried to sound noncommittal even though she felt like turning backflips like a gymnast on espresso. "Perhaps."

Mackenzie took a sip of her caipirinha, giving Kenya time to admire her jaw-dropping beauty. Mackenzie's father was African-American and her mother was Italian. As a result, she looked like a cross between Lena Horne and Sophia Loren. Kenya imagined tracing a finger across Mackenzie's full lips, then running her hands through Mackenzie's short, wavy brown hair as their mouths met in a kiss. The glint in Mackenzie's hazel eyes said she knew exactly what Kenya was thinking, though she didn't comment on it.

"Pierce, Jackson, and Smith is one of the best PR firms in Miami," Mackenzie said instead. "I admire your work."

Kenya made a concerted effort to keep the nervous quaver out of her voice. Making a good first impression was always important, but never more so than now. She felt like Cinderella meeting Princess Charming for the first time—and praying the clock wouldn't strike midnight. "I wish I could take credit for the company's success, but the art department is more responsible for that than I am."

Mackenzie started shaking her head well before Kenya finished her sentence. "I beg to differ. Where would the firm be if you didn't select the right personnel? Success begins with the right hire. And that starts with you." She leaned forward. "I could use someone like you on my team."

Kenya's spirits flagged at the prospect Mackenzie had sought her out for professional reasons rather than personal ones. "Are you planning to make me an offer?"

Mackenzie leaned even closer. "I'm planning to do a lot of things to you. If you'll let me, that is."

Kenya felt her face flush, along with other body parts slightly farther south.

The emcee called out a five-minute warning for the speed dating to begin. Nearly a dozen women—some eager, some nervous—began to take their seats at the long, conference-style table that had been set up on what was normally the dance floor.

"We don't have much time," Mackenzie said. "I'd better say what's on my mind before someone has a chance to steal you away from me. Safe Space's spring fundraiser is right around the corner. This year, they're holding a ballroom dancing contest instead of their usual boring sit-down dinner. I signed up ages ago, but I still don't have a partner. Are you interested?"

"In more ways than you know."

Mackenzie arched a perfectly manicured eyebrow. "But?"

"I have two left feet." Kenya had sneaked an occasional peek at a popular TV show that paired B-list celebrities with professional dancers, but she had never felt skilled—or brave— enough to try to replicate their moves. "I'm better at the Electric Slide than the Viennese waltz. If you want to win the contest, I suggest you choose someone else."

Mackenzie reached across the table. "Winning the dance competition would be nice, but right now, I'm more interested in winning you." She drew circles on the back of Kenya's hand with her thumb. The sensation made Kenya's heart rate quadruple. "I'd like to spend more time with you. Someplace quieter so I can get to know all the things you won't have time to tell me in ten minutes or less. Would that be okay with you?"

Kenya tried to keep from nodding like a bobblehead doll. Mackenzie seemed like a great catch. The perfect catch, in fact. She was smart, gorgeous, and wildly successful. What was there not to like? But Kenya didn't want to agree to her proposal without thinking it over first. Mackenzie had been quoted more than once as saying she didn't plan to settle down anytime soon, if ever. Tonight, it seemed that not only had she had a change of heart, but her heart was set on Kenya. But that had to be too good to be true. Mackenzie had been on the prowl for years. Kenya doubted she could ever truly be tamed. Making the attempt might be a heartache waiting to happen. But if Mackenzie was as sincere as she seemed to be, she could very well be the woman of Kenya's dreams. And if she wasn't, agreeing to spend time with her could be the stuff of nightmares.

"Sorry to interrupt, boss," the emcee said when she came over to them, "but we're two minutes away from show time and we're now short a person."

"That's my fault." Mackenzie ran her free hand over her paper name tag, which looked like a last-minute addition to her carefully accessorized outfit—suede Gucci loafers, a black Prada suit, and a Patek Philippe watch even more expensive than a tricked-out sports car. "You guys did such a good job advertising the event that I decided to join in rather than observe. See if one of the staff members will volunteer to help fill out the field."

"Someone already did."

Kenya turned to see Simone standing behind her. Simone had ditched her work clothes in favor of a white button-down shirt, a pair of fashionably distressed jeans, and a set of well-worn black motorcycle boots. It was the kind of outfit celebrities wore when they wanted to seem approachable. But Simone didn't have to pretend to be down-to-earth. She already was.

"Is there room at the table for one more?" Simone asked.

"Sure," Mackenzie said, finally letting go of Kenya's hand. "Have a seat."

As Simone grabbed a chair and altered the seating arrangement, Kenya could already feel herself being forced into a decision she didn't want to make. Mackenzie—beautiful, intelligent, and financially stable—was the kind of woman she was looking for, but Simone—charming, sexy, and so wrong for her in so many ways—was the kind of woman she craved. The kind she had tried to avoid ever since her last relationship had ended so acrimoniously. Simone was sweet at the center but rough around the edges. Hungry for everything life had to offer but not blessed with the means to make her dreams come true. Was she willing to work for what she wanted, or was she looking for someone to hand it to her? Kenya wasn't looking to be anyone's sugar mama. She had done it before, but that was a mistake she had vowed not to repeat. No matter how tempting the prospect.

"Are you ready?" Mackenzie asked as the emcee announced the start of the event.

Kenya tried to muster a smile. "As ready as I'll ever be."

❖

Promptly at eight o'clock, club DJ Crystal cut the music and held an upraised finger between her mouth and the microphone to amplify her voice, a trick, Simone noted, Crystal had picked up from watching too many of Jay-Z's performances. Her outfit had been cribbed from Hova, too: baggy jeans, a plain white T-shirt, a puffy down vest, and an oversized medallion dangling from a white gold chain around her neck. That was the difference between her and Crystal. Simone didn't want to be the headlining act. She wanted to be the producer behind the scenes. The one who created the music, not the one who performed it. The initial paycheck wasn't as good, but the shelf life was a whole lot longer and the influence extended far beyond a photo on an extra-large T-shirt or a poster on a wall.

"I can see you're anxious to get started, ladies," Crystal said, "so I'm not going to stand in your way. Not for long, anyway." The diamonds in her blinged-out necklace reflected the bright lights trained in her direction. "After I remind you of the rules, the floor is yours. For you brave souls who have decided to participate, you have ten minutes to get to know the lovely lady sitting across from you. When the buzzer sounds, that will be your cue to play musical chairs. The ladies seated to my left will shift to their right until they've spent time with all ten—excuse me, *twelve*—women who have signed up to meet them."

Simone had positioned herself so she would be the last woman seated in front of Kenya when the final buzzer sounded. Mackenzie would have the chance to make the first impression, but she wanted the opportunity to make the one that counted the most. When it came time for Kenya to decide who she wanted to spend more time with after the mini-dates were concluded, her encounter with Simone would be freshest on her mind.

"Good luck, ladies," Crystal said. "Your search for love begins now."

Simone felt her adrenaline surge. There were a lot of attractive women seated at the table. On any other night, she would have asked at least four for their phone numbers. Tonight, though, only one woman truly piqued her interest.

As she spoke with a legal secretary from Hialeah, she kept one ear tuned to the conversation Kenya and Mackenzie were having a short distance away. Mackenzie's questions almost made her roll her eyes. The whole what's your sign, what's your favorite color thing was so played out. Was Mackenzie trying to get to know Kenya or put her to sleep? She perked up when Mackenzie asked what was the one place Kenya most wanted to visit. Because the answer told her how large an obstacle she would have to face if she hoped to win Kenya's heart.

"There's a restaurant on the outskirts of Venice called Per Due," Kenya said. "It's the most exclusive restaurant in the world. Like its name suggests, it seats only two people. A private car picks you up from your hotel, drives you into the mountains, and drops you off at an intimate restaurant reserved exclusively for you and your dining companion. The price is astronomical, the food is extraordinary, and the experience is one you're bound to remember for the rest of your life. Or so I've heard."

Simone could work until she was a hundred years old and never be able to afford to take Kenya on a trip like that, but Mackenzie didn't bat an eye before she said, "I'm all about making dreams come true. Tell me when you want to go and I'll make it happen. We could stay at my villa in Milan and make a day trip to Venice. How does next weekend sound?"

"Are you allergic to cats?" Barbara the legal secretary's question forced Simone to focus on her own conversation instead of someone else's. "Because I have three."

"I prefer dogs." Simone thought of the stray she had taken in when she was younger. The mutt was a mixture of so many breeds she didn't know what to call him, but he had been unfailingly loyal and obviously grateful to finally have a home of his own. "Cats love you only as long as they need something from you. Dogs love you no matter what."

"Oh." Barbara wrinkled her nose as if she smelled something unpleasant. "So you're one of those."

"Yeah," Simone said with an apologetic shrug, "I guess I am."

"Then I don't think this is going to work out." Barbara reached across the table to give her a limp handshake. "It was nice meeting you," she said, though her tone hinted the opposite was true.

Kicked to the curb in less than two minutes, Simone thought as she waited for the buzzer to sound. This might be harder than I imagined.

❖

Kenya couldn't help but smile at the awkward exchange between Simone and the first of her mini-dates. It was the kind of encounter one could expect to have with a complete stranger, even in a setting as faux intimate as this one. Fortunately, she wasn't having the same experience. Mackenzie didn't feel like someone she had just met. She felt like someone Kenya had known all her life. Someone she wanted to know for the rest of her life.

"I'm having a White Party on my yacht tomorrow and I'd love it if you could come," Mackenzie said as the ringing buzzer signaled the end of their allotted time. Surely their ten minutes weren't up already. Not with so much still to be said. "Can I count on seeing you there? I promise not to twist your arm about pairing up with me for the Safe Space event, but I can't guarantee the subject won't come up at least once."

Despite her reluctance to pour herself into a ball gown and step well outside her comfort zone, Kenya didn't hesitate to accept Mackenzie's invitation. She wanted to get to know Mackenzie better, and attending a party on a luxury yacht sounded a whole lot better than her normal Saturday afternoon routine of doing laundry. "It's a date."

"Excellent. Find me when this is over so we can exchange contact information. If I'm lucky, I might even be able to talk you into grabbing a nightcap. Does that sound good?"

The prospect was beyond thrilling. It had been a long time since she had taken a chance on something—someone—new.

"Yes," Kenya said. *On both counts.*

Mackenzie moved one seat to her right, putting her directly across from the cat lover who'd had issues with Simone's fondness for dogs. Mackenzie said she was far too busy to look after pets of any kind so she didn't fare any better than Simone had. Kenya's luck wasn't much better. Almost from the opening salvo, she found she didn't have anything in common with the architect she found herself paired with or the high school guidance counselor who followed. A few women caught her attention, including an artist in paint-splattered jeans who invited her to check out her gallery sometime, but she didn't feel the same chemistry she had felt with Mackenzie. The all-important desire to see what might happen next was missing. As she tried to hold up her end of her conversations with the various women who sat opposite her, both her brain and her body were still buzzing from her mini-date with Mackenzie—and the very real possibility that there was more to come tonight, tomorrow, and perhaps the day after.

She was trying to figure out whether to wear something comfortable or something sexy to Mackenzie's party when Simone claimed the vacant seat across from her.

"We meet again," Simone said. "And this time, I get to ask the questions." She rubbed her hands together as if she'd been waiting for the opportunity all night, making Kenya wonder what she had in store for her.

"I thought this experience was supposed to be about give and take."

"That didn't work so well for me last time so I decided to change things up. If that's okay with you, of course."

Kenya tried not to smile. Simone was so self-confident she didn't seem to need much encouragement. Yet Kenya found her persistence appealing rather than off-putting. And it would have helped matters a great deal if she didn't find it—or Simone—quite so irresistible. "I'm in your hands."

Simone looked skeptical. "I doubt you intend to make it that easy for me, but I'll remember you said that." She cleared her throat as if preparing to deliver a speech. She had been all smiles all night, but she certainly wasn't smiling now. "Before we begin, I want you to promise me something."

"What?" Kenya asked warily. She wasn't in the habit of making promises she couldn't keep—or signing contracts without giving them a thorough read-through first.

Simone reached into the back pocket of her jeans, pulled out a folded sheet of notebook paper, and smoothed the wrinkles with the heel of her hand. She looked like she was about to pass Kenya a note asking her to check yes or no if she wanted to go steady, but it was much too soon to be making or accepting proposals of any kind. "I have twenty-one questions for you. We can't get through all of them in ten minutes, obviously. Promise me that once we start, you'll allow me to finish. No matter how long it takes. Do we have a deal?"

Simone reached across the table, and Kenya looked at her outstretched hand. Simone was obviously interested in her, but did she feel the same? Simone was attractive and funny, but the two of them were at different stages in life. Kenya was established in her career. Unless her lifelong dream was to be a bartender, Simone was still finding her way. What kind of future could they have?

If she agreed to Simone's request, Kenya would be opening herself up to temptation by agreeing to see Simone again. And she might damage her chances of possibly making a go of it with Mackenzie, provided Mackenzie's invitation to drinks turned into something more. But Simone's proposition intrigued her and she was curious to see how the experiment might play out.

"Yes," she said, taking Simone's hand in hers, "we have a deal."

❖

Simone took a deep breath to calm her nerves. Part of her had expected Kenya to turn her down. Again. Instead, Kenya had said yes. Now she was truly on the spot. It was time to put up or shut up.

She scanned the list of questions before her. Which one should she ask first? Which should follow? And, most important, what would happen after she asked the last one? Would she and Kenya fall for each other as promised, or would the end of the list mean the end of them as well?

"Okay," she said, trying to kick herself into gear as the timer clicked inexorably toward zero, "let's get started." She decided to save the heavier queries for later and selected something reasonably innocuous to break the ice. "Question one. If you could have dinner with any person, living or dead, who would it be?"

"Hmm." Kenya sat back in her seat, her expression a mixture of fascination and confusion with a hint of surprise thrown in for good measure. "That's a good question."

Simone felt like patting herself on the back for having chosen wisely, but she didn't have time for self-congratulation. She was too busy waiting to hear Kenya's response to her question. When Kenya leaned forward as if she were about to spill a deep, dark secret, Simone moved closer in order to receive it.

"It would be tempting to name someone I've always considered a hero, but I would be reluctant to actually break bread with them for fear they wouldn't live up to my expectations. If they didn't turn out to be the person I thought they were, then who would I have to look up to?"

The wounded look in Kenya's eyes hinted she had experienced a similar disappointment firsthand. Simone resolved not to provide the same letdown.

"With that in mind," Kenya said, "I'd have to say I would prefer to have dinner with the man who conducted my first job interview. I was fresh out of college and eager to take on the world. I put on my best suit and showed up fifteen minutes early so my potential employer would be impressed by my appearance, my punctuality, and my work ethic. He started yawning halfway through the interview, barely glanced at the résumé I'd worked so hard to perfect, and told me in no uncertain terms I didn't have what it took to make it in a corporate environment. He even suggested I should reconsider my career goals. I walked out of his office feeling like I wanted to cry."

"What did you do?"

"I got angry."

Simone couldn't blame her. If she had been in the same situation, she would have been escorted out of the building in handcuffs instead of allowed to leave on her own. She didn't like to settle arguments with her fists, but sometimes words could only get you so far. Her parents said there were other ways to get respect without having to fight for it. Maybe one day she'd be able to figure out how.

"Whether it was his intention or not," Kenya said, "his rejection increased my drive to succeed. I don't know if I would be where I am now without him. I've always wanted to thank him for that."

"Before or after you told him to kiss your ass?"

"I wouldn't put it in quite those terms," Kenya said with a Mona Lisa smile, "but I would definitely remind him of our previous encounter at some point during the evening. What about you? Who would you like to have dinner with?"

"You."

Kenya looked skeptical. "Out of anyone in the world, you would choose me? Why?"

"For the same reason you gave. The guy you just told me about underestimated you and you want to show him the error of his ways. I want a chance to do the same with you."

"Simone—"

Simone held up a hand to stop Kenya's protests before they could begin. "I'm not asking for a lifetime commitment, Kenya. All I'm asking for is a chance. Will you give me one, or have you already made up your mind about me? If you have, give me the opportunity to prove you wrong. I'm not just a bartender. I'm more than you think I am."

"I'm sure you are, but—"

Kenya flinched when the buzzer chimed. Simone couldn't tell if she was startled by the dissonant sound or the probing questions.

"Time's up, ladies," Crystal said over the PA system. "Thank you for participating in our event. How many love connections were made tonight?"

As hands shot up all around them, Kenya pushed herself out of her seat as if she couldn't wait to get away. "I have to go. Thank you for an interesting evening."

"It doesn't have to end here."

"Yes, I'm afraid it does." Kenya glanced toward Mackenzie, who was slowly making her way toward them with her assistant in tow. "Mackenzie and I have plans."

"I see." Simone thought she had made progress with Kenya during their mini-date. Gotten to see the real woman behind the polished corporate façade. But Kenya had apparently been humoring her because it was obvious she had decided Simone wasn't worth her time. Simone wasn't old enough, smart enough, or rich enough. In short, she wasn't Mackenzie Richardson. She gathered her things and prepared to head back to work while Kenya and Mackenzie prepared to spend a night on the town.

"Thanks for stepping up the way you did," Mackenzie said, giving Simone a fist bump. "I owe you one."

"Just doing my job, boss. Have a good time tonight." She turned to Kenya. "Don't forget I have twenty questions left."

And she intended to make each one count.

❖

"Twenty questions?" Mackenzie asked. "What did she mean by that?" She placed a hand in the small of Kenya's back and guided her away from the crowd of people milling around the dance floor. "I don't have competition for your affections already, do I?"

Kenya shook her head. "She made a play, but I told her I wasn't interested." Even though the statement was true, it felt like a lie. Kenya was more interested in Simone Bailey than she was willing to admit. Nothing could come of a relationship with Simone, but that didn't stop her from imagining the possibility. However brief the encounter might turn out to be.

"Simone doesn't give up easily," Mackenzie said. "Then again, neither do I."

"Good to know." Kenya leaned into the pressure of Mackenzie's hand, finding comfort in the security it offered—and a bit turned on by the tremendous power it wielded. "Are you ready for that nightcap you promised me?"

Mackenzie grimaced. "I'm afraid I'll have to reschedule, if you don't mind." She introduced the woman at her side, a young redhead who seemed more interested in texting on her smartphone than taking part in the conversation. "This is Gabby Dawson, my assistant." Gabby nodded hello, but her flying fingers barely paused as she continued pecking away at her touch screen. "She's just alerted me to a situation at my San Francisco property that needs my urgent attention. I don't know how long it will take me to resolve the issue, so I wouldn't dare ask you to wait around while I try to put out the fire. I will see you tomorrow for the White Party, though, won't I?"

"Yes, of course." Kenya felt like her former lovers must have each time she got caught up in a meeting that ran long or had to be on call to solve an unexpected crisis. Abandoned.

"Excellent." Mackenzie gave Kenya a kiss on the cheek. Kenya breathed her in. Mackenzie smelled like citrus groves and sunshine. Like a warm breeze wafting over the Mediterranean. Kenya couldn't get enough. She wanted more. She wanted. God, how long had it been since she was able to say that? Then Mackenzie pulled away and handed her a business card. "Here's my contact information. My yacht is named *La Dolce Vita* and it's docked at South Beach Marina. The party officially starts at five, but I'll be on board most of the day to supervise the setup, so feel free to drop by whenever you like."

"I'll do that." Kenya fingered the embossed letters on the business card, impressed by the clean, understated design. It was both classy and classic. Just like Mackenzie herself. "Do you mind if I bring a friend?"

"Of course not. The more, the merrier."

"Good."

Because Kenya needed backup for something like this. She needed someone with a level head to make sure she didn't lose hers. She needed Celia. Bridget would not only allow her to do something stupid but encourage it in her ongoing attempt to get Kenya to loosen up. Celia's well-honed maternal instincts, however, would prevent her from doing something she might enjoy tomorrow but regret the next day. She called Celia while she waited for the valet to retrieve her car.

"Tell Juan he's babysitting the kids tomorrow. You and I have a party to attend."

❖

Simone felt restless after her shift. She started to find an after-hours club and a willing partner so she could dance herself into a better mood, but she decided not to. Tonight, she didn't want to listen to music. She wanted to make it.

Music had been her salvation for as long as she could remember. It had gotten her through the bad times, chronicled the good ones, and made her believe the best moments were still to come.

Tonight, she needed music more than ever. An opportunity had slipped through her fingers and she knew it. The question was, would she ever get the chance again?

After she helped lock up at Azure, she climbed on her motorcycle and headed over to Liberty City Records. Andre "Dre" Williams, the label's owner, had so many artists on his ever-growing roster that he practically worked around the clock. Simone knew that, despite the late hour, he would probably be huddled over a soundboard while a hungry rapper spat rhymes or a wannabe diva channeled her inner Beyoncé.

Simone made backing tapes for Dre in her spare time and remixed some of the artists' singles so they could receive airplay on a wider variety of stations than the hip-hop and R & B-focused ones that normally played Liberty City Records' music. She got a thrill each time she heard her music on the radio. She wished she could have that feeling all the time. Even though her family knew how much she loved music, they didn't want her to make it her career because the music industry was anything but a sure thing. Artists and styles went in and out of favor all the time, they reasoned. The recipes for classic cocktails never changed. Simone could mix drinks anywhere, but could she anticipate music lovers' tastes and give them what they wanted even before they knew they wanted it?

"There's my girl," Dre said after Simone submitted to the mandatory pat down at the studio's front door. Liberty City Records was named for the rough-and-tumble Miami suburb most of the label's artists called home. Some performers brought the 'hood with them when they walked through the door, resulting in the occasional shootout, stickup, and loud displays of machismo. Simone had learned long ago how to keep her head on a swivel in order to avoid danger. Because she wasn't about to let anyone stop her from achieving her dreams.

"What's up, Dre?" Simone gave him a hug and handed him a CD she had burned. "Here's the remix I promised you."

Dre cued up the CD and nodded his shaved head to the beat as the music poured through the oversized speakers mounted in each corner of the room. In the recording studio on the other side of the thick reinforced glass, a skinny kid whose gold crucifix weighed more than he did practiced his flow while his posse of friends passed a lit blunt back and forth. The smoke was so thick the room looked like it was being fumigated.

"That's hot," Dre said. "I love the reggae flavor you added to it. Keep that up and you're going to start making some serious bank." He reached into the pocket of his voluminous jeans and peeled five bills off a roll of hundreds. After a slight hesitation, he peeled off five more.

"What's with the extra paper?" The thousand dollars in her hand would pay her rent for the next two months, which meant she could use her paycheck to buy the electronic drums she'd had her eye on since she spotted them in the music store a few weeks ago. But did the cash come with a catch?

"Consider it an advance." Dre handed her a CD labeled *Reagan*. "Reagan Carter is my newest artist. She's only twenty-two, but you can tell she's already been through some shit and come out the other side. She sounds like someone twice her age."

Simone pocketed the money before Dre could change his mind and ask her to return it. Like most payments she received, this one was practically already spent. "What's the problem?"

"I can't find a signature sound for her. I need you to come up with a beat that highlights her voice instead of drowning it out. I don't want her to sound like everybody else on the radio. I want her to sound like herself. When people hear one of her joints start playing, I want them to know it's her right off the bat like Timbaland did for Missy Elliott and Aaliyah before her. I want this girl to shine. She could be the one who puts us all on the map."

Dre said the same thing each time he signed someone new. This time, though, he truly seemed to mean it. When she took the CD home and gave it a listen, Simone understood why. Reagan's voice was pure, but it had a raw quality to it, too. Like an uncut diamond before it finds its way into the hands of an expert jeweler. Despite her relatively young age, Reagan already had a style all her own. All she needed was the music to match. Simone wanted to be the one who created it for her.

She picked up some callaloo and pickled mackerel from the all-night Jamaican restaurant near her apartment to fortify herself. Then she parked herself in front of her digital keyboard, tossed the handful of phone numbers in her pocket into the trash, and put her frustrating encounter with Kenya Davis behind her. Then she lost herself in the one lover she could always depend on: music.

CHAPTER THREE

Kenya stood in front of her open walk-in closet and tried in vain to find something to wear. She had plenty of clothes, if the vast array of blue, gray, and black power suits were any indication, but thanks to the all-white dress code, her options for today were limited to little more than a camisole, four T-shirts, and a pair of linen pants she hadn't worn since a vacation to St. Lucia that had helped bring her previous relationship to an ignominious end. The pants were a definite no-go. She didn't want that kind of bad mojo following her around today. Now that she was finally trying to make a new start, she needed to put the past behind her. She pulled the pants off the hanger and set them aside until she could swing by Goodwill and deposit them in the donation drop box.

Celia poured herself a glass of white wine while she admired the view of the Miami River from the balcony outside Kenya's bedroom. "Tell me everything that happened last night and tell me slow. I don't want to miss anything."

"I already told you once."

Celia had oohed and ahhed over her account of last night's events like she was listening to the recap of a soap opera. Kenya felt a bit like she was starring in one. If that was the case, she wasn't looking forward to the requisite cliffhanger. The last thing she needed was for someone she had thought long dead to come back from the grave or to discover she had a secret evil twin, two tried and true plot devices soap writers kept turning to time and time again in order to please their steadily dwindling audiences.

"I know you *said* you told me the whole story, but you must have left something out. Otherwise, I wouldn't be wondering how you left the office yesterday with no women in your life and less than twenty-four hours later, you have two beating down your door."

"Correct me if I'm wrong, but the only person beating down my door today is you. And the last time I checked, you weren't on the list of prospects."

Celia shrugged as she sipped her chardonnay. "I don't like office romances."

"Or sex with women."

"I don't know. A few more nights like the ones I had in college and I might be persuaded to join the team."

"Do I need to keep my eye on you today?" Celia didn't party often. But when she did, she really let loose. And reeling her in was often no easy feat.

"It might be wise to keep me on a short leash. I haven't had more than one glass of wine since the twins were born and I have a feeling the booze is going to be flowing pretty freely after we arrive. This party isn't clothing optional, is it?" She pointed to her full breasts. "If it is, the girls might come out to play."

"Make sure you tell them they aren't invited. I don't want to have to bail you out after the three of you get arrested for indecent exposure."

"Like I said, short leash." Celia closed the patio door and came back inside. "So which one are you more interested in, Mackenzie or Simone? Because both of them sound pretty hot."

Kenya considered the question. Even though the answer seemed obvious, she couldn't come up with it. Mackenzie and Simone both had their strong points. And their weak ones, too. Mackenzie had a thriving career but a spotty romantic track record. Simone was easy to talk to but her job situation was less than ideal. Mackenzie was the easy choice, but was she the right one?

"I'm not ready to pack up the U-Haul and park it outside anyone's house right now, let alone someone I just met."

"What about getting horizontal? Are you ready for that?"

"I'm not sure."

Kenya hadn't allowed herself to be intimate with anyone since she caught her lover of four years fucking a maid in their hotel room bed. Ellis's betrayal had been the last straw in a relationship that had been on shaky ground for months before finally crumbling under its own weight—and the dozens of exorbitant purchases Ellis had made on her credit card when Kenya had been lovestruck enough to trust her with the valuable piece of plastic. Not to mention the other cards Ellis had maxed out post-breakup after she "borrowed" Kenya's social security number to complete the applications.

Kenya supposed she could have taken legal action after she discovered what Ellis had done, but what would have been the point? There was no way Ellis could have paid her back, and trying to make her learn from her mistakes would have been an exercise in futility. The damage to her financial standing was reparable. The resulting damage to her reputation, if the scandal became public, wasn't. As for the effect on her heart, well, that was still to be determined.

She should have known Ellis was wrong for her. She was too wild. Too irresponsible. Too everything. But the untamed quality Ellis exuded had been part of the attraction. After they ended, it was easy to look back and say, "I told you so." But while they were together, the relationship had felt like a risk worth taking. Kenya was still paying for her decision to assume that risk. In more ways than one. Ellis's betrayal had bankrupted her emotionally and had nearly had the same effect financially. Monetarily, she was finally back on her feet. Emotionally, she wasn't so sure.

She had dated a few times since she'd told Ellis they were through, but none of the relationships had made it past the embryonic stage. Her fault. And she knew it. She kept judging her prospective partners based on the low bar Ellis had set rather than allowing them to pass or fail on their own merits. Things were different with Mackenzie. And so was she.

She had felt comfortable with Mackenzie from the moment they met. At ease. Yet she had also felt a spark of something electric whenever Mackenzie touched her. Something carnal. She was well aware of Mackenzie's playgirl reputation, but Mackenzie hadn't made her feel like she wanted her to become just another notch on her bedpost. Mackenzie had made her feel like she wanted her to become something more. Or maybe she was reading more into the situation than was really there. Either way, she wanted to explore it further.

Simone had pitched her case, though not well enough for Kenya to buy what she was selling. As for Mackenzie, today would go a long way toward answering the question of whether she was truly interested in Kenya or simply on the hunt for her next conquest. Perhaps it would also determine if Kenya was ready to open herself up to someone again or if she was destined to remain as she was now—closed for business.

"I can tell you're fascinated by Mackenzie and everything she brings to the table," Celia said. "The two of you would probably go to sleep whispering the latest business news into each other's ears instead of sweet nothings. But Simone got to you, didn't she?"

Kenya temporarily put her search for the perfect outfit on hold and sat on the edge of her queen-sized bed. Simone's questions—even the ones that hadn't come from a list—had challenged her. Made her think. Now she was filled with questions of her own. Was Simone right? Had she underestimated her? Should she give Simone what she had asked for, a chance to prove her wrong? But Kenya didn't have any room in her life for second-guessing. Otherwise, she'd never be able to make a decision and stick to it. In her professional life or her personal one. If everything went well over the next few weeks, saying yes to Mackenzie and no to Simone might turn out to be the best decision she had ever made.

"You don't do office romances," she said, resuming her search, "and I don't do short-lived ones. Now help me find something to wear."

"Give it up. You're not going to find what you're looking for in there. That's why I brought two outfits with me instead of one." Celia set her wine glass on the dresser and tucked two stray locks of her long brown hair behind her ears before she unzipped the garment bags she had tossed on the bed when she had arrived half an hour ago. "Take your pick."

Kenya inspected the contents of the garment bags. The first bag contained a vintage Versace blouse and a pair of cream-colored sailor pants, a high-end combination that made her wonder if Celia's salary was still within the prescribed pay scale for her position. The second bag contained a slightly more casual outfit: a pair of white jeans and a white T-shirt embellished with interlocked Chanel logos in black sequins.

"How much are we paying you?"

"Enough," Celia said with a cheeky grin, "but I wouldn't turn down a raise. Diapers aren't cheap, you know. So do you want to wow in Versace or be understated in Chanel?"

Kenya reached for the T-shirt and jeans. "I'll leave the wowing to you, thanks."

"I figured you'd say that. My mother loves to say classy beats trashy, but I don't see anything wrong with adding a little spice every now and then."

"I know. Remember that mini-dress you wore on our last girls' night out?"

"How could I forget? Nine months after Juan saw me in it, I ended up giving birth to twins." Celia pulled a gold chain link belt and a pair of stiletto heels from an overnight bag. "Thankfully, that's not going to happen today."

"Are you sure? Every time Juan so much as breathes on you, you end up peeing on a stick and watching it turn blue."

"That's why I plan to turn myself from a diva back into a soccer mom before I head home tonight. Four kids are enough."

Celia was so serious at the office Kenya had forgotten how much fun she could be when she was away from it. As they began to get ready for the party, Celia made her laugh until she cried. She had to redo her makeup twice when her waterproof mascara proved to be anything but. "I haven't had this much fun since—"

"You were still getting some?"

Kenya pursed her lips in mock disapproval. "I was going to say since I was a teenager, but thanks for reminding me how long my drought has been."

"In a few hours, your drought may be officially over. Just give me a heads-up if I need to catch a ride home, okay?"

"In that outfit, I think you'll have plenty of volunteers."

"So will you." Celia looked her up and down. "Why does understated look frumpy on me but sexy on you?"

Kenya regarded her reflection in the floor-length mirror. She wasn't vain enough to rate herself a perfect ten, but she didn't think she looked half-bad, even in borrowed clothes. "Let's hope Mackenzie feels the same way."

❖

Simone checked her station to make sure it was sufficiently stocked. She had two bottles of vodka, a bottle of gin, a bottle of bourbon, two bottles of tequila, two bottles of white wine, and two bottles of red wine, along with various mixers and garnishes. That should get her through the two-hour trip at sea, but with Mackenzie's friends, too much was never enough. Deciding it was better to be safe than sorry, she grabbed another bottle of tequila to make sure she didn't run out before she could hit the supply truck for more.

"All set?" Amanda asked, struggling under the combined weight of the two ice-filled five-gallon buckets she was carrying.

"Yeah, I'm good. Let me help you." Simone grabbed one of the buckets and dumped its contents into an oversized cooler filled with sodas, energy drinks, and bottled water.

"Thanks." Amanda emptied her bucket and shook her arms as if they'd gone numb during her long trek from the storeroom two decks below. "What's today's cause for celebration?"

"Does there have to be one?"

"Right. I forgot who we work for. In her world, every day is cause to celebrate. If I were in her shoes, I'd probably do the same thing. When you've got it, flaunt it, right?"

Simone stirred the ice with her hands to make sure all the drinks were equally covered. "I just want to get it. Flaunting it can wait."

The assortment of silver bracelets adorning Amanda's wrists sparkled in the afternoon sun as she hitched up her low-slung jeans. "Do you mean to tell me if your music career took off, you wouldn't start making it rain all over town?"

"I've worked too hard to get where I am. If I broke big, I wouldn't waste my money on expensive toys. I'd put it in the bank to make sure it worked for me instead of the other way around. After I traded in my broke-down Kawasaki for a tricked-out Harley Fat Boy like Arnold Schwarzenegger rode in *Terminator 2*, of course."

"If Linda Hamilton came with the bike, I'd get one, too." Amanda ran a hand through her black hair. One side of her 'do was cut close to her scalp, while the rest spilled past her shoulders. An elaborate tattoo of a dragon crept up the side of her neck, completing the edgy look her physician parents disapproved of. "But speaking of impossible dreams, how did things work out during your mini-date with Miss Old-fashioned last night?"

"They didn't."

"I told you she was out of your league. Face facts, girl. You can't compete with the boss." Amanda poured two shots of vodka and handed Simone one, their traditional way to mark the beginning of a shift and celebrate the end of one. "So do yourself a favor and stop trying."

Simone had almost managed to do just that by the time she got home last night. After she had worked on her music for a few hours, she had nearly gotten Kenya Davis out of her head. But when she saw Kenya board the boat looking fine as hell in tight jeans and a form-fitting Chanel T-shirt, she realized some things were worth fighting for.

❖

Celia let out an appreciative whistle as she craned her neck to see *La Dolce Vita* in all its beauty. "This is some sweet setup. If you don't marry Mackenzie, I will."

"You're already married, remember?"

"Once he got a look at all this, I'm sure Juan would understand."

"Whatever, Celia." Kenya laughed at the absurdity of the idea. Aside from Bridget and Avery, she had never seen a couple as blissfully in love as Celia and Juan. Even after fifteen years together, they still only had eyes for each other. "I'm going to look around. Do you want to come?"

"What you really mean is you're going to look for Mackenzie. Go ahead. I don't want to cramp your style. Besides, I want to find your hot bartender from last night. I bet she's here somewhere."

Kenya had assumed Mackenzie had hired a caterer for today's event, but it would make better economic sense for her to use her own staff. She could showcase her brand to any potential investors on board while being assured of providing a quality experience for her guests.

"Savvy way to optimize brand management and maintain quality control," she said. "I admire her business acumen."

Celia pursed her Cupid's bow lips. "I'm sure that's not all you admire about her. Now go spend some quality time with her before she has to start playing happy hostess for half of Greater Miami."

Kenya got a sinking feeling in the pit of her stomach. She had seen that look on Celia's face before, and she knew nothing good could come of it. "What are you going to do?"

"I have a date with a hot bartender."

Celia jerked her head toward the starboard side of the boat. When Kenya looked in the direction Celia had indicated, she spotted Simone standing behind a portable bar laden with bottles of high-end liquor. Simone was wearing a white Azure-branded tank top, white cargo shorts, and white high-top tennis shoes. Around her neck, a white bow tie sat jauntily off-center. The bill of her all-white Miami Heat snapback hat pointed in the opposite direction. The outfit was unconventional but suited her somehow. Kenya had to agree Celia's description of Simone as "the hot bartender" was an apt one indeed.

"I've seen this look in your eye before, C. What are you planning to do?"

"Nothing," Celia said innocently. "Can't a girl get a drink without being given the third degree? And don't you have somewhere to be?" She pushed Kenya toward the stairs leading to the lower decks. "Tell Mackenzie I said hello."

Kenya watched Celia make a beeline toward Simone. Heaven only knew what Celia had in mind, but she wasn't sticking around long enough to find out.

"With friends like this, who needs enemies?"

La Dolce Vita was a pleasure craft in every sense of the word. The one-hundred-fifty-foot boat had more rooms than some people's houses and was packed with more top-of-the-line amenities than a five-star hotel. Kenya clutched the railing as she headed to the lower deck. The smooth wood beneath her fingers was polished to so high a sheen the walnut almost gleamed brighter than the gold hardware holding it in place.

She smelled something wonderful coming from what must be the galley and turned sideways to allow some of the crew members to ferry trays of food up to the main deck.

"If you're looking for Miss Richardson," one of them said, "you're in the wrong place. Her suite is on the main deck on the forward part of the ship."

"Thank you."

Kenya continued her impromptu tour before she headed back upstairs. The engine room, crew's quarters, and five guest cabins were on the lower deck. The dining room and another five guest rooms were on the main deck. Like Goldilocks, Kenya was tempted to test the beds to see if they were too hard, too soft, or just right, but she decided to wait until she received an invitation to do so rather than taking it upon herself. When she reached Mackenzie's suite, she heard muffled voices coming through the thick wooden door. She knocked twice and waited for a response.

"Come," Mackenzie said.

Kenya opened the door to find Mackenzie sitting behind a wide desk. Mackenzie's demeanor was businesslike as she signed a series of checks and handed them to Gabby one by one.

"I'm not interrupting, am I?"

Mackenzie looked up and broke into a broad grin when she saw Kenya standing in the open doorway. "You made it."

"I can come back if you're busy."

"No. Stay. I was just finishing up." Mackenzie signed the last check with a dramatic flourish and handed it to Gabby. "Hold on to those until we get back to shore, then you can pay everyone for today. Now go have some fun."

"Sure thing." Gabby locked the checks and checkbook register in a safe and nodded at Kenya on her way out.

Mackenzie came around the desk and greeted Kenya with a warm hug and a kiss on the cheek. "You look amazing. Though I'm sure I don't need to tell you that, do I? Thank you for coming."

"Did you think I wouldn't?"

"After last night, I wasn't so sure." Kenya must have looked as confused as she felt because Mackenzie led her to a plush leather couch and fixed her with an earnest expression after she took a seat. "I don't have to put out fires often. Normally, my general managers are up to the task and I don't have to hear about problems until they're solved. Last night was a special circumstance. I didn't want you to think I was blowing you off when I asked for a rain check on our nightcap."

"The thought never crossed my mind. I've had to cancel plans under similar circumstances. Believe me, I understand."

Mackenzie looked relieved. As if she had been expecting a scene that hadn't materialized. Was she already that invested? Perhaps Kenya should buy stock as well.

"So I can cancel the order for a dozen roses I planned to have sent to your office?" Mackenzie asked.

"I didn't say that. Receiving flowers at work is always a pleasant surprise. Even if, as in this case, I'll already know they're coming."

"I thought you were bringing a friend." Mackenzie rested her hand on Kenya's arm. Her skin was cool, but Kenya felt her own begin to warm. "Is she with you, or do I have you all to myself today?"

"She went to grab a drink from the bar. I'll catch up to her later."

Mackenzie's all-white ensemble perfectly complemented her olive skin. The material of her silk blouse begged to be touched, but Kenya forced herself to keep her free hand in her lap.

"Tell me something about you I wouldn't find in your business bio," Mackenzie said.

Kenya tried to think of something that wasn't common knowledge and was interesting enough to share. "I find Italian accents unbelievably sexy."

"Fortunately for me, I happen to have one of those. What else?"

"In high school, I was voted Most Likely to Succeed."

"No surprise there. I think I was voted Most Likely to End up on the Front Page of a Scandal Rag. Mission accomplished on both our parts."

Kenya couldn't imagine having her mistakes chronicled for the public's entertainment. "What's it like living your life in the public eye?"

"Public," Mackenzie said with a world-weary sigh. "That's why I enjoy moments like this. Spending time one-on-one with someone who doesn't want anything from me and only wants to be with me."

"How do you know I'm not a gold digger in disguise?"

"Because you don't have the right amount of desperation in your eyes. When I look at you, I don't see dollar signs reflecting back at me."

"What do you see?"

"An intelligent, successful woman who has never been truly appreciated. But I intend to change that."

The idea thrilled Kenya, but it was too new to sink in. She and Mackenzie had met less than twenty-four hours ago and hadn't even had an official date yet. They hadn't covered enough ground for either of them to stake a claim on the other. But she couldn't deny the idea held tremendous appeal. "You move fast, don't you?"

"I'm a businesswoman," Mackenzie said matter-of-factly. "When I see what I want, I don't stop until I get it. And I want you. I've wanted you for months. And I'm not going to stop until I get you."

Mackenzie moved closer. Kenya's breath hitched in anticipation as Mackenzie's mouth moved toward hers. It had been so long since she'd been touched by someone other than herself, one kiss was probably all it would take to send her over the edge. Her body gave her the green light to continue, but her head flashed a warning sign. Everything was happening too fast. She needed to slow down.

"Wait." She held out a hand to hold Mackenzie at bay. Mackenzie frowned. "Is something wrong?"

"I haven't been in a relationship in a while and I'm woefully out of practice. Can we—"

"Take things slow? Of course we can." Mackenzie skimmed her knuckles along the line of Kenya's jaw, sending shivers down her spine. "Take as much time as you need. When you're ready, I'll be waiting for you."

Kenya leaned into the pressure of Mackenzie's hand. "It's been my experience that most people who seem too good to be true usually are."

"That's because you hadn't met me."

And now that she had, Kenya doubted her life would ever be the same.

❖

After Kenya went downstairs, presumably to meet up with Mackenzie, the woman she had arrived with made her way over to Simone.

"I hear you mix a mean drink," the woman said in a slight Cuban accent. "May I have one?"

"Sure. What would you like?"

The woman put a hand on her hip. "You tell me. That's your specialty, isn't it?"

Simone did a double take. Her ability to guess someone's favorite drink wasn't exactly common knowledge. "Have you and Kenya been talking about me?"

"What would you do if I said yes?"

The needle on Simone's gaydar hovered in the Curious zone, but she didn't think the woman was flirting with her. More like running reconnaissance, which meant she must have made an impression on Kenya after all. She felt a flicker of hope take hold. "If you say yes, I'll make you the best white wine spritzer you've ever had."

The woman's full lips quirked into a smile. "Damn. You *are* good."

"How do you and Kenya know each other?" Simone asked as she added lemon-lime soda and a dash of peach schnapps to a glass of sauvignon blanc.

"She's my boss."

"Are you often your boss's plus-one at parties?"

"Only when no one else is available. I'm the proverbial stick in the mud no one wants to have around."

"I somehow doubt that." Simone set the finished drink on the bar. "Everything about you screams life of the party, not wallflower."

"Your tip is getting bigger by the second." The woman smiled as she sipped her drink, then stuck out a manicured hand. "Celia Torres. Nice to meet you."

"I'm—"

"The woman who's got Kenya's panties in a bunch."

"You must have me mistaken for someone else." Simone adjusted the fit of her hat, lifting and resetting the flat bill until it achieved the desired angle. "My name's Simone Bailey, not Mackenzie Richardson."

"I know exactly who you are."

"Yeah? Who might that be?"

"The woman who's going to be waking up next to Kenya for the foreseeable future."

"Do you know something I don't?" Simone's heart skittered at the thought, but she couldn't afford to get too far ahead of herself. Hearing Kenya might be interested in her was all well and good, but it didn't really count unless she heard it from Kenya.

"No, but I do know Kenya. Better than she knows herself sometimes. That's the mark of a good assistant. Now tell me what I can do to help."

Simone mixed an old-fashioned, wrote a note on a cocktail napkin, and handed both to Celia.

"You can start by giving her these."

❖

La dolce vita meant "the sweet life" in Italian. As Kenya sat on the sundeck listening to Mackenzie describe her idyllic if nomadic childhood—boarding school in Switzerland, summers in the Italian countryside or on the beaches of south Florida— she realized she was living a very sweet life indeed.

"You grew up in Tallahassee, didn't you?" Mackenzie asked.

"Wow. You've really done your homework. Did you have your assistant run a background check on me?"

"Nothing quite so drastic. Like I said last night, I make it a point to know something about all the beautiful women in my orbit. That includes you. What brought you here?"

"I received a scholarship to the University of Miami, fell in love with the area, and never left. My parents are Seminole fans, so they've never forgiven me for picking the Hurricanes, a fact they remind me of every time Florida State defeats them. You went to Harvard, didn't you?"

"Yes. My father's alma mater. I initially resisted the idea of following in his footsteps."

"Why?"

"For two reasons. I wanted to blaze my own path, and I wasn't looking forward to the brutal New England winters. Swallowing my pride turned out to be a wise move. My father's name might open doors for me, but all the things I learned in the Ivy League keeps me sitting at the table."

Mackenzie's father, Michael Richardson, was a Donald Trump-style real estate mogul with a similar financial profile but better hair. His investment had allowed Mackenzie to open her first restaurant, but she had made it a success all on her own. Eventually, one restaurant had become two. Now she owned properties from coast to coast.

"Have you thought about going international?" Kenya asked.

"As a matter of fact, I'm drawing up plans to open my first resort property, but I haven't decided on the ideal location. Mexico and the Caribbean are on the verge of becoming overdeveloped, but I think there's room for—" Mackenzie scowled as she looked over Kenya's shoulder. "Don't look now, but I think someone is trying to get your attention."

Kenya looked out the window and saw Celia waving at her like a flagman signaling a jumbo jet.

"Is that your friend?" Mackenzie asked. "If so, invite her up."

Kenya beckoned for Celia to join them. A few minutes later, Celia walked into the room with a drink in each hand. She gave Kenya the old-fashioned and kept the white wine spritzer for herself.

"I thought you might be thirsty after all that…talking," Celia said. She turned to Mackenzie. "I would have brought you one, too, but I only have two hands."

"That's quite all right," Mackenzie said. "I think I know the way to the bar."

Kenya provided introductions. "Mackenzie Richardson, I'd like you to meet Celia Torres. Celia and I work together."

"I actually work *for* her, not *with* her," Celia said, "though she's much too modest to point that out." She tossed a wink in Kenya's direction. "Drink up. Mackenzie and I can handle it from here."

Celia handed Kenya a cocktail napkin before she drew Mackenzie aside and began peppering her with questions about the restaurant business. When Kenya unfolded the napkin so she could place it under her drink to soak up the condensation dripping down the side of the glass, she saw something written on the thin paper.

"Question #2," the note read. "What would you consider a perfect day?"

Kenya folded the napkin inside out so the words were no longer visible. The note could only have come from Simone. The question was, had Simone asked Celia to do her bidding, or had Celia volunteered? Either way, Celia was thoroughly enjoying watching her squirm.

"I think you've had too many wine spritzers," she said after Mackenzie excused herself to check on the party preparations.

"Actually, I'm just getting started," Celia said. "This party is even more fun than I thought it would be. So what did Simone ask you?"

"Like you don't already know."

"Okay, I admit I may have sneaked a peek." Celia's eyes glittered with excitement. "What's your answer? What do you want me to tell her?"

"I thought you were on Mackenzie's side. Why did you switch allegiances?"

"I'm not on anyone's side. I just want you to be happy."

"And you think Simone can make me happy?"

"No, I don't."

"Then why are you passing messages for her like she's double-oh seven and you're auditioning to be a Bond girl?"

"Because it's fun. Look, I hate to get all Dr. Phil on you, but since this is my second glass of wine on an empty stomach, I will. No, I don't think Simone can make you happy. I don't think Mackenzie can, either. Because only you can make you happy, Kenya. Happiness begins and ends in here." Celia placed a hand over her heart. "No one else should be tasked with the responsibility of providing it for you. Sharing it? Yes. Providing it? No, that's on you. And to be frank, you've done a piss poor job of it the past few years. Yes, Ellis hurt you, but there are plenty of women out there who won't. Get off your ass and take a chance on one. Falling in love is like a trust exercise. At some point, you have to let go of your fears and trust the other person to catch you before you hit the ground."

Kenya felt her temper flare. She wasn't used to being upbraided, in her professional life or her personal one. Even though Celia meant well, her words had bite. Unfortunately, they also held a hint of truth. She had been holding back for so long she didn't know how to let go. Mackenzie had promised to take things slow. To let her set the pace. What more incentive did she need?

"As much as it pains me to admit it," she said, "you're right."

Celia blew out a sigh of relief. "So I'll still have a job come Monday?"

"For the moment. If you have one more glass of wine, though, we might need to reevaluate your employment status."

"Point taken. Now what do you want me to tell Simone?"

Even though Simone had managed to earn Celia's seal of approval, that wasn't enough to convince Kenya to start seeing her behind Mackenzie's back. That would feel too much like cheating and she knew from experience how devastating that sensation could be.

"Nothing," she said. "I'll tell her myself."

❖

"Uh oh," Simone said when she saw Kenya marching toward her like she was Oprah Winfrey preparing to give Whoopi Goldberg the infamous You Told Harpo to Beat Me speech in *The Color Purple*. "This can't be good."

"Good luck," Amanda said, beating a hasty retreat. "I'm going to return to my station before I get caught in the crossfire."

Kenya waited until Simone served a hurricane and a tequila sunrise to a couple of Mackenzie's friends before she brandished the note Simone had asked Celia to give her. "Are you soliciting my friends to help you now?"

"I'm willing to do whatever it takes to get your attention."

"You've got it. Now what?"

God, Kenya was sexy when she was angry, but Simone needed to chill her out before the smoke coming from her ears erupted into flame.

"Simple. Tell me what constitutes your perfect day."

Kenya crossed her arms across her chest as she tapped a sandal-clad foot. "I'm here to see Mackenzie, not you. You know that, right?"

"You've made it very clear how you feel," Simone said, keeping her voice steady like a professional negotiator in the middle of a crisis, "but you also promised to answer my questions. *All* of my questions."

"What do you expect to accomplish?"

"I'm not expecting anything, but I am hoping to get to know you."

"That's all?" Kenya asked skeptically.

"No strings, remember?" Simone spread her arms to indicate she didn't have a hidden agenda. "Now tell me. What's your perfect day?"

Kenya still looked dubious, but she dutifully answered the question. "It would begin with breakfast in bed and end with a moonlit stroll on the beach."

"And in between?"

Kenya unfolded her arms as her voice took on a dreamlike tone. "I would shut off my phone, tune out the world, and get lost in the woman I love."

"I feel you."

Simone wanted to live the fantasy Kenya had just described. She wanted to wake up next to the woman she loved, spoil her madly, and spend an entire day showing her just how much she valued her. She wanted to live the life love songs and romance novels were written about. If only for twenty-four hours.

"What would you do on your ideal day?" Kenya asked, seeming to warm to the subject.

"I would spend it making music and making love. Both come from the same source of inspiration. When done right, it's impossible to tell them apart."

Kenya's expression softened. "Are you a musician or simply a music lover?"

"Both. I play drums, guitar, and piano. And given sufficient time, I could name you every single Prince ever released, including the B-sides. Which brings me to question number three. When was the last time you sang to yourself or someone else?"

"I sing to myself in the shower every morning," Kenya said with a slightly embarrassed laugh, "but subjecting my lack of vocal skills on an unsuspecting victim would be tantamount to assault."

"A little Auto-Tune and you'll be fine. Just ask Britney Spears or that blonde who used to be on *Real Housewives of Atlanta.*"

Kenya's eyes widened ever so slightly. "You watch that show?"

"I know it's not *Masterpiece Theater*, but I never miss an episode." Simone figured the admission might cost her points with Kenya. Reality television was probably too lowbrow for her sophisticated tastes.

"Neither do I. I'm glued to my TV every Sunday night to see what they'll do or say next. Who's your favorite cast member? If you say the wrong one, I will throw what's left of my drink in your face."

"Don't. That would be alcohol abuse of the highest order." Simone held up her hands to prevent such a calamity from occurring. "I like Kandi. She's the only one who keeps it real every week and doesn't seem to be playing a part. Plus I love the songs she and her group sang back in the day."

"I like her, too. I especially like the fact she's built an empire based on more than just music. She has her hands in everything from songwriting to Internet talk shows to clothing stores to sex toys."

"I've tried out a few products from her line and I can truly say I'm a satisfied customer."

"I'll take your word for it."

"What other shows do you like?"

"Thursday is my favorite night of the week."

"Shonda Rhimes night, right?"

Kenya nodded. *"Scandal* sandwiched between *Grey's Anatomy* and *How to Get Away with Murder.* The other networks might beg to differ, but that's what I call must-see TV. *Grey's* is a little long in the tooth but still capable of delivering an emotional punch, especially when Christina left and Derek died. The other two shows are just one OMG moment after another. I can't get enough."

Simone could feel Kenya start to relax and open up. To trust her. She wanted to continue the conversation—to dig deeper and see what else they might have in common—but Mackenzie chose that moment to address the crowd.

"Ladies and gentlemen," Mackenzie said into a cordless microphone, "I would like to welcome you aboard and thank you for agreeing to spend the afternoon with me and my crew. The agenda for today is simple. Captain Mendoza is going to take us for a spin around the harbor. Once we're away from the marina, we'll crank up the music and have a little fun. Does that sound good?"

Naturally, the crowd whooped and raised their glasses in agreement. Whether you had seven figures in your bank account or one, free booze was free booze.

"Before we raise anchor," Mackenzie continued, "I would like to ask a very important question." She held her hand over her eyes to shield them from the rays of the sun. "Kenya Davis, I know you're out there somewhere. Where are you?"

Beside Simone, Kenya nearly choked on her drink but quickly regained her composure and raised her hand as the guests craned their heads in her direction. "I'm right here."

"While I have everyone's attention, I'm going to ask you a very important question." Mackenzie placed a hand over her heart in a gesture of sincerity. "Will you be my partner?"

A few people gasped and, for one surreal moment, Simone thought she was witnessing a marriage proposal. Then she reminded herself Mackenzie hadn't flashed a ring or gotten down on bended knee, two vital prerequisites for popping the question.

Kenya looked none too happy about being put on the spot. "As I said before, I'm not a ballroom dancer."

"You don't have to be," Mackenzie said. "I'll teach you everything you need to know. Just say yes. I promise you won't regret it."

Simone finally copped to the fact Mackenzie was asking Kenya to partner up with her in the dance contest her favorite charity was putting on, not asking Kenya to marry her. She hoped Kenya would say no just to show Mackenzie she couldn't always get what she wanted. But despite her apparent misgivings, Kenya relented.

"Okay, I'll do it."

"Excellent," Mackenzie said over a loud round of applause. "And that brings me to the other reason we're here today. Safe Space is a wonderful organization that does amazing things for our community. Tickets for their upcoming fundraising event will be on sale today. If you can't attend the event, please make a donation. The individuals at Safe Space—and the kids they serve—can use all the help they can get. Thank you for coming."

Mackenzie handed the microphone to Crystal and bounded over to Simone and Kenya through a sea of well-wishers.

"What would you have done if I'd said no?" Kenya asked.

Mackenzie grinned. "Picked my face off the floor and kept begging until you said yes. Thank you for not forcing me to grovel in front of fifty of my nearest and dearest friends."

"You're not off the hook yet. You have to promise me something."

"Name it."

"The next time you ask me to be your partner—if there is a next time—promise me you'll do it in a much more intimate setting."

Mackenzie drew a cross over her heart. "I promise. How much trouble am I in?"

"Let's just say it's going to cost you a lot more than a dozen roses."

Mackenzie squeezed Kenya's hand. "I'm good for it. Now dance with me. I could use the practice."

"You? I thought you were the expert."

"I've never been ballroom dancing in my life. This will be a first for both of us." Mackenzie twirled Kenya in a circle as she drew her away. "The first of what I hope will be many shared experiences."

On the dance floor, Kenya swayed in Mackenzie's arms as Crystal played something slow and sensual. And Simone could only stand on the sidelines as she watched Kenya begin to fall in love.

CHAPTER FOUR

On Monday morning, Kenya was swamped with work. She needed to schedule the next round of employee training, review a paid intern's workers' compensation claim that seemed more like a desperate grab for much-needed cash than a legitimate charge, and sift through the sixty-plus résumés she had received in response to the online posting for the company's open position in the graphic design department. Memories of the weekend, however, left her unable to concentrate.

From the beginning, Mackenzie had gone out of her way to make her feel comfortable. Appreciated. Desired. At the same time, Mackenzie hadn't shied away from keeping her on her toes. Keeping her guessing. Kenya was still trying to decide if the surprise tactic Mackenzie had used to get her to team up with her for the Safe Space dance competition was charming, manipulative, or both. She would have probably said yes the next time Mackenzie asked, but she wished she hadn't had to make a decision with dozens of strangers watching her mull it over. She had agreed partly because she didn't want to make Mackenzie look bad in front of her guests but mostly because she was thrilled by the idea of spending the next month in almost constant contact with her. She was still terrified by the prospect of channeling her inner Ginger Rogers, but at least she wouldn't be going it alone. Mackenzie would be just as lost.

"What have I gotten myself into?" she asked herself.

Their first practice session was scheduled for tonight, when she and Mackenzie would meet with a choreographer to go over their routine. Afterward, they planned to grab dinner. They hadn't decided where yet, but Kenya was fine with whatever was closest to the dance studio where they were meeting for rehearsal. It wasn't the food she cared about but getting to know Mackenzie. She kept telling herself it wasn't a date so she wouldn't psych herself out. Deep down, however, she knew the meal represented far more than a casual get-together. It was the resumption of the life she had put on hold while she gave herself time to heal from the wounds Ellis's infidelity had inflicted. Not only was she moving on, she was doing it with Mackenzie-flipping-Richardson.

Was this real? Were she and Mackenzie actually becoming a thing? The local gossip columnists seemed to think so. Kenya had woken up on Sunday morning to see her face splashed on the inside pages of several newspapers, reporters referring to her and Mackenzie as the new It couple around town. Someone had even coined a nickname for them. Just as Jennifer Lopez and Ben Affleck had morphed into Bennifer and Brad Pitt and Angelina Jolie had become Brangelina, she and Mackenzie were now known as Mackenya. The attention felt inappropriate, but asking for a retraction wasn't worth the effort. No matter what she said or did, people were going to believe what they chose to believe. It was the way of the world. Especially when it came to gossip. Besides, there were worse things to be called than Mackenzie's latest bed warmer—even if the designation was not only inaccurate but premature.

Celia knocked on Kenya's office door and let herself in. "These flowers just arrived for you."

Kenya looked up, expecting to see Celia brandishing the dozen roses Mackenzie had said she'd ordered to make up for breaking their date Friday night. Instead, Celia was carrying a potted plant. A beautiful pale blue hydrangea in a container designed to look like a vintage watering can.

"I bet I know who this is from," Celia said in a singsong voice as she placed the vase on the corner of Kenya's desk.

"Why? Did you read the card?"

"No, I didn't have time to steam it open." Celia plucked the card from its plastic holder and handed it to Kenya. "I'll let you do the honors this time."

Kenya reached for a letter opener. "Cut flowers die so quickly," she said as she regarded the thriving plant. "It was thoughtful of Mackenzie to give me flowers I won't have to throw out after only a few days. I can think of her every time I look at them."

Except the flowers weren't from Mackenzie. The note inside the tiny envelope she sliced into was from Simone. It said, *Question #4: If you could live to be a hundred and keep either the mind or body of a thirty-year-old for the last seventy years of your life, which would you want?*

"Is something wrong?" Celia asked with a concerned frown.

Kenya showed her the note. "Did you put her up to this?"

"I didn't have to. She's doing just fine on her own." Celia took a seat in one of the two chairs angled in front of Kenya's desk. "Have you called Bridget yet?"

"No."

"Why not? You know how much she'd love to hear all the gory details."

"I haven't called her because, one, she's on vacation and, two, there's nothing to tell. With a six-hour time difference between Miami and Maui, the two of us would end up playing phone tag rather than conversing anyway. We can play catch-up when she gets back."

Kenya had been best friends with Bridget Weaver since their days at the University of Miami, when an attempted make-out session at a freshman mixer had devolved into a fit of giggles and a bond that had only strengthened over time. Kenya shared everything with Bridget and vice versa, but she couldn't share this. Not until she knew what *this* was.

She was looking forward to spending time with Mackenzie, but she was starting to look forward to receiving Simone's questions, too. To seeing what Simone would come up with next. Something humorous or deadly serious, but always thought provoking. She still didn't see the point of the whole exercise, but did it really matter? She didn't have to know the end game to enjoy the process. And if she made a new friend along the way? Even better.

She liked the way Simone's mind worked. Nimble, sharp, and quick to come up with a witty retort. And her passion for music was almost palpable. Her whole body thrummed with excitement when she talked about her favorite artists. The only thing Kenya had ever been as passionate about was carving out a successful career. Now that she'd made it to the top of the heap, what was left to get her juices flowing? Love? Romance? Until Friday night, she thought those things were meant for other people. Now, perhaps, she'd been granted a second chance to find both.

"Are you going to call her or what?" Celia asked.

"Who?" Kenya blushed, hoping she hadn't missed out on a work-related question while she was daydreaming about her personal life.

"Simone, of course. To thank her for the flowers."

"I would, but I don't have her number."

"I do."

"Since when?"

"Since none of your business." Celia jotted what looked like a cell phone number on a Post-It note. "Call her and give her an answer. Because I'm already primed to hear question number five."

"You and me both."

Kenya felt an unexpected surge of anticipation as she reached for her phone. Like she was eschewing a strict diet in order to allow herself a decadent treat. If Simone was so bad for her, why did being around her feel so right?

❖

For Simone, the worst part of working nights was sleeping during the day. It messed with her circadian rhythms something fierce. So when she had a day off like today, she ended up yawning at noon and feeling wide-awake at midnight. She walked to the coffee shop a few blocks from her apartment to get a double shot of espresso. If an extra potent infusion of caffeine couldn't perk her up, nothing could. She added a turkey sandwich to her order to make sure her hands weren't shaking by the time she took the last sip. Otherwise, she wouldn't be able to read the music she hoped to write while she was out. She was close to finding the right sound for Reagan—something street, yet supple and sexy like her voice—but she needed to give the demo Dre had given her a few more listens first.

She took a seat in her favorite booth and put in her earbuds so she could focus on Reagan's vocals and tune out the other customers' conversations, but her phone rang before she could press Play. She didn't recognize the number printed on the display. She reflexively reached for the Decline button, but instinct told her to hold off.

"This is Simone," she said after she pressed Accept.

"Simone, hello. It's me, Kenya."

Simone's stomach did a somersault when she heard Kenya's voice. She hadn't expected to hear from her so soon—if at all. "This is an unexpected surprise. Did you get my flowers?"

"I did."

Simone pushed her steaming coffee aside. She didn't need it now. The jolt of adrenaline she had received from hearing her name come out of Kenya's mouth had managed to banish her lethargy. "So what's your answer?"

"If I could live to be a hundred and keep the mind or body of a thirty-year-old for the last seventy years of my life, I would choose to keep the body, but not for the reasons you might think. It's not a matter of vanity but maturity."

"How do you mean?"

"Even though it was only six years ago, I remember how much growing up I still had to do when I was thirty. I was just starting to find myself. I thought I knew it all, but I quickly realized I still had a lot to learn. I still do. I wouldn't want to be an overgrown adolescent for the rest of my life. I would want the wisdom that comes with age—without the physical ailments that normally accompany it. It would be the best of both worlds."

"In other words, you're vain."

"That's not what I said."

"But it's what you meant isn't it?"

"Well, maybe a little bit." Kenya laughed at being called out. "What about you? Which would you choose?"

"The mind. I'm not looking forward to my first gray hair or my first set of wrinkles," Simone admitted, "but I would want to stay as sharp as I am now without having to worry about senior moments."

"Sounds reasonable. The flowers are beautiful, by the way. Unnecessary, but beautiful."

"Why unnecessary? I had to get a message to you somehow, didn't I?" Even though Kenya had agreed to answer her questions, she hadn't given her any contact information. Then Celia had come along. She hadn't offered to divulge Kenya's private information, but at least she had agreed to take Simone's "just in case." In a battle with so much at stake, it was good to have an ally. Especially one on the inside.

"Try email. It works faster and it's less expensive. Now that you have my number, you could also text me."

Simone reminded herself to add Kenya to her list of contacts as soon as they ended their call. "What would Mackenzie say if she knew I had your number?"

"She has no reason to have cause for concern."

"She's half-Italian. She might be the jealous type. If I were her, I wouldn't want another woman talking to my girl behind my back."

"I'm not her girl, and you are I are just friends, right? No strings. Isn't that what you said?"

"Yes." *But I'm not so sure it's what I meant.* Simone couldn't deny her attraction to Kenya, but could she control it? Could she settle for being her friend instead of her lover? The question wasn't on her list, but she knew she would have to answer it sooner or later. "Does this mean I can call you sometime?"

"I don't see any other way to get through the rest of your list. Unless, of course, I become a barfly and stop by Azure every night so you can ply me with drinks while you pepper me with questions."

Simone liked the idea of Kenya becoming a regular. Of seeing her walk into Azure at her preferred time and having her drink waiting for her when she arrived. "I don't see a problem with that."

"But I do."

"Because of Mackenzie?"

"No, because of me," Kenya said, suddenly serious. "You say you understand when I tell you it would never work out between us, but I don't think you do. I think you're hoping if you bide your time long enough, I might see the light. I don't want to hurt you or lead you on, Simone."

"I'm a big girl. I know what I'm doing. If you want to be with Mackenzie, fine. I'm not trying to stand in your way. I just want to ask you some questions."

And hope against hope that the answer to the last one—whatever it might be—is yes.

❖

Kenya watched choreographer and dance instructor Anton Simms demonstrate the various types of the tango. Even though he called each one out before he performed it—from Argentine to American to Finnish to contact to ballroom to *nuevo*—she couldn't tell them apart. In some versions, Anton and his partner kept space between them at all times. In other versions, they stood so close they were practically sharing the same pair of underwear.

No wonder tango is known as the dance of love.

"The style I'm going to teach you is queer tango," Anton said. "It's especially popular in the gay community since the rules allow dancers to break free from heteronormative standards. In queer tango, the decision of who will lead and who will follow isn't based on gender. Which of you wants to lead?"

Kenya was about to suggest they flip a coin, but Mackenzie volunteered before she could.

"I'll do it."

"Open or closed embrace?" Anton asked. "In the open position, you'd have constant contact from your chest to your pelvis. In the closed position, you'd stand slightly apart. Beginners usually prefer the closed embrace because it's not as intimate. Which would you like?"

Mackenzie turned to her. "I'm not afraid of a little intimacy. Are you?"

Kenya felt the heat from the fire in Mackenzie's eyes. She shook her head, not trusting herself to speak.

"Then it's settled," Anton said. "Val and I will demonstrate the routine I've choreographed for you, then we'll start teaching you the steps."

He nodded toward one of his assistants, who pressed Play on a boom box resting on the polished hardwood floor. Acoustic guitar-driven music with a staccato rhythm filled the room. Anton and Val moved as one, their facial expressions as passionate as the movement of their limbs. Kenya and Mackenzie applauded wildly when they were done.

"Your turn." Anton beckoned them to move forward.

"Do you really expect us to do that?" Kenya asked.

"Not tonight, no. Tonight, we'll focus on the basics—framing and footwork. We'll slowly add in additional elements over the coming weeks. By the time the contest rolls around, you'll be experts."

"I doubt that," Kenya said.

"It's only eight steps repeated over and over with a few theatrical flourishes thrown in," Mackenzie said with a shrug. "How hard can that be?"

Harder than Anton and Val had made it look.

Kenya positioned her arms the way she had seen Val do when he was demonstrating her portion of the dance, but she must have done it wrong because he started correcting her right away.

"Lift your head, hold your elbows higher, and move closer. Tango is about passion, desire, and lust. Act like you like her. Like you can't live without her."

He positioned Kenya and Mackenzie so their bodies touched up and down. Their breasts, stomachs, and pelvises pressed against one another's. When Mackenzie slid a hand down her back and pulled her even closer, Kenya thought she might spontaneously combust.

So much for acting.

"Aren't you glad you said yes?" Mackenzie asked.

Kenya felt goose bumps form as Mackenzie's breath kissed her skin. Her heart was beating out of her chest, and she wondered if Mackenzie could feel it. She wanted to kiss her. To run her hands over the hard nipples and firm breasts pressing against hers. Mackenzie ground their hips together, exerting exquisite pressure on her rapidly swelling clit. Kenya bit back a moan and tried to listen to Anton's and Val's instructions, but she was lost. Lost in the moment. Lost in Mackenzie. Before she knew it, the two-hour rehearsal was over and Anton was congratulating them for a good first session, but she couldn't remember a single thing she had just been taught. She could only remember how incredible it had felt to be in Mackenzie's arms.

"Let's get out of here," Mackenzie said.

Kenya couldn't remember the last time she had received such a tempting offer.

Try never.

"Even though we have our pick of restaurants in this area," Mackenzie said, "I thought we could go to my place for dinner. My chef can prepare us something while we're soaking our sore muscles in the hot tub."

Kenya imagined sinking into bubbling water up to her neck while she and Mackenzie sipped champagne and waited to dine on a five-course meal prepared by a private chef, but there was one small problem. "I brought a change of clothes, but I didn't bring a swimsuit."

"You won't need one. You can borrow one of mine. But if you ask me, you'd look even better wearing nothing at all."

Mackenzie's voice was husky with desire. Kenya had asked for and received permission from her to take it slow. But now all she wanted to do was speed up. She wanted to feel Mackenzie's hands on her bare skin. She wanted to touch Mackenzie's in return. She wanted to take the lessons she had learned tonight and put them to use. She wanted to take Mackenzie to bed and show her she didn't always have to take the lead. She wanted to show her how good it could feel to follow. She wanted to trace the curves and planes of her body and commit every inch to memory so when she closed her eyes, her mind would be able to reproduce the image. And she wanted to taste her. God, how she wanted to taste her. She wanted to drink from her until she'd had her fill, then go back for more.

But not tonight. The next time she made love with someone, she wanted it to be about more than fulfilling a need. She wanted it to be about more than simple physical release. She wanted it to mean something. She wanted to feel the rush of emotion that occurred when two people of like minds came together. More than anything else, she wanted it to happen with someone she loved, not someone she met three days ago. Except Mackenzie was starting to feel like both.

"Let's go," she said. "I'm starving."

Chapter Five

S imone usually powered off her cell phone and stashed it in her locker before the start of each shift. Not by choice, though. During her last employee evaluation, Jolie Winters, her manager, had asked her to focus on her customers while she was on the clock instead of posing for selfies with her coworkers. Tonight, however, she decided to break the rules. After she clocked in, she slipped her cell into her pocket instead of storing it away.

Two days had passed since she and Kenya had talked. She had texted Kenya the fifth question this afternoon. She hadn't thought the question was that difficult and had expected an immediate reply. Almost five hours later, she was still waiting for a response. Was Kenya mulling the question over, was she ignoring her, or was she too busy being wined and dined by Mackenzie to check her messages?

"Got a hot date?" Amanda asked after Simone checked her phone for the third time in the last ten minutes.

"I wish."

She put her phone in her pocket and resolved not to take it out again until the end of her shift. Or maybe not for another hour. Whichever came first. She made a Midori sour for a corset-clad femme clearly on the hunt for companionship for the night and wished her good luck as she slid the drink toward her.

The femme licked her MAC-covered lips and adjusted the fit of her corset so her full breasts rode even higher. "In this outfit, I won't need luck."

She walked away on heels so high they made Simone's feet hurt just looking at them. Based on the number of heads that craned in her direction as she walked past them, the femme wouldn't lack for volunteers to rub away the ache. Simone was tempted to fight for a place in the growing line, but her phone vibrated as she prepared a tray of pineapple margaritas for a group of tourists staying at the spa hotel down the street. She smiled when she saw Kenya's name on the screen.

"Can you cover for me, Amanda?" she asked, handing the tray of drinks to one of the servers. "I've got to take this call."

"You got it."

"Thanks, buddy. Text me if you start to get slammed."

Amanda kept mixing drinks without missing a beat. Simone didn't expect Amanda to call for help. The busier it got, the more focused Amanda became. It was only when the crowds started to thin that her mind began to wander. That's when the trouble began. When she started looking for new, creative ways to have fun instead of doing her job. More often than not, Simone was right there with her. Playing drinking games, cracking jokes, flirting with customers. Whatever it took to make the shift go faster—and life more enjoyable.

Simone answered her phone before the call went to voice mail and headed to the alley out back so she could talk someplace quiet. Quiet being a relative term. The only place to find peace in rowdy South Beach was inside a sensory deprivation chamber. And she was fresh out of those.

"Sorry it took me so long to get back to you," Kenya said, "but I had a meeting that ran long, then I had a two-hour practice session that turned into three. I'm just getting home. I was about to nuke myself something to eat and head to bed when I saw your message."

Simone checked her watch. "It's after nine. You haven't had dinner yet?"

"Mackenzie invited me to her place, but I begged off."

"Getting bored already?" Simone asked hopefully.

"No, but her personal chef insists on turning every meal into an event. He says food should be experienced, not simply consumed. Tonight, I was too wiped to make it through the appetizer, let alone all the way to dessert."

"Is Mackenzie there with you?" Mackenzie was still putting in as much face time at Azure as ever. Simone hadn't realized she and Kenya were spending so much time together, which meant they were becoming even more serious than they had been on *La Dolce Vita* over the weekend.

"No. She said she was going to head home and crash, too. Anton, our choreographer, really put us through the wringer tonight. We need it. The competition's a little over three weeks away and we're nowhere near ready."

"You shouldn't push yourself so hard. Do you want to win that bad? I mean, it's all for charity, isn't it?"

"That's why I'm taking it so seriously. I don't care if Mackenzie and I come in first or last. I just don't want to look like a klutz while we're doing it. Especially for such a worthy cause."

"I might not know a mambo from a merengue, but I bet you'll be great."

"Thanks." Kenya sounded genuinely touched. "I appreciate that."

"Don't mention it." Simone pushed herself off the wall before she got too comfortable. "I have to get back to work and you need to get some sleep, so I won't keep you long. What's your answer to question number five?"

Kenya paraphrased the question Simone had posed earlier. "Before I make a phone call, do I rehearse what I'm going to say? Short answer? It depends on who I'm calling. If I'm conducting a job interview, I follow a script and ad-lib as needed. If I'm talking to someone I care about, I speak from the heart."

"And when you're talking to me?" Simone was curious about where she stood on the spectrum.

"With you, I never know what to expect so I try to prepare for every possible eventuality."

"I'll take that as a compliment." Kenya chuckled, her voice as warm as the feeling that flowed through Simone's body when she heard the sound. "Now go to bed before you fall asleep standing up."

"I intend to. Good night."

A limo pulled into the mouth of the alley as Simone ended the call. She paused, waiting to see if a VIP needed to be escorted inside without being mobbed by the crush of people outside the front door. She didn't recognize the glammed-up redhead in the tight bandage dress and sky-high designer heels who exited the limo first. She did, however, recognize Mackenzie, wearing a bespoke pinstriped suit and a smug, just-got-fucked expression.

Simone snapped a picture with her phone while Mackenzie and the glamazon played an action-packed round of tonsil hockey.

"So much for going home and crashing."

Mackenzie and the glamazon took separate entrances so they wouldn't be seen together. Simone opened her text messages so she could forward the photo she had just taken to Kenya, but she hesitated before initiating the upload.

Even with photographic evidence, would Kenya believe Mackenzie was cheating on her so soon? Kenya was so sprung, Mackenzie could probably tell her the sky was green and she would believe her. For a skilled player like Mackenzie, explaining away the photograph would be child's play. Because Kenya would most likely choose to believe her, not her own eyes.

Simone hated to see Kenya being played for a fool, especially by someone who was so good at it, but she had never inserted herself in Mackenzie's romantic entanglements before and she wasn't going to start now. No matter how much she wanted to.

She deleted the message, turned off her phone, and reluctantly returned to work.

If she tried to point out Mackenzie's shortcomings, Kenya would probably think it was just a case of her airing sour grapes. In order to believe the truth, Kenya needed to discover it on her own. The only thing Simone needed to do was make sure she remained the one thing Mackenzie wasn't: honest.

❖

Bridget returned from Maui sporting a deep tan and an ear-to-ear grin. Thanks to scheduling issues, she and Avery had been forced to take their honeymoon before they said, "I do."

"It doesn't take a rocket scientist to know what you and Avery were doing when you weren't lounging by the pool," Kenya said when she and Bridget met for brunch on Saturday.

"That's what vacation in paradise is all about, isn't it? Eating too much, drinking too much, getting too much sun, and having way too much sex. On second thought, strike the last part. There's no such thing as too much sex. Too little, perhaps, but not too much."

"If you say so."

"Would you like something to drink?" the waiter asked.

"A pitcher of mimosas," Bridget said. "And keep them coming."

Kenya spread her napkin in her lap as she perused the menu. "Are we celebrating something?"

"Yes, the merciful end to your dry spell. A little bird told me you're seeing someone. To be specific, Mackenzie Richardson."

Kenya rolled her eyes, suddenly painfully aware of why Bridget had asked her to meet her today. "Is that little bird named Celia?"

Bridget flashed a smile as wide—and as inscrutable—as the Cheshire cat's. "A good reporter never reveals her sources."

"You're an editor, not a reporter," Kenya pointed out. "You spend your days whipping other people's words into shape, not crafting your own."

"Same difference. Now tell me about you and Mackenzie. On second thought, don't. I already know all about her. Tell me about the hot bartender you're seeing on the side."

"I'm not seeing anyone on the—" Kenya held her head in her hands. "Remind me to fire Celia after we're done here."

"Don't blame her. She was just trying to keep me in the loop after my so-called best friend cut me out of it."

"Stop being so dramatic."

"Fine. Now tell me what I've missed."

While they dined on eggs Benedict and stuffed French toast, Kenya told Bridget about the events of the past week. Everything from her panic attack outside Azure before the speed dating event to the White Party on Mackenzie's yacht to her nightly dance lessons to her agreement to answer Simone's list of questions.

"Have you slept with Mackenzie yet?"

Kenya nearly did a spit take. Bridget never hesitated to ask in-your-face questions, but there was a time and place for everything. This was neither. "No, I haven't."

"That has to be some kind of record for her. Her relationships typically have the average life-span of a fruit fly."

Kenya pushed her empty plate away from her. "That's comforting."

Bridget lifted her broad shoulders and slowly let them fall. "I'm not telling you anything you don't already know is true. We read the same gossip columns, remember? I know because we've compared notes more than once. What about the hot bartender?" she asked after she refilled their glasses. "Are you dating her, too, or is that wishful thinking on Celia's part?"

Kenya took a sip of her fresh drink. "Simone and I are friends."

"In the way you and I are friends or the way Romeo and Juliet were friends?"

"Thank you for the unexpected literary reference, but Simone and I are not having an epic romance, doomed or otherwise."

"What are you having?"

"An extended conversation."

"So that's what the kids are calling it these days. When do I get to meet her?"

"Mackenzie?"

Bridget shook her head. "Been there, done that. I met her at a business luncheon the paper sent me to when no one else was willing or able to attend."

"What did you think?" Kenya asked, anxious to hear Bridget's take on a woman she thought she could very easily fall for. If she hadn't already.

Bridget wagged her hand from side to side. "Meh."

Kenya felt a prickle of concern. Bridget was an excellent judge of character, and Kenya valued her opinion. "What do you mean by that?"

"She's drop-dead gorgeous, but I found her a bit oily. She reminded me of a car salesman. Too focused on the sale at the expense of the experience. When our conversation ended, I checked my wallet to make sure it was still there." Bridget grimaced as if she'd gone too far. "But that was years ago. She might have changed since then. For your sake, I hope so."

"Why for my sake?" Kenya resented the implication she was somehow fragile and in need of protection. Vulnerable, yes. She would readily admit to that. But fragile? Not by a long shot.

"Your relationship with Ellis had other issues," Bridget said, "but you ended it for the most part because she cheated on you. Now you're dating someone with a reputation for being a serial philanderer. Surely you see the irony."

"I do. Which is why I'm not rushing into anything. Mackenzie is beautiful and sexy and charming, but I'm not going to sleep with her unless it feels right. Until I feel I can trust her."

"Good. Because I don't want to end up in prison for going medieval on her ass. Now when do I get to meet Simone? I know," Bridget said before Kenya could respond. "You, Celia, and I should go to Azure for drinks tonight. It's been forever since the three of us had a girls' night out."

"Celia and I had one last week. Sorry you missed it."

"On a one-hundred-fifty-foot yacht, no less. Don't rub it in."

"I'll call Celia to see if she's free tonight, but I doubt she'll be able to talk Juan into watching the kids two weeks in a row."

"She already did. And I've already cleared it with my other half, too, so Celia and I are all set. We're just waiting on you."

"What if I have plans?"

"Even if you did, Celia and I would go without you."

"I'm sure you would." Kenya tossed her napkin on the table and signaled for the waiter to bring the check. "In that case, count me in. I don't want you and Celia roaming around Miami without a chaperone."

"We'll try not to embarrass you too much."

"Uh huh. I'll believe that when I see it."

❖

Simone was intrigued when Kenya, Celia, and a tall, imposing woman with a close-cropped Afro and the relaxed look of someone who had recently spent time basking in the tropical sun walked into Azure a little before nine. After they came over to the bar, the woman with the fresh tan—Kenya introduced her as Bridget something or other—didn't ask Simone to guess her favorite drink (Scotch on the rocks), but she did proceed to spend the next thirty minutes asking her practically everything else. Before long, Simone started to feel like she was being given the third degree.

This must be the best friend Celia warned me about.

She had already been asked to confirm she was gainfully employed, didn't have a criminal record, and wasn't "a drug-addled whack job." What was next? Was Bridget planning to throw an arm around her shoulders and ask her to state her intentions, or take her out to the proverbial woodshed and kick her ass?

"That's enough, Bridge," Kenya said at length. "Give her a break. She's got work to do."

"I suppose I have what I need," Bridget said before adding a pointed, "for now."

"I'll buy us another round," Kenya said. "Why don't you and Celia find a table?"

"A woman after my own heart. Just don't tell Avery I said that." Bridget stuck out her hand. "Nice to meet you, Simone."

"Likewise." Simone waited until Celia and Bridget were out of earshot before she turned to Kenya and asked, "Is she always like that?"

"Only when she likes someone."

Simone started preparing a fresh round of drinks. "If that was her demonstrating how much she likes me, I'd hate to see what she'd do if she detested me."

"Yes, you would. Believe me, it's not pretty."

"Has she always been so protective?"

"Yes. Which is what makes her such a good friend. Do you have any friends like that?"

"Yes, but they're the kind who would rather defend my honor with their fists rather than their wits."

"Bridget went through a phase like that. Thankfully, she grew out of it."

Simone hoped the comment wasn't meant to be a subtle reminder she still had some growing up to do. She was twenty-eight, not twelve. She added the garnishes to Kenya's old-fashioned and reached for a bottle of white wine to make Celia's spritzer.

Kenya was wearing a low-cut little black dress and strappy heels that made her legs look even lovelier and longer than usual. A gold choker, elegant and understated, matched the small hoop earrings dangling from her earlobes. She looked not only sexy but classy, too. The combination left Simone feeling lightheaded.

"This is as good a time as any for question six, don't you think?" she asked.

"Hit me."

Kenya took a seat at the bar and crossed her legs, giving Simone a peek at her shapely thighs. Simone felt her mouth fall open like the detectives interrogating Sharon Stone in *Basic Instinct*. Though her view wasn't as R-rated as the one Michael Douglas's character had enjoyed in the movie, it was just as memorable.

"Would you like to be famous?" she asked when she finally recovered her ability to speak. "If so, for what?"

Kenya raised her right hand as if swearing on the Bible. "I can unequivocally say I have no desire whatsoever to be a household name."

"Andy Warhol once said everyone is destined for fifteen minutes of fame. Don't you want your share?"

Kenya shook her head emphatically. "I want to be respected, not recognized."

"Then why are you dating someone as famous or infamous or whatever you want to call it as Mackenzie?"

Kenya's answer was as simple as her accessories. "Because I like her."

"I like you, too," Mackenzie said as she slipped her arms around Kenya's waist and planted a kiss on her cheek. Kenya closed her eyes and leaned into Mackenzie's embrace.

Simone had been so focused on Kenya she hadn't seen Mackenzie approach. Now she couldn't turn away. Kenya looked so peaceful in Mackenzie's arms. She looked like she felt she belonged there. Yet she deserved so much more than

Mackenzie could give her. She deserved more than someone who could buy her fancy things and take her on exotic trips but couldn't be faithful to her. She deserved someone who would respect her and treat her right. Mackenzie wasn't that kind of person. Simone was. But Kenya wasn't willing to even consider the idea, let alone accept it.

"Are you here alone?" Mackenzie asked.

Kenya spun on her bar stool. "No, I'm here with friends." She pointed out Celia and Bridget, who waved from the table they had claimed across the room.

"Why didn't you tell me you were coming? I would have reserved you a booth in the VIP section."

"We aren't going to be here that long," Kenya said. "We only popped in for a quick drink."

Mackenzie snapped her fingers the way she always did when she was trying to get someone's attention. The demeaning habit made Simone and her fellow employees feel like they were pets being reprimanded, though none of them had been able to convince Mackenzie to see it that way. "Simone, whatever they're drinking is on the house. As a matter of fact, send over a bottle of Dom with my compliments."

"You got it, boss." Simone grabbed a bottle of Dom Perignon and a bucket of ice.

"I recognize Celia," Mackenzie said, peering at Kenya's friends. "Who's the woman with her?"

"Bridget Weaver," Kenya said with a frown. "She said she met you at a business luncheon a few years ago. Don't you remember?"

"No," Mackenzie said hesitantly. She looked taken aback. Like she had been caught in a lie. Before Simone had a chance to gloat, Mackenzie laughed and said, "But I meet so many people it's hard to keep track."

Unless you're trying to sleep with them, Simone thought. Then you have a mind like a steel trap.

"Would you like for Bridget and me to get reacquainted," Mackenzie asked, "or am I your dirty little secret?"

Simone couldn't stand to see Kenya being manipulated, but what could she do? "Here are your drinks. Would you like me to carry them to the table for you?"

"I can take care of Kenya," Mackenzie said. "You just keep doing what I'm paying you to do."

Simone clenched her teeth, having been not-so-politely put in her place. Did Mackenzie know she was interested in Kenya, or was she trying to make herself look big by belittling someone else?

I guess money can buy everything but class.

❖

Mackenzie picked up the tray of drinks and motioned for Kenya to precede her. "Lead the way. I've got this."

As Kenya ran point through the growing crowd, she tried to figure out why Mackenzie had claimed not to know Bridget when Bridget was certain they had met. Kenya didn't know which one to believe, but why would either have reason to lie?

Mackenzie wasn't exaggerating when she said she met a lot of people. People vied for her attention all the time. For business and for pleasure. But Bridget, a six-foot African-American woman with a crew cut, left a distinctive impression which made her hard to forget. The nerves Kenya had felt about having Bridget meet Simone paled in comparison to the ones she felt now. According to Bridget, her first meeting with Mackenzie had been inauspicious. What if tonight's was even less so? If this encounter was anything like the last one, it might make future get-togethers awkward at best.

Kenya mentally chided herself for jumping too far ahead. She and Mackenzie were dating, not engaged to be married. There was still time to work things through before they got in too deep.

Mackenzie placed the drinks on the table, kissed the back of Celia's hand, and reached to shake Bridget's. "Kenya tells me you and I have met, but for the life of me, I can't remember where. Please refresh my memory."

Bridget popped the cork on the bottle of champagne and poured everyone a glass. "It was a couple of years ago at a networking luncheon hosted by the Better Business Bureau. You introduced yourself and asked if I knew one of the women seated at my table."

Mackenzie thought for a moment, then her face lit up in recognition. "Ah, yes. The one who looked like Halle Berry. *Her*, I remember."

Bridget's eyes flashed, but a corner of her mouth quirked up into a smile. "So do I. Last week, she agreed to marry me."

"Congratulations." Mackenzie raised her glass in a toast and wrapped her arm around Kenya's shoulders. "It goes to show we both have great taste in women."

"That we do," Bridget said evenly. "It's the one thing I've always admired about you."

"But not the only thing, I hope," Mackenzie said.

Bridget sipped her drink in uncharacteristic silence.

Kenya felt trapped. Like she was caught between warring factions locked in a battle in which she wanted no part. When Mackenzie had said she wanted to get reacquainted with Bridget, Kenya had hoped they would take to each other. Now the best she could hope for was that each survived the next few minutes unscathed. Tonight hadn't turned out like she expected, but surely things could only get better from here. They had to, because they certainly couldn't get much worse.

"I need a do-over," Mackenzie said as she and Kenya sat in her office at the end of the night. Bridget and Celia had already left, and Mackenzie had offered to drive her home. "I think I screwed that up."

"Why do you say that?"

"Because the only person at your table who seemed to like me was you."

Kenya tried to make light of the tense situation. "Since Celia's married and Bridget's engaged, that isn't such a hardship, is it?"

Mackenzie pulled Kenya into her lap. "I'm being serious, Kenya. These are your friends we're talking about. If I'm going to be in your life, I want them to be as comfortable with me as they are with you. It's just—" She faltered, apparently unsure of what to say. "What I feel for you, I've never felt for anyone else. I don't want to lose that—or have anyone else try to take it away. Since I've met you, no other woman exists for me. You're the only one I want. The only one I need. I think I might be falling for you, Kenya."

Each time Kenya doubted her, Mackenzie gave her more reason to trust her, not less. It was obvious Mackenzie had changed. She wasn't the amoral cad she used to be. Between working, rehearsing, and getting to know Kenya, she didn't have the time—or the inclination—to pursue other women. After years of playing the field, it seemed she was finally ready to embark on a real relationship. A relationship with Kenya.

"I feel the same way."

"What about your friends?" Mackenzie asked.

"When they see how happy you make me, they'll come around."

Mackenzie stretched her neck for a kiss. Kenya bent to oblige her. The moment her lips met Mackenzie's was electric. She could feel the crackle in the air. A surge of power. Of passion. Of lust. All the things she and Mackenzie were supposed to pretend to feel when they were dancing. When Mackenzie slipped her tongue into her mouth, she felt them in earnest.

"You asked me to let you know when I was ready to take our relationship to the next level," Kenya said when they finally came up for air.

"Are you there?" Mackenzie asked eagerly.

"Yes, I am. Please take me home."

❖

Mackenzie hustled Kenya out of Azure with an unmistakable sense of urgency. Simone tried to think of an excuse to thwart their escape—a faulty tap, a disgruntled customer, even a report of a stopped-up toilet—but she couldn't come up with anything that would stand up to closer inspection.

She pulled out her phone and opened the picture of Mackenzie in a lip-lock with someone other than Kenya. She should have forwarded the photo when she had the chance and let Kenya sort it out for herself. But she hadn't been willing to inflict such pain on Kenya or jeopardize her place in Kenya's life over what Mackenzie would probably have claimed was a misunderstanding. Now it was too late.

She hoped Kenya knew what she was doing. That she was climbing into bed with Mackenzie with an open mind and not just an open heart. Because if she wasn't, her heart was bound to be broken.

CHAPTER SIX

K enya's hands were shaking so badly she could hardly fit her key in the lock. "This is it," she said when she finally managed to get her front door open. "Welcome to my humble abode."

Mackenzie stepped inside, gave the condo a quick once-over, and nodded appreciatively. "This place is gorgeous. Clean lines. Open spaces. My compliments to your interior decorator."

"That would be me." Kenya hadn't felt the need to pay someone to tell her which accessories to buy and how to place them, so she had eschewed the unnecessary expense and done the job herself. The decision had proved fortuitous after Ellis's deception made money—or, more accurately, the lack of it—such an issue.

"A woman of many talents, I see."

Mackenzie kissed the side of Kenya's neck, making her knees go weak. When Mackenzie drew her into her arms, Kenya nearly lost all sense of reason. Mackenzie's embrace was like a refuge. A place where nothing and no one else mattered. She was not only safe there but desired.

"Thank you for the tour," Mackenzie said. "What I've seen so far is wonderful. When do I get to check out the view from your bedroom?"

Kenya's heart was racing so fast she couldn't think clearly. It had been so long since she'd made love with someone for the first time. Six years, in fact. When Mackenzie kissed her, she trembled at her touch.

"What's wrong?" Mackenzie asked.

"I'm nervous." Kenya lowered her gaze, feeling like the inexperienced virgin she once was. "I haven't been in this position in a while. I think I've forgotten how to act."

"Let me remind you."

Mackenzie kissed her again. Softer this time. Almost tentatively. Now she was the one holding back, throttling down and waiting for Kenya to catch up. Kenya felt something stir inside her. A fire that had nearly gone dormant flickered back to life. She felt the warmth slowly build inside her.

"My bedroom is this way." She took Mackenzie's hand and led her there.

"Beautiful," Mackenzie said.

Kenya joined her by the window. Below them, the lights in the harbor twinkled like stars. "The view is one of the main reasons I bought this place." And the reason she had fought so hard to hold on to it.

Mackenzie turned to her. "I was talking about you, not the view." She held Kenya's face in her hands. "You don't have to be afraid. I'm not going to hurt you."

"I know," Kenya said with certainty. The little warning light in her head had finally stopped flashing. She could not only see how much Mackenzie wanted her. She could feel it, too. And the feeling was very much mutual.

"Then let me show you."

"No." Kenya unbuttoned Mackenzie's suit jacket and pushed it off her shoulders. "Tonight, it's my turn to lead. Are you willing to follow me?"

Mackenzie smiled. "Just tell me where you want to go."

Kenya loosened the knot in Mackenzie's silk tie and slowly pulled it free. Using the tie as a restraint, she bound Mackenzie's wrists. Loose enough to avoid cutting off circulation, but tight enough for Mackenzie to feel the restriction. Mackenzie's eyes danced as Kenya lay her across the bed and straddled her body.

Kenya unbuttoned Mackenzie's shirt and slid her fingertips against her skin. Mackenzie arched her back, making it easier for Kenya to reach underneath her and unhook her bra. "Yes," Mackenzie hissed when Kenya flicked her tongue against her nipple. "I would follow you anywhere." Kenya moved lower, skimming her lips over the smooth skin of Mackenzie's stomach. Mackenzie squirmed beneath her. "Kenya, you're killing me. Please." Kenya looked up. The desire she saw in Mackenzie's eyes fueled her own. She ripped Mackenzie's zipper down and pulled off her pants. She removed Mackenzie's boxer briefs with her mouth, taking care to graze her teeth against the sensitive skin of Mackenzie's inner thigh.

She could smell Mackenzie's arousal. Oaky and earthy like a fine wine. But when she ran her tongue from Mackenzie's opening to her clit, she discovered she was as sweet as nectar. She used her lips and tongue to bring Mackenzie to the edge, then finished her with her fingers as she explored Mackenzie's mouth with her tongue.

"That was amazing," Mackenzie said after she caught her breath, "but now it's my turn to show you what I'm capable of."

She shook off her restraints, flipped Kenya on her back, and spent the next several hours showing her she was capable of a great many things.

Kenya woke up the next morning happy, satiated, and alone. A note and a single rose rested on the nightstand. She held the rose against her lips as she read the note Mackenzie had left behind.

You're beautiful when you sleep. I would have loved waking up with you, but I promised my father I would meet him for an early round of golf today. Looking forward to our next round of Follow the Leader—M

Kenya covered her face with her hands, unable to suppress the girlish giggles that welled up from within. When her phone buzzed, she thought it was Mackenzie texting her to say she had changed her mind about going golfing and was coming back to pick up where they had left off. Instead, the message was from Simone.

"Question number seven," she read. "Which is more important in a relationship, honesty or passion?"

Seeing the word passion in print reminded Kenya of the lust-filled night she had spent, but she took a moment to formulate a thoughtful response rather than a reflexive one.

"Passion has its merits," she eventually wrote, "but a relationship built on anything other than honesty isn't a relationship at all."

Thankfully, the relationship she was crafting with Mackenzie was built on both.

❖

Simone's heart sank when she read Kenya's answer to her question. Kenya seemed to think she was living a dream, but a nightmare awaited her. A nightmare in the form of whatever fine piece of ass next caught Mackenzie's eye.

Simone ached to call Kenya and tell her everything she knew about Mackenzie, but she didn't want to hear the joy in Kenya's voice replaced by pain. Joy that was bound to be short-lived if Mackenzie stuck to her usual patterns.

"What are your plans for the day?" she typed instead.

A few minutes later, her phone beeped with Kenya's reply. "I'm just waking up. I haven't planned anything yet. I'll probably catch up to Mackenzie at some point, but the rest of the day is up for grabs. Why do you ask?"

"I'd rather ask you question eight in person." She could have asked over the phone or by text, but she needed to see Kenya face-to-face. She needed to see if Kenya was as hung up on Mackenzie as her words made her sound. "Can we meet somewhere?"

"Sounds good. Any particular location?"

Simone wanted to show Kenya the Miami she knew. Not the playground for the filthy rich or the hunting ground for thieves and hustlers. The Miami populated by immigrants in search of the American Dream and ordinary Joes struggling to make sure their dreams didn't end up deferred. The Miami she had grown up in and the one in which she continued to live.

"I thought we could check out the street art in the Wyndham Art District," she wrote. "The Wynwood Walls is an outdoor museum that has over forty permanent murals on display. There are hundreds of other murals in the area, too, and it's all free and open to the public. If you work up an appetite from all that walking, we could head over to the Caribbean Food Festival and stuff ourselves with jerk chicken and fried plantains while we listen to some reggae, dancehall, and soca."

"Sounds like fun. What time do you want to get together?"

Now.

"If you text me your address, I could pick you up around noon. We can check out the art for a couple of hours, then head over to Alice Wainwright Park for the festival."

"I'm looking forward to it."

Not as much as I am.

❖

Kenya loved the idea of spending the afternoon looking at art, but she balked at Simone's suggested mode of transportation: a battered motorcycle that sounded like it was about to cough up a lung. "You don't actually expect me to ride that thing, do you?"

"Well, yeah, that's kind of why I brought the extra helmet."

The protective headgear emblazoned with an elaborate photo-realistic illustration of a human brain made Kenya worry even more about getting hers scrambled. "I don't ride anything that has less than four wheels," she said, holding her ground. "By my count, you're two short."

"I've been riding motorcycles for ten years. I haven't had an accident yet." Kenya eyed the dent in the rear fender. "That wasn't my fault," Simone was quick to point out. "Someone backed into my bike while it was parked outside the post office and didn't stick around long enough to exchange insurance information."

"Uh huh."

Simone grinned and tightened the chin strap on her helmet. "Where's your sense of adventure?"

"When I was in college, one of my fantasies was to ride with the Dykes on Bikes during a Pride parade."

Simone gunned the idling engine. "What do you say we hold our own parade?"

Kenya felt her resolve begin to weaken. "You're a bad influence, you know that?"

"I may have heard that a time or two. Now get on."

"Here goes nothing." Groaning at her foolhardiness, Kenya strapped the helmet in place and straddled the motorcycle, leaving plenty of space between her body and Simone's.

"Come closer. I'm not going to bite."

Kenya reluctantly slid closer until Simone's firm, round ass was nestled against her crotch. She felt awkward being in such an intimate position with someone she wasn't sleeping with, but she didn't know any other way to ensure she wouldn't fall off the back of the bike once Simone began to pick up speed. Simone showed her where to put her feet but didn't direct her where to put her hands. She tentatively slipped her arms around Simone's waist, vaguely registering the feel of Simone's washboard abs pressing against her fingers.

She wasn't prepared for the excitement she felt when Simone hit the gas. As the wind whipped in her face and the warm sun shone down on her skin, she finally understood why adrenaline junkies had a need for speed.

"I didn't realize you were a backseat driver," Simone said after she parked the bike and they made their way through the entrance to the Wynwood Walls. Huge murals—some more than forty feet high—loomed before them. Kenya loved the bright colors and the artists' clever ways of utilizing the buildings' architectural elements in their work. "I could feel you leaning into the turns and squeezing me like you were the one working the accelerator."

"Too much ballroom dancing, I'm afraid. When you lead, you're supposed to squeeze your partner's hand or side to let them know which direction you want them to go."

"That explains the bruises." Simone rubbed her narrow waist as if to erase the marks Kenya had left behind. "How's rehearsal going?"

"Better. I'm still nervous about the competition, but I'm more confident than I was a few days ago. Mackenzie is a wonderful partner."

"In more ways than one?"

Kenya felt herself begin to blush. Were the events of the night before written on her face? Or was Simone better at reading her emotions than anyone else? "How did you know? Did she tell you?"

"No, I saw you leaving the club last night and put two and two together." Simone shoved her hands in the pockets of her shorts as she slowed her pace. "Do you love her?"

"Is that the question you wanted to ask me?"

Simone stopped in front of a mural of one-time rap rivals Tupac Shakur and Notorious B.I.G., two supremely talented young men who had died while in the prime of their careers. "No, but it's a good place to start."

Kenya's feelings for Mackenzie were growing by the day. But had they blossomed into love? She had felt so close to Mackenzie last night. Even before they'd had sex. Mackenzie had listened to her concerns, assuaged her fears, and promised to remain faithful. She had done everything short of swearing on a stack of Bibles. In the end, she had convinced Kenya that her present—and her future—had nothing in common with her past.

Kenya didn't know if she was ready to use the L word yet in reference to Mackenzie. But when she was, Mackenzie deserved to be the first to hear it, not someone else.

"She's a remarkable woman," she said diplomatically as she regarded a mural depicting famous antiheroes from American cinema. Marlon Brando as Vito Corleone in *The Godfather*. Robert De Niro as Max Cady in *Cape Fear*. Al Pacino as Tony Montana in *Scarface*. Jack Nicholson as Jack Torrance in *The Shining*. When she resumed walking, Simone fell into step beside her.

"Code for none of my business. Got it."

"I'm not trying to shut you out, but—"

"No, Kenya, it's cool. When I start a new relationship, I don't want to talk about it, either, until I know I'm not going to screw it up. I'm just happy that you're happy."

Simone sounded sincere. Like she genuinely meant what she had said and wasn't simply paying lip service. She was a loyal friend. Kenya admired that about her and hoped she would remain in her life long after their question-and-answer session ended. Lovers came and went, but friends were forever.

"Here's a question I hope you do answer," Simone said, almost as if on cue. "Question eight: if you found a magic lamp and the genie inside granted you three wishes but said you couldn't use any of the wishes on yourself, what would you wish for?"

"Peace on Earth, goodwill toward men—"

"No, seriously." Simone put a hand on her arm. Kenya stopped in her tracks, rooted in place by both the tenderness of Simone's touch and the intensity in her eyes. "What would you wish for?"

Kenya felt an unexpected surge of emotion. Her heart swelled in her chest as she thought of all the things she would bestow upon other people if given both the means and the opportunity. "I would wish that my friends and family could live long, healthy, and happy lives. I would wish that Pierce,

Jackson, and Smith would continue to be successful for years to come. Not for my benefit but for the sake of the talented agents and artists who work there. And I would wish that you could meet someone who's as passionate about you as you are about music."

Simone looked startled. "You'd waste a wish on trying to find me a girlfriend?"

"I wouldn't consider it a waste at all."

"That's because you're in that zone where you're in a new relationship and you're blissfully happy and you want everyone else to be happy, too. You're going to drive all your friends crazy trying to get them hooked up, you know that, right?"

"Including you?"

Simone regarded her as if sizing her up. "Do you consider me a friend?"

"I do," Kenya said honestly. "I like having you around."

"Good." Simone sighed as if she had been holding her breath while she waited to hear Kenya's answer. "Because I wasn't planning on going anywhere. I could drag out these questions for years if I want to."

The comical expression of exasperation on the face of a woman on a nearby graffiti-covered wall seemed to sum up Kenya's feelings perfectly. "What have I gotten myself into with you?"

Simone's smile faded and her expression turned serious. "Nothing you can't get out of if you want."

"That's just the thing. I don't want to. I like what we have. I don't know how to define it, but I like it." And whatever it was, she didn't want to be without it. "Now what's your next question?"

"Question nine: what do you value most in a friendship?"

"Oh, that's easy." Kenya was glad to finally have a question she could answer without hesitation instead of one she needed to ponder for several minutes before formulating a response. "I place the highest value on the same thing in a platonic relationship as I do a romantic one: honesty. Loyalty is good, but I don't want someone to support me just because she's my friend. If I'm wrong, tell me I'm wrong. Don't take my side just because you think you have to. And if I ask your opinion, give it to me. Don't spare my feelings."

"But what if…a friend knew something that would hurt you and kept quiet in order to keep you from being hurt? Would you hold their silence against them?"

The question didn't sound entirely hypothetical. Kenya briefly wondered if Simone knew something she didn't. Something she might not want to know. But, fully cognizant of how much stock she placed in open, honest communication, how could Simone ever keep anything from her?

"It would depend on what they were holding back. If I ask you if my ass looks fat in a particular pair of jeans and you say no when we both know the answer's yes, I could overlook that. But if you know something that, if revealed, would have a direct effect on my life and you keep it from me? Yes, I would have a problem with that. Why? Do you have something to tell me?"

"No," Simone said quickly. Too quickly? "I was just curious. Come on, friend. Let's go to the park and listen to some tunes."

"Sounds good to me," Kenya said, but the sudden change of subject made the issue at hand feel tabled instead of resolved.

Simone draped her arm across Kenya's shoulders and steered her toward the exit. Kenya slid from her grasp. Not because Simone's touch was unwanted but because it was. What did it mean that an innocent gesture from Simone could excite her just as much if not more than an intimate one from Mackenzie?

Coming here today—agreeing to be with Simone like this—was probably a mistake. Kenya was dating Mackenzie, which meant her relationship with Simone had to remain strictly platonic. Having been cheated on, she could never bring herself to cheat on someone. She didn't want to give anyone the impression she and Simone were more than friends. What if someone saw them together and got the wrong idea? Even worse—what if she did? For a moment, she realized with a start, she had wanted to lean into Simone's embrace rather than pull away from it.

"Sorry." Simone raised her hands as if she were being held at gunpoint. "I forgot for a second you were spoken for."

"I'll let you slide this time," Kenya said, but the attempted joke sounded hollow even to her own ears.

❖

As she blended a Blue Hawaiian, Simone hummed along to the Bob Marley song that had been stuck in her head since she and Kenya had attended the Caribbean Festival that afternoon. She couldn't remember the last time she'd had so much fun. Sampling wares from all the food vendors, dancing to the wide variety of music, and spending time with someone she cared about. She had hated to see it come to an end. Even if the joy she had felt hanging out with Kenya was offset by the guilt she felt for keeping Mackenzie's betrayal a secret from her.

Kenya had said if something had a direct effect on her life, she would want to know about it. Mackenzie's cheating certainly qualified. But Simone couldn't bring herself to break the news to her.

She supposed she could ask Bridget for advice—Bridget had known Kenya longer and would have a better handle on her feelings than she did—but turning to someone else felt like a cop-out. She had to figure this out for herself. And, hopefully, spend a few more days like this one in the process.

Amanda took a long look at her as she tossed the ingredients for a lemon drop martini in a cocktail shaker. "You look happy. What did you do this afternoon? Or, to be more exact, *who* did you do?"

"I didn't do anyone. I went to the Caribbean Festival."

"With?"

"A friend," Simone said cagily.

"A friend, huh? Anyone I know?"

Simone ran her fingers across her mouth as if zipping her lips. "Mum's the word."

"You can try to keep her identity a secret if you want, but I'm going to find out. I always do."

"I hate to break this up just when it's starting to get good," Crystal said as she squeezed between them to grab a bottle of mineral water from the cooler. "I want to know who you're hooking up with as badly as our inquisitive little friend here, but the boss wants to see you."

Simone didn't know whether to be thankful or wary. She was glad she could escape Amanda's incessant questions for a few minutes, but she wasn't looking forward to having face time with Mackenzie. Nothing good could possibly come of it. Unless, of course, she received a long-overdue raise. That would certainly be worth the stress of making the long walk to Mackenzie's office with the other employees' eyes boring holes in her back the whole way.

When she stepped into Mackenzie's office, Mackenzie was standing in front of the wall-length one-way mirror that allowed her to keep tabs on the action in Azure without being seen. She whispered something to Gabby, who suddenly found a need to be elsewhere.

"You wanted to see me?" Simone asked.

Mackenzie slowly turned away from the view. "Are you happy here?" she asked as she tugged at the cuffs of her five-thousand-dollar suit. She took a seat but didn't motion for Simone to do the same, so Simone remained standing, which made her feel even more like she was being called on the carpet.

Not an auspicious start to the conversation.

"I love it here. My coworkers are like family. This is the best job I've ever had."

"Then tell me why I shouldn't fire you."

Simone's stomach dropped. She couldn't afford to lose her job. She had bills to pay. A mouth to feed. Namely, hers. Aside from the grand Dre had fronted her, she didn't have a lot of money in the bank. Her parents had always told her she should set something aside for a rainy day, but she had been too busy living in the moment to plan for the future. Now what was she supposed to do?

"I know I've been late a time or two," she said, confessing her faults, "but, even with the worst hangover, I've never called in sick. I don't bail in the middle of my shifts, I don't overpour, and the customers like me. I might not be a model employee, but I'm willing to compare my performance to anyone else's. I'm one of the best bartenders you have."

"Exactly. You make me a lot of money. Which is why I would hate to see you go." Mackenzie steepled her fingers under her chin and leaned back in her chair. "Yet how can I afford to keep you around?"

"I don't understand."

"I'll make it simple. I want you to stay away from Kenya."

Simone nearly laughed out loud.

"That's what this is about? You called me in here because my spending time with Kenya makes you feel insecure? Just because you're sleeping with her doesn't mean you can control her. She can see who she wants. What's good for the goose is good for the gander. Isn't that how the saying goes?"

"If you're trying to imply something, don't beat around the bush. Spit it out. Confession is supposed to be good for the soul."

Simone told herself not to take the bait, but it proved too tempting to resist. "I'm not trying to imply anything. I'm saying I saw you last week. The night you told Kenya you were heading home after rehearsal, you met up with someone else. I saw you in the alley."

Mackenzie's eyes widened as recognition set in. She tried to play it cool, but Simone saw beads of sweat form on her upper lip. The first crack she had ever seen in Mackenzie's usually impenetrable façade. "Have you told Kenya what you *think* you saw?"

"No."

Mackenzie's shoulders slumped in apparent relief. She unscrewed the cap on an expensive fountain pen and reached for her checkbook. "How much would it take for you to keep this between us? A hundred thousand would go a long way toward financing your musical ambitions, wouldn't it?"

Simone felt her eyes nearly bug out of her head. One hundred thousand dollars would allow her to quit her job, buy the remaining equipment she needed to complete her home studio, pay off every debt she had, and lay back and make music while she took her sweet time finding another gig. She started to grab the check and cash it before Mackenzie could change her mind, but she couldn't. One hundred thousand dollars was a lot of money, but no amount was high enough to convince her to betray a friend.

"I don't want your money, Mackenzie. I haven't told Kenya what I saw because, unlike you, I don't want to see her hurt. I was protecting her, not angling for a potential payout from you."

"Do you think you're the only one who has her best interests in mind?"

"Were you thinking of her best interests when you were French kissing some bimbo out back, or were you only taking yours into consideration?"

"Not that it's any of your concern, but Fernanda and I aren't seeing each other anymore. She and I had an affair. The fire burned quickly, it burned brightly, but now it's gone. This is why Kenya doesn't need to know about any of it."

Simone found herself in the same uncomfortable position as the rest of the women in Mackenzie's life: listening to her tell a lie and hoping it was the truth. "That's debatable, but she won't hear it from me."

"Good." Mackenzie finished writing the check and slid it across the desk. "Here's a little something for your loyalty."

Simone stared at all those zeroes. She might not ever see that much money at one time in her life. How could she possibly walk away from a piece of paper worth six figures? Because if she took it, she knew she would never be able to live with herself. Or without Kenya. She picked up the check, ripped it into shreds, and let the pieces fall on Mackenzie's desk. "Are we done here? Because if I'm still your employee, I've got drinks to serve."

After Mackenzie waved a hand to indicate she was dismissed, Simone walked out of Mackenzie's office and sagged against the door. Money was the root of all evil, and she had nearly succumbed to its allure. She had come uncomfortably close to compromising her principles. And for what? The financial security Mackenzie's bribe would have afforded her wasn't worth the price she would have to pay in order to accept it.

Even though Kenya hadn't come right out and said it, it was obvious she didn't want to take a chance on a relationship with her because she didn't think she was worth the risk. The more Simone thought about it, the more she realized she hadn't done much to refute Kenya's argument. She was going to be thirty in a couple of years and what did she have to show for it? No house, no car, minimal savings, and a fistful of dreams but no concrete plans on how to achieve them.

"I've got to make some changes in my life," she said to herself as she headed back to a job that seemed glamorous from a distance but paid less than minimum wage. "And the time starts now."

CHAPTER SEVEN

I want you to meet my parents."

Kenya and Mackenzie were just waking up—or trying to—after spending another long night exploring each other's bodies. This time in Mackenzie's palatial mansion in one of the most exclusive neighborhoods in Miami. There were so many helipads in the area the residents practically needed their own air traffic control tower.

Kenya rubbed her eyes and yawned, squinting from the glare of the early morning light streaming through the blinds. Mackenzie had insisted on leaving them open last night so she could take Kenya against the window "for all the world to see." Kenya was far from an exhibitionist, but she had been so turned on by the thrill of the forbidden she had eagerly agreed to Mackenzie's proposition. Her body still felt the effects from last night's sexual gymnastics.

Mackenzie was a wonderful lover. Highly skilled, attentive, and eager to please. When she was with her, Kenya had never come so hard or so often. Despite their obvious chemistry in bed, however, she felt like something was missing from their relationship. Something she couldn't quite put her finger on. She told herself she was being too cautious. Mackenzie could give her everything she had ever wanted in a relationship—passion, stability, and mutual financial security. So why was she trying to find fault where there was none?

"I must still be asleep," she said, "because I could have sworn I just heard you say you want me to meet your parents."

"I mean it." Mackenzie moved closer. Kenya loved the contrast between the warmth of Mackenzie's bare skin and the cool of the silk sheets. "Let's have dinner with them tonight. I want to introduce you."

"We've been dating less than two weeks. Do you always invite women to family dinner this soon?"

"You're the only woman I've ever invited to my parents' house."

Suddenly Kenya was wide-awake. Mackenzie's invitation now seemed less like a lark and more like the start of something permanent. The sheets rustled as she untangled their limbs so she could roll over and face Mackenzie. "Why me? Why now?"

"Because you're not like anyone I've ever been with."

Mackenzie never talked about her feelings except in vague generalities. This time, Kenya needed her to go deeper. She wanted to know what made her laugh and what made her cry, not just what made her come. And she wanted Mackenzie to know all those things about her, too. But once she had gotten her into bed, Mackenzie had stopped trying to figure out what made her tick. Didn't she want to know her better, or did she think she already knew enough? Perhaps inviting Kenya to have dinner with her parents was her last step before taking the most important one of all. The one that led to marriage and commitment. Two things Kenya had always wanted but had begun to fear she would never have.

"In what way am I different?" she pressed.

"Because you're a woman."

Kenya barely resisted rolling her eyes. "I think the rest of the women you've been with were women, too."

"But they weren't like you." Mackenzie raked a hand through her tousled hair, but her short curls resisted taming.

"They were flighty and immature. I could take them to a White Party, but not a black-tie event. And a business function? Forget it. I could have fun with them, but I couldn't make a life with them. They were someone I could date. You are someone I could marry. And that's what I love about you." Mackenzie slowly ran the tip of one finger across Kenya's collarbone, causing goose bumps to form in its wake. Or perhaps her body was reacting to Mackenzie's words instead of her touch. "I also love this spot right here." She gently maneuvered Kenya onto her back and kissed the valley between her breasts. "And this spot right here." She moved lower and kissed Kenya's navel. "And," she said, spreading Kenya's legs, "I especially love this spot right here."

Kenya sighed as Mackenzie ran her tongue along the length of her clit. Then her sighs quickly turned into moans as the tantalizing movements of Mackenzie's tongue stripped away her ability to think clearly.

"So is that a yes?" Mackenzie asked afterward as Kenya lay boneless in her arms.

Kenya tried to catch her breath. "With an inspired pitch like that, how could I say no?"

❖

"She wants me to meet her parents."

Simone had barely finished reading the mysterious text message before her phone rang. Kenya's number was printed on the display.

"Please ignore the message I just sent," Kenya said. "It was meant for Bridget. I sent it to you by mistake."

"I gathered that." Simone leaned back on her couch and propped a foot on the edge of her refuse-covered coffee table. She had stayed up late working on her music and had the empty burger and candy wrappers to show for it. Not to mention the bags under her eyes. One day, though, all her hard work and long nights would be worth it. Provided, of course, she didn't keel over from exhaustion first from burning the candle at both ends. She munched on a cold French fry until she could get her hands on some real food. "I assume the 'she' in your email is Mackenzie. If she's inviting you to meet her parents, you must be getting serious."

"To be honest," Kenya said with a sigh, "I don't know what we are. Everything is a blur right now."

Simone felt the same way. She had been in a daze ever since Mackenzie had tried to buy her silence. Even if she hadn't gotten paid for it, perhaps keeping quiet was the right thing to do. Kenya was happy and Mackenzie was apparently doing right by her. For once.

"Are you nervous?" Simone asked.

"I'm petrified. She's never invited anyone she was dating to meet her parents. I'm the first. I'm not sure I'm ready to be a trailblazer."

"Just be yourself and you'll be fine. Her folks put their pants on one leg at a time just like everyone else. Unless they pay someone to do it for them."

"Are you trying to make me more nervous or less? Because you're not helping."

"Sorry," Simone said, trying not to laugh.

She couldn't blame Kenya for being so spun out over the idea of having dinner with Mackenzie's parents. The Richardsons were people you wanted to impress, especially if they might become your in-laws one day. The concept of Mackenzie being in a serious relationship that might lead to marriage was so foreign Simone still couldn't wrap her head around it. Mackenzie played the field. She didn't leave it behind. But she had apparently decided to do so for Kenya. And who could blame her? Kenya was worthy of that kind of commitment. Simone just hoped Mackenzie was worthy of her.

"What are you doing?"

Kenya's question pulled Simone out of her reverie.

"Working on a project that's had me stumped. This morning, I think I finally managed to pull it together."

"What is it?"

"A track for a new artist I hope to produce. Would you like to hear it?" she asked hesitantly. She wanted Kenya's opinion, but she was leery of possibly receiving negative feedback on something that meant so much to her.

"I'd love to."

"Here. Let me put you on speaker." Simone pressed the appropriate icon on her phone and held the microphone near her laptop. Then she began playing the new version of one of Reagan's songs. She hadn't altered the vocals in any way, but she had gotten rid of the original music and replaced it with her own. "It's still raw, but—"

"Shh," Kenya said sharply. "Let me listen."

Simone bit her lip as she waited for the song to finish. As she waited to hear what Kenya had to say about what she had heard.

"You wrote that?" Kenya asked after the last note sounded.

"Not the lyrics, no. I wrote the music. Did you like it?"

"I love it."

Kenya's enthusiastic response made Simone's chest swell with pride. It was one thing for her friends to say her music was dope. Friends were supposed to be loyal that way. Hearing it come from Kenya, someone who sought out talent for a living, meant a whole lot more. It meant she was good. It meant music didn't have to be a dream. It could be a career.

"It reminds me of yesterday," Kenya said. "Of being at the Wynwood Walls in the middle of a riot of color, then inundated by a cornucopia of sights, sounds, and smells at the Caribbean Festival."

"That was my inspiration. I tried to replicate everything we saw and did because I wanted the track to sound like a mix of all those influences."

"You've succeeded."

"I hope the guy I'm doing this for feels the same way." She couldn't allow herself to get too excited until she heard what Dre thought of the track. Since he was the one paying the bills, that gave him final say. "If he approves and the artist likes my direction, I may be asked to produce the rest of the album. It's only a five-song EP, but it's a start."

"If the rest of the songs sound as good as the one I just heard, it could be the start of something big. And one day, I'll be able to say I knew you when."

"From your mouth to God's ears." Kenya's praise felt good, though a bit bittersweet. The more Kenya got wrapped up in Mackenzie's world, the less likely she would remain part of hers. Yesterday was one of the best days of her life. She hated the idea that it might never be repeated. "Do you have time for question ten, or do you have to go get gussied up for your big date?"

"I have time."

"Question ten: what's your ultimate fantasy? The one thing you've always dreamed of doing but never have."

"In bed or out?"

As much as Simone wanted to hear all the things Kenya wanted to do to someone sexually or have done to her, she didn't want to imagine her doing them with Mackenzie. "Out."

"I once read an article about a woman who retired, sold her house, and now lives on a cruise ship. At last count, she had visited over a hundred countries. I would love to spend the rest of my life on permanent vacation."

"You still could."

"On my salary? I don't think so. If I want to pay six figures a year to live a life of luxury, I need to start buying lottery tickets."

Kenya either didn't seem to realize or didn't want to admit she had already hit the jackpot. She didn't need to work when her girlfriend made more money in an hour than most people did in a year. Simone liked the fact that Kenya wanted to earn her rewards rather than having them given to her. Working for something always made it taste sweeter in the end.

"Have fun at dinner tonight."

Kenya growled in frustration. "Ugh. Dinner. Don't remind me. Quick. Ask me a question to take my mind off of it."

Simone smiled at Kenya's reluctance to end their conversation. To break their connection. "Instead of asking a question, I'd rather make a request. Tell me about your ex."

"Ellis? Why?"

Simone had seen the damage the end of her relationship with Ellis had caused Kenya, but she was curious about the relationship itself. Did they have more good times than bad, or had it been rocky from the beginning? "What drew you to her?"

"The same thing that drove us apart," Kenya said with a hint of sadness in her voice. "She was impulsive, free-spirited, and spontaneous. Everything I wasn't. She often acted on a whim and I like to think things through first. When I was with her, I loved not knowing what to expect. Until I walked in on something I should have seen coming."

"Aside from the obvious, how did that make you feel?" Simone felt like she was channeling Dr. Phil, but she wanted to know more about Kenya's past in case she was lucky enough to be part of her future.

"I was disappointed, I was angry, and, in a way, I was relieved it was over."

"Why?"

"Until then, I thought I could fix us, but we were over long before I walked into that room. I just didn't want to admit it. I tried so hard to hold on when I should have let go."

"Why didn't you?"

"I was afraid. Afraid of hearing 'I told you so' from everyone who kept saying Ellis wasn't right for me. Afraid of feeling like a failure for trying to prove them wrong."

Simone couldn't imagine how someone as confident and successful as Kenya seemed to be could harbor such deep-seated doubts. "Do you still feel that way?"

Kenya's silence hinted the answer might be yes. Her attempt to use humor to sidestep the issue confirmed the fact. "At the moment, the only thing I'm afraid of is using the wrong fork at dinner."

"Outside in," Simone said. "I think that's the rule."

And in her case, it also referred to her role in Kenya's life. On the outside looking in.

❖

Simone's questions usually left Kenya feeling vaguely unsettled as they forced her to confront thoughts and feelings she hadn't examined before. Today, however, Simone's line of questioning had left her shaken. Had fear of being alone compelled her to accept the advances of the first person who had shown more than a passing interest in her since she left Ellis? Was she settling for Miss Right Now instead of waiting for Miss Right? She couldn't be. Because if that was the case, she would be dating Simone instead of Mackenzie. She would be settling for something temporary instead of planning a future.

She needed to gather her brain trust. She needed to sit down with Bridget and Celia and talk through the situation. But what was there to talk about? With Simone, she could have a few laughs and a few interesting conversations. With Mackenzie, she could have a life. But if everything was so black-and-white, why did she keep seeing gray?

She called Bridget first, then got Celia on the line.

"Bridget, you and I haven't had a chance to talk since girls' night, and, Celia, you and I haven't talked about anything except work during that time. What did you guys think of Mackenzie? Be honest."

"She's beautiful, charming, and rich," Celia said. "What's not to like?"

"Her wandering eye, for one," Bridget said. "She's got a lot going for her, but she's a player, Kenya. I thought that would be a major red flag for you."

"It was at first, but she says she's changed and I believe her."

"What makes you so sure?" Bridget asked.

"The sound of her voice when she whispers my name. The feel of her touch when she—"

"La, la, la," Celia said. "Stop right there. I don't want to imagine any of my friends having sex, let alone my boss. When you're with her, you feel like you're the only one. Is that what you're trying to say?"

"Precisely. Work gets in the way sometimes—for both of us—but I believe her when she says she isn't seeing anyone else. That she doesn't *want* to see anyone else. A few hours ago, she asked me to meet her parents."

"She did what?" Bridget asked. "Way to bury the lead, Kenya. This is a big deal. Especially for someone with her reputation. If you plan to love 'em and leave 'em, you don't take them home to meet Mommy and Daddy first."

"When was the last time someone you were seeing asked you to meet her family?" Celia asked. "Juan asked me after our second date."

"Try never for me," Kenya said. "Ellis wasn't close with her family. The only times we saw them were at weddings and funerals. Even then, she introduced me as her roommate instead of her lover because, after she came out, her mother asked her not to tell the rest of the family she was gay."

"And that was okay with you?"

"Of course not, but I loved her. You know how it is. When the person you love asks you to do something, you occasionally say yes to keep the peace even though doing so tears you up inside." Kenya paused to remember how much she had hated being relegated to the sidelines. Being asked not to mention her relationship with Ellis made her question its legitimacy. When they met, Ellis was working as a clerk in a convenience store. Had she pursued a relationship with Kenya because she was interested in her or the things her money—and good credit score—could buy? "Now, instead of being shoved in a corner, I'm being put in the spotlight. I'm thirty-six years old and I feel like I'm embarking on my first real relationship. What if I blow it?"

"You won't," Celia said reassuringly. "As long as you don't spend the evening with a piece of food stuck in your teeth or a giant booger hanging out of your—"

Kenya interrupted Celia before she could finish painting the unpleasant picture. "I get the gist. Thanks."

While Celia provided comic relief, Bridget countered by being the voice of reason. "Relationships are always harder when you have something at stake," she said. "That's when they matter the most. This one obviously matters to you. And if it matters to you, it matters to me. Good luck tonight. I'll be rooting for you."

Despite four years of togetherness, Kenya's relationship with Ellis had existed in name only. What she was building with Mackenzie felt real. It felt right. Her heart warmed at Bridget's show of support.

After she had walked in on Ellis and the woman Ellis had risked their relationship for in order to pursue a few moments of cheap thrills, she had lost her ability to trust. Then she had met Mackenzie, who had managed to convince her to trust again. And, perhaps, to love. If her trust was betrayed this time, she feared the toll would be much higher than a broken heart. The cost could be her soul.

❖

"Let's see whatcha got." Dre reached for the CD containing Simone's version of Reagan's single. "Is it as good as the last track you mixed for me?"

"Better. I hope."

Simone wiped her sweaty palms on the frayed hems of her khaki shorts. She hadn't felt this nervous since the first time she had screwed up enough courage to ask a girl to go on a date. Then, she'd felt like her whole life was on the line. Now, it truly was. Dre held her future in his hands. If he liked what she'd done to this song, he might trust her with even more. More work meant more money and more exposure. She held her breath as she waited for the music to start pumping from the speakers.

When Dre liked a song, you knew it right away. Hell. Everyone within a fifty-mile radius could hear his whoop of approval as he bobbed his head to the beat and pumped a fist in the air like he was working an invisible speed bag. As Reagan's song played, Dre nodded his head a time or two but remained uncharacteristically silent. Simone kept waiting for him to give her some kind of sign, but he didn't give anything away.

"Well?" she asked after the song ended.

Dre regarded her as he leaned back in his chair. "Are you still working at that club in South Beach?"

"Azure, yeah," Simone said, a bit confused by why Dre had chosen this moment to ask about her employment status. "What about it?"

"How much are they paying you?"

Simone shrugged. "Enough to pay the rent and keep the lights on, but I could always use more." She didn't mention the fact that she'd had a chance to get her hands on a hundred grand. Accepting Mackenzie's bribe would have caused more problems than it had solved. And as far as she was concerned, the subject was closed. Permanently.

"I feel you." Dre's worn leather chair creaked as he leaned forward. "I can't pay you South Beach money, but I want you on my squad. Full-time, not just a track or two every now and then. Because this shit right here"—he pointed to the CD she had given him—"is the best thing I've heard in a *long* time. Reagan has something special, and you can help her tap into it. Not just her. I have a whole string of artists who could use your magic touch."

"Are you asking me to become a producer? Because that's, like, my dream job."

"I know. It's what you've been talking about for years. We can make it happen. The money might not be that great starting out, but once we get some airplay and the royalty checks start rolling in, it'll be peaches and cream after that. Then, once your name gets out there and people start beating down the door to work with you, you can jack up your fees as high as you want. What do you say? Are you ready to stop dreaming about doing what you love and start making those dreams come true?"

Simone thought it over. What Dre was asking her to do was risky. She would be walking away from a steady paycheck and great tips in favor of a career in which she was only as good as her last release. Should she stick with a sure thing or take a chance on the unknown? While her friends would be supportive, her parents would lose their minds. But it was her life and she had only once chance to get it right.

"Let's do this."

❖

Mackenzie's cell phone rang as her chauffeur drove her and Kenya away from the crowded city center to the less-populated gated communities in the moneyed suburbs. She glanced at the display, sent the call to voice mail, then turned off her phone.

"Was it business?" Kenya asked.

"Yes," Mackenzie said with a weary sigh.

"You should have taken the call. It might have been important."

With so many businesses under her belt, Kenya didn't know how Mackenzie kept track of them all. If she had that many plates spinning at the same time, there would be broken china everywhere. But Mackenzie managed to keep them going without so much as a wobble.

"If there's a problem tonight, my general managers can handle it." Mackenzie placed a hand on her knee. "Tonight, the most important thing in my life is you." She reached into her jacket's inside pocket and pulled out a telltale robin's egg blue box. "This is for you."

Kenya untied the white ribbon securing the box and ran a finger over the Tiffany's label etched into the square cover. She gasped when she opened the box and saw a diamond and platinum bangle bracelet resting inside. "I can't," she said, trying to return the box.

"Why not?"

"Do you have any idea how much this costs?" Kenya didn't know the exact price, but she was willing to bet the bracelet was valued at over twenty thousand dollars. Four times the price of the first car she had ever owned and almost as much as the salary from her first job.

"Naturally. I paid for it." Mackenzie pulled the bracelet out of the box and clasped it around Kenya's wrist. "It looks beautiful on you."

The bracelet reflected the glow of passing streetlights. Despite its obvious beauty, Kenya didn't feel right wearing it. Did Mackenzie intend to buy her an expensive bauble every time she needed reassurance when only a few words of comfort were what she really wanted?

"I'm sorry, Mackenzie, but I don't feel comfortable accepting such a lavish gift."

"Don't you want me to spoil you? Like I said the night we met, I like making dreams come true. And I want to help you fulfill yours. Will you allow me to do that?"

Kenya decided to concede defeat rather than press the issue. "I can't stop you, can I?"

"You could try, but I don't know how successful you'd be." Mackenzie looked out the window as the car pulled to a stop in front of a sprawling Italianate mansion. "We're here."

As she looked at the multimillion-dollar home and the lush surrounding grounds, Kenya felt in over her head. Everything was happening so fast. Too fast. She wanted to slow down, but she didn't know how. Meeting Mackenzie's parents was the next logical step in their relationship, but why was she so reluctant to take it?

"Relax." Mackenzie turned Kenya to face her and kissed her so tenderly it nearly brought tears to Kenya's eyes. "My parents will love you as much as I do."

It took a moment for the import of Mackenzie's words to register. "Did you just say—"

"Yes, I love you. After we have dinner, I intend to take you back to my place and show you how much. Is that okay with you?"

As she stroked Kenya's cheek, Mackenzie's eyes glowed with affection. With love. For her. A gift even more precious than the one circling her wrist. "It's perfect. Just like you."

Mackenzie smiled. "My parents are waiting to tell you I'm far from perfect, but you're free to ignore everything they say."

Kenya leaned into the pressure of Mackenzie's hand. "I'm looking forward to hearing all their stories about you."

"Let me spare you the trouble. I was a bratty child, a bratty teenager, and an even brattier adult. But you make me want to be better in every way. Better than I've ever been. Better than I ever thought I could be." Mackenzie fingered the bracelet. "That's more than worth a minor investment."

Kenya felt lightheaded. Like she was breathing rarefied air. "I'm just a girl from a blue-collar family in Tallahassee. I'm not used to such luxury, such extravagance, such—"

Mackenzie silenced her with a kiss. "Get used to it. Because as far as I'm concerned, this is just the beginning."

When she'd gone speed dating a few weeks ago, Kenya had been in search of a new beginning. In Mackenzie, perhaps she'd found her Happily Ever After as well.

A distinguished African-American man in a charcoal gray suit opened the limo door and stuck his head inside. "Are you planning to sit in the driveway all night, or will you be joining us for dinner?"

"We were on our way, Dad," Mackenzie said.

"Of course you were." He offered his hand to Kenya and helped her out of the car. "You must be Kenya. I'm Michael Richardson."

"It's a pleasure to meet you, sir."

He held Kenya's hand in both of his. "I assure you the pleasure is mine."

"I can see where Mackenzie gets her charm." As well as her height and her sexy alto voice.

"Fortunately, she got her looks from her mother. In every other way, though, she is her father's daughter."

He wrapped his arm around Mackenzie's shoulders and pressed a kiss to her forehead. Kenya was touched by the obvious affection between them. She had never seen Mackenzie look so unguarded or carefree. Out of bed, anyway.

"How was your golf game last week?" she asked as they walked toward the house. "Mackenzie hasn't told me who won."

"Golf game?" Michael furrowed his brow. "Mackenzie detests golf. I tried to teach her when she was younger because some of the best business deals are made with a handshake after a round, but she would rather chase a fuzzy yellow ball around a tennis court than hunt for a dimpled white one in a bunker."

Kenya turned to Mackenzie for an explanation. The morning after they had made love for the first time, Mackenzie had left her a note saying she couldn't stay because she had to meet her father for an early morning round of golf. But according to

Michael, Mackenzie hated the sport. Why would she lie? Was it the only thing she had lied about, or was she harboring other secrets? Had she, despite her many assurances she had changed, reverted to her old ways?

"Thanks for ruining my cover story, Dad." Mackenzie turned to Kenya. "I know what you're thinking, but don't. I left you that morning so I could arrange to buy you the present I gave you a few minutes ago. I wanted to surprise you."

"Mission accomplished." Kenya felt like kicking herself for being so quick to believe the worst. She trusted Mackenzie implicitly on the dance floor. If they were going to make a life together, she needed to be able to trust her after the music stopped. "I'm sorry I doubted you," she whispered as Michael led them inside.

Mackenzie curled an arm around her waist and drew her closer. "I'll give you a chance to make it up to me later."

Mackenzie fixed her with a look that left no doubt how she expected to be compensated, and Kenya couldn't wait to begin paying her debt.

❖

Simone hung up the phone after her call to Jolie went to voice mail. She needed to give two weeks' notice at Azure before she made the jump to Liberty City Records, but she didn't want to do it by leaving a message. She decided to do the right thing. The responsible thing. She would give her notice face-to-face rather than resorting to the impersonality of a phone call.

As she dressed for work, she felt an odd sense of relief knowing her time at Azure was limited. She would miss getting paid to hang out with her friends and she would miss interacting with the customers, but she definitely wouldn't miss the drama that swirled around the club like a toxic cloud. No more watching the revolving door to Mackenzie's office to see who would walk through it next. No more jilted lovers crying in their Technicolor drinks. And, perhaps, no more Kenya.

Unlike Mackenzie's other paramours, Kenya had a mind of her own. And a life filled with more important things than partying and keeping track of the latest trends. Simone doubted her friendship with Kenya would end after she quit Azure, but part of her wondered if it would survive Mackenzie's wrath. She hadn't intended to call Mackenzie out on her cheating, but she hadn't been able to resist an opportunity to wipe the smug expression off Mackenzie's face after Mackenzie called her into her office. To let her know that her money and power didn't make her a better person than she was. It just meant her bank balance had a lot more zeroes on the end. Not a trade Simone was willing to make. She might not drive a six-figure sports car or be able to jet off to Europe on a whim in a private plane, but she had integrity. One thing Mackenzie's money couldn't buy.

She grabbed her keys and prepared to head out, but her doorbell rang before she could leave her apartment. She opened the door to find a nervous-looking young woman standing on her doorstep. Her visitor was wearing camouflage cargo shorts and a tie-dye T-shirt with a picture of a ganja-smoking Bob Marley on the front. Her hair was teased into an oversized Afro that would have put Angela Davis' iconic one to shame. Her soulful brown eyes searched Simone's face as she shifted from foot to foot.

"Are you Simone Bailey?"

"Yes, I am. May I help you?"

The young woman visibly relaxed and extended her hand. "Hi, I'm Reagan Carter. Dre told me where to find you."

As she shook Reagan's hand, Simone made a mental note to remind Dre not to give out her home address. She didn't want any stalkers or irate artists showing up on her doorstep unannounced. But she supposed she could make a one-time exception in this case. "It's a pleasure to finally meet you." She opened the door wider. "Come in. Would you like something to drink?"

Reagan blew past her, her musk-scented perfume wafting in the breeze. "Sure," she said with what sounded like false bravado. "Whatever you're having is fine."

While Simone headed to the kitchen to grab a couple of ginger beers from the refrigerator, Reagan sat cross-legged on the couch and tucked her worn tennis shoe-clad feet under her thighs.

"I listened to your version of my song," she said as Simone popped the tops on the sodas. "I just wanted to tell you I thought it was dope, and I'm looking forward to working with you."

"Cool. I'm glad you like it." Simone hadn't expected to see someone barely out of her teens exhibit such a professional attitude. She took a seat opposite her. "How long have you been singing?"

Reagan's face lit up. "All my life. I had my first solo when I was three during an Easter pageant at church. I caught the bug for performing then. Now all I want to do is get up on a stage and blow. I don't care if there are two people in the audience or twenty thousand. I just want my voice to be heard."

Simone had a feeling Reagan was speaking figuratively rather than literally. "What's your story?"

Reagan's smile faltered. "What do you mean?" she asked defensively.

"As Dre put it when he first told me about you, you're young, but your voice sounds like you've been through some things and come out the other side."

"I grew up in the 'hood," Reagan said with a shrug. "You can guess the rest. My story's no different from anyone else out here trying to make something from nothing. What about you? With that accent, I bet you grew up sipping fresh coconut milk on the beach rather than hiding in the bathtub while someone did a drive-by on your block."

Simone nearly laughed at the absurdity of the suggestion, but she held her mirth inside so Reagan wouldn't think she was laughing at her. She had a feeling Reagan didn't make friends easily—that she'd had to force herself out of her comfort zone to come here today—and she didn't want her to shut down when she was trying to open up. To forge a connection.

"My parents left Jamaica when I was six years old," she said. "We didn't have much except for the clothes on our backs. Our first place was a cramped two-bedroom apartment. My parents had one bedroom, my sisters shared the other, and I slept on the pullout in the living room. It was a tight squeeze for the five of us, but the apartment had more room than the shanty we left behind. Plus it had running water and indoor plumbing. Two things we didn't have back home. So, yeah, I've seen some things, too."

"Maybe we were meant to work together."

Reagan's smile was so infectious Simone couldn't help but smile back. "Maybe so. We should set up a time to compare notes and figure out what direction we want to take."

"How about now?"

Simone glanced at her watch. "I appreciate your enthusiasm, and I can't wait to start putting some polish on your raw talent, but I have to be at work in half an hour. That's not nearly enough time to do much more than scratch the surface."

"I'm sorry. I didn't know you had to be somewhere. I should have called first to see if you had some free time. Why did you let me ramble on like that?"

Reagan bolted out of her seat. Simone felt like a cowboy trying to corral a bucking bronco. She placed a hand on Reagan's arm to ground her.

"I let you 'ramble on' because I wanted to hear your voice. Isn't that what you want?"

Reagan nodded fervently. "Yes, I want that more than anything."

Any doubts Simone might have had about putting Azure in her rearview vanished when she saw the hunger in Reagan's eyes. Reagan had talent to spare and the drive to match. And she had the chance to nurture both.

"Meet me tomorrow at noon at the coffeehouse down the street. We've got work to do."

❖

Kenya leaned back so the butler could clear her plate from the last of her five courses. She felt like she had wandered into an episode of *Downton Abbey* minus Maggie Smith's withering putdowns. The Richardsons didn't seem to be as hung up on decorum as the title-bearing family in the popular BBC series, but the opulence surrounding them was on the same level. Kenya was tempted to pinch herself to make sure she wasn't dreaming. This was a fairy tale, not real life. And she was Cinderella, praying the clock wouldn't strike midnight.

Rafaella Cocconi Richardson, Mackenzie's mother, dabbed the corners of her mouth with her napkin and pushed her chair away from the table. "Kenya, would you like to take a walk with me?"

The request sounded more like a command than a question. Kenya felt compelled to respond in the affirmative. "Of course."

Michael and Mackenzie stood in unison. "I think that's our cue to fire up some Cohibas, don't you?" he asked.

"Sounds good to me."

Apparently sensing Kenya's discomfort, Mackenzie caught her eye and gave her a nod. Kenya felt a growing sense of solidarity. Whatever this was, at least she and Mackenzie were in it together.

Rafaella had been a ballerina before she met Michael and abandoned hours spent at the barre for a life of luxury. Kenya could see the lasting influence of Rafaella's former profession in the straight lines of her back and shoulders and the gracefulness in her gait as she walked from the dining room to a glass-filled sunroom bathed in lunar rather than solar light. Rafaella flipped a switch that added muted artificial light to the room. When Kenya looked at the stars overhead, she felt like an astronaut floating in space.

"It's so peaceful here."

"Isn't it?" Rafaella sat on an overstuffed divan and invited Kenya to do the same. "Don't worry. I didn't bring you in here to bombard you with a slew of personal questions that are none of my business. Mackenzie doesn't involve Michael and me in her personal affairs and, to be frank, I prefer it that way. She's a grown woman. She's free to do what she wants."

"Then why am I here?"

Rafaella's smile was filled with a mixture of pride and love. "Mackenzie and Michael are so much alike they could be clones. If I didn't have the stretch marks to prove I carried her inside me for nine months, I would be tempted to believe he gave birth to her instead of me." She folded her hands in her lap like she was performing the lead role in *Swan Lake*. "I brought you in here to give them time to smoke a cigar or two and compare their latest acquisitions." She eyed the bracelet on Kenya's arm. "Is that what you are, Mackenzie's latest acquisition?"

Kenya bristled at the question. "I'm not for sale," she said, fighting to keep her voice steady.

Rafaella looked at her long and hard. "No, I don't think you are. I've never tried to dictate whom Mackenzie should and shouldn't date, but I have made it clear I would prefer if she spent time with someone of substance rather than the steady procession of models, actresses, and image-conscious fashionistas who only want to receive a few trinkets and get their pictures in the paper while they dream of a lavish wedding that will never take place. Those relationships are disposable and Mackenzie treats them as such. I'm not surprised. She's addicted to conquest. Always has been. Her father's influence, I'm afraid. He's like a junkie chasing the next high. For him, his drugs of choice are the next property, the next business deal, and the next woman."

Kenya was surprised to hear Rafaella use the present tense instead of the past. "But you've been married for almost forty years. Didn't his skirt-chasing end when he met you?"

Rafaella barked a laugh that sounded even more toxic than a smoker's cough. "Michael has money and power, two aphrodisiacs that are potent enough to compel more than a few women to ignore the wedding band on his finger. I'm not foolish enough to think I'm the only woman in his life. I'm just the one he comes home to. And Mackenzie, as has been proven many times over, is her father's daughter. Before you commit to a life with her, I advise you to be sure it's one you're willing to live with. Do you love her enough to share her with someone else? Because believe me when I say there will always be someone else."

The warning bells that had gone silent in Kenya's head began to blare louder than ever before. Was Mackenzie with her because she wanted to be, or because she wanted someone "acceptable" on her arm so she could please her parents?

"Are you okay?" Mackenzie asked after they bade her parents good night and climbed into the back of the limo.

"No, we need to talk."

"You're scaring me." Frowning, Mackenzie took her hand in hers. "What did my mother say to you?"

"Nothing I haven't heard before, but there are some things I need to hear from you."

"Of course. I have to swing by Azure to address an issue that just came up, but it shouldn't take more than a few minutes. Then we can talk for as long as you want."

Kenya didn't know whether to go or stay. She didn't want to walk away from a relationship that had seemed to hold such promise at the outset, but she didn't want to be a trophy wife in constant competition for Mackenzie's affections. She couldn't spend each day wondering if the business meeting Mackenzie said she was attending was nothing more than a cover story for a romantic tryst with someone new. She didn't want to be the other woman. She wanted to be the only one. If Mackenzie couldn't give her that assurance, she would find someone who could. No matter how long the search might take.

❖

The light had gone out of Kenya's eyes. That was the first thing Simone noticed when Kenya and Mackenzie walked into Azure. The second was the gorgeous bracelet around Kenya's wrist. A piece of bling like that must have cost Mackenzie a pretty penny. Based on the look on her unsmiling face, however, Kenya was the one paying the price.

"Old-fashioned?" she asked after Kenya made her way to the bar.

"Make it a double."

"Rough night?" Simone reached for a bottle of bourbon. She wanted to ask Kenya how dinner with Mackenzie's parents had gone, but the answer seemed pretty obvious. Not well. Not well at all.

Kenya blew out a sigh. "Ask me again when it's over."

Simone almost offered to serve as a sounding board, but she could tell from the uneasy vibe coming from Kenya that Mackenzie was the one she needed to talk to, not her.

"I hear congratulations are in order," Mackenzie said when she finally joined them. "My loss is Liberty City Records' gain."

Kenya looked from Mackenzie to Simone and back again. "Am I missing something?"

Mackenzie looked almost gleeful when she said, "According to the text I received earlier tonight, Simone has turned in her notice. She's leaving the fold to take a crack at the music biz. Didn't she tell you?"

Kenya didn't answer. Instead, she posed a question of her own. "When did you decide this?"

"Today," Simone said. Unlike Mackenzie, she wasn't keeping anything from her. Well, one thing, but she had almost managed to convince herself that not mentioning Mackenzie's dalliance with Fernanda was for Kenya's own good. Almost. "Dre offered me a producing gig and I couldn't turn it down."

"Will he be paying you more than I do?" Mackenzie asked as if she thought a raise might provide enough incentive to convince her to stay.

"Not at first, but some things aren't about money."

"Don't be naïve," Mackenzie said. "When it comes down to it, everything's about money. But if you're willing to make less of it in order to do what you love, that's your decision. For your sake, I hope it won't be one you'll end up regretting."

"I'm happy for you," Kenya said genuinely. "It takes a lot of guts to follow your dreams."

"What's your dream?" Simone ignored their audience and focused on Kenya. "Question eleven. What do you want most out of life?"

Kenya's eventual response was directed at Simone, but it seemed to be more for Mackenzie's benefit.

"I want to love someone and be loved in return. I want to give my heart to someone without worrying about having it broken. And I want to prove that happy endings can exist outside of children's books, romance novels, and cheap massage parlors."

"I hope all your dreams come true," Simone said, but she hoped even more that Kenya wasn't counting on Mackenzie to help her fulfill them.

❖

As she walked through the foyer into the living room, Kenya felt like she was seeing Mackenzie's house through new eyes. Compared to the tasteful Old World charm of her parents' home,

Mackenzie's screamed *nouveau riche*. She had bought it from a former member of the Heat, the professional basketball team that called Miami home. The house had been put on the market after the four-time All Star had opted out of his contract with the Heat in search of a better deal with the Lakers. Mackenzie had snatched it up when the exorbitant price tag was sliced in half after the sprawling house spent more than a year on the market. She had done some redecorating, but she had left most of the oversized bells and whistles intact, including the eight-foot tall walk-in showers, thirty-seat movie theater, four-lane bowling alley, and Olympic-sized pool. The beds were new, but each was large enough to accommodate an NBA center—or several regulation-sized women.

Kenya tried to tell herself the women who had preceded her in Mackenzie's bed didn't matter. She tried to tell herself that she would be the last woman in the seemingly endless string. But, as she recalled the conversation she'd had with the woman who knew Mackenzie best, she had a hard time believing either argument.

"Do you love her enough to share her with someone else?" Rafaella had asked. "Because believe me when I say there will always be someone else."

Kenya cleared her throat to get Mackenzie's attention. Mackenzie had been glued to her cell phone since they left Azure. If she wasn't sifting through emails or typing texts, she was making calls to put out feelers for a new bartender to take Simone's place. A few hours ago, she had promised to let her general managers handle any issues that arose tonight. That promise was already being broken. How many others might follow?

"Mackenzie, we need to talk."

"I know." Mackenzie continued to peck away at the digital keyboard on her phone. "I'm almost done. Gabby already has a lead on a potential replacement for Simone. If it works out, I'll get to steal a valued employee from one of my competitors and fill a need at the same time. I call that a win-win situation. For me, at least. Scotty might not feel the same way when she finds out her most popular bartender will be coming to work for me, but she'll get over it in time." She shook her head as if in disbelief. "I still find it strange Simone didn't tell you she was quitting. The two of you are practically joined at the hip. Sometimes I wonder if there are three of us in this relationship instead of two. I'm not opposed to a *ménage* down the line if you're interested, but I'd rather keep you to myself for a while."

"How generous of you." Kenya pulled the phone from Mackenzie's hands and powered it off. "Speaking of relationships, your mother had some interesting things to say about the one she and your father share."

"I assume she told you about their 'understanding.'" Mackenzie put air quotes around the word. "If she did, that would explain why you looked so shell-shocked after your meeting with her. I'm sure you weren't expecting to hear she and my father have an open relationship. I would have told you myself, but I didn't expect the subject to come up tonight."

"Is that the kind of relationship you want? One that exists in name only?"

"My parents' marriage might not seem conventional by most people's standards, but I assure you it's real," Mackenzie said hotly. "You don't spend forty years with someone you don't love. My father might have a weakness for beautiful women—and who can blame him—but he loves my mother to the moon and back. She feels the same way about him. If she didn't, she wouldn't have agreed to marry him in the first place."

"You make falling in love sound like a business deal."

Mackenzie shrugged. "Everything's open for negotiation, especially love."

Kenya refused to take a clinical view of a subject that provoked such passion. She and Mackenzie seemed to have so much in common. How could they be so far apart on the one thing that counted the most? "You and I view relationships differently. I get that. Whether one view is better than the other is a matter of opinion."

"And you've made your opinion abundantly clear. But do me a favor. Leave my parents out of this. The issue you're having at the moment is between me and you. Or should I say the issue lies with you?"

"Me? How?"

"I've owned up to my past rather than trying to deny it. I've told you that I've changed. Other than strap on a chastity belt, I don't know what else I have to do to convince you I'm not running around on you. I'm not your ex, Kenya."

"I'm not comparing you to Ellis."

"Aren't you?"

Kenya took a breath to keep the situation from spinning completely out of control. Once—just once—she wanted a relationship that was drama-free. She would gladly do without the mind-blowing make-up sex if it meant she could avoid the disagreements that preceded it and the inevitable heartache that followed. "I'm not trying to start a fight with you, Mackenzie," she said evenly. "I just want some answers. Are you seeing me because you're interested in me or because you need me to make you look respectable? Are you looking for the kind of relationship where you're free to see who you want while I sit at home wondering if the next affair might turn into something more, or do you want something different? Because if we don't want the same things, we should cut our losses now and end this before either of us gets in too deep."

"Too late. I'm already in deeper than I've ever been." Mackenzie pulled Kenya into her arms and held her tight. "Would you be amenable to an open relationship?"

"No," Kenya said without hesitation.

"Then why would I ask you to change who you are in order to be with me?"

"Because you're your father's daughter."

"Yes, I am, but I'm also my mother's."

"Which means?"

"I can't perform a decent *plié* to save my life, but I can make my own pasta."

Mackenzie's smile was endearing, but Kenya refused to let down her guard. "I'm serious."

She tried to pull away, but Mackenzie held her fast.

"So am I. You're good for me and I don't want to lose you. Stay with me, Kenya. I can give you everything you've ever wanted."

"Yes, but—"

"No buts." Mackenzie gently pressed a finger against Kenya's lips. "After we win the dance competition next weekend, we should celebrate with a bottle of red wine and a plate of my homemade manicotti, followed by breakfast in bed."

Kenya had become more comfortable performing the routine she and Mackenzie had been practicing for weeks, but she wasn't looking forward to performing it for an audience. If given a choice, she would prefer to spend next Saturday night in Mackenzie's kitchen instead of on the dance floor. "Why don't we skip the competition and dive straight into the wine and manicotti?"

"Because I don't want all our hard work to go to waste. And I want to show you off. Everyone in the room will be drooling when I walk in with you on my arm, but at the end of the night, you'll be going home with me."

When she was with Mackenzie, Kenya had never had felt so desired. One look—one kiss—one touch from Mackenzie was all it took to set her body on fire. It was when they were apart that the doubts crept in. Was Mackenzie in this relationship for the right reasons? Was she? She should end this before—

When Mackenzie kissed her, Kenya felt her resolve weaken. She felt her misgivings about their relationship fade. Just like they always did each time Mackenzie's lips met hers. As the kiss deepened, she tried to convince herself to stop worrying about the past and the future and live in the moment.

"Yesterday is history, tomorrow is a mystery, and today is a gift," she said, looking into Mackenzie's eyes. "That's why we call it the present."

"I'd like to unwrap my present now, if you don't mind." Mackenzie pulled Kenya toward her bedroom. "I want you naked except for the bracelet I bought you."

Kenya couldn't think of a better way to put the evening to rest. If she was lucky, perhaps her mind—and her heart—would follow suit.

CHAPTER EIGHT

A re you seeing anyone?"

Simone nearly choked on her green tea. "Excuse me?"

"I'm not trying to get with you, if that's what you're wondering," Reagan said. "We're going to be spending a lot of time together, and I want to make sure some jealous girlfriend, wife, or significant other doesn't show up at the studio wanting to put the beatdown on me because I'm cutting into your quality time with her."

"I invited you here to talk about your career, not my personal life."

"You're the boss."

Simone never dreamed she'd hear that particular B word used in relation to her. She liked the sound of it. She flipped to an empty page in the notebook she was using to keep track of her thoughts and impressions during the informal meeting. "What kind of career do you want? Do you want to stay in the game for decades like Aretha Franklin and Patti LaBelle, or do you want to have a few hits, make your money, and retire to Switzerland like Shania Twain?"

Reagan thought it over. The first time she'd been quiet for longer than two minutes at a stretch since they'd taken their seats. Simone hadn't invited Reagan to her apartment because she wanted to keep her home and work lives separate. She thought meeting with her artists in a public place would be cheaper than renting office space, but the way Reagan was putting away the food and drinks, she would end up paying about the same. She chalked it up to the cost of doing business on her own terms rather than someone else's. And that was a price she was more than willing to pay.

"I know he hasn't been around that long," Reagan said at length, "but I want to pattern my career after Sam Smith, the British guy who went from an unknown to a superstar a few years ago. Even though he was open about his sexuality from the beginning, he wasn't marginalized as a gay artist, his first album ended up winning a bunch of Grammys, and he was given the honor of recording the theme song for a James Bond movie. Only someone with true staying power is asked to do something like that. Now he has the Oscar to prove it. That's the blueprint I want to follow."

Simone hoped Reagan would avoid the vocal cord hemorrhage and subsequent surgery that had threatened her idol's career.

"Does Dre know you're a lesbian?" she asked. Dre didn't care who she slept with, but she was behind the scenes, not on the album cover. It was her job to make records, not sell them—and herself—to the public.

"I told him the first time he said he wanted to sign me as an artist. I wanted to make sure he was on the up-and-up and wasn't trying to dangle a contract in front of me just so he could get in my pants. When he mentioned I'd be working with you, I jumped at the chance."

"Why?" Simone couldn't hide her surprise. She wasn't a household name. Yet.

"Because I knew I could be myself with you."

For a brief moment, Reagan reverted into the shy girl who had appeared on Simone's doorstep the day before. Then she smiled and Simone saw the confident young woman she'd heard on record. The one whose voice could strike a chord in any listener, reminding people of their similarities rather than pointing out their differences.

"I admire your desire to be honest about who you are," Simone said, "but that's a lot of pressure to take on at twenty-two. Are you ready to be someone's role model? There are a few openly gay R&B and hip-hop artists making music underground, but there aren't any in the mainstream. Except for the ones who claim they're bi or bi-curious when they're publicity-hungry newcomers, but turn straight as an arrow once the hits start coming. Are you sure you want to be the first who stays the course?"

Reagan sipped her iced chai tea latte. "Are you asking because you're worried about album sales, or are you asking because you're worried about me?"

Simone thought of all the artists who had crumbled under the pressure of fame. Judy Garland. Janis Joplin. Jimi Hendrix. Jim Morrison. Kurt Cobain. Amy Winehouse. Whitney Houston. "I want you to be a success, not a cautionary tale."

"So do I. If given a choice, I'd rather do it being myself than pretending to be someone I'm not."

They hadn't spent a second in the recording studio, but Simone could already tell her collaboration with Reagan would be a productive one.

"Even though your EP won't hit the streets for a while, we need to start getting the word out about you. I have a friend who works for a marketing company. I'll give her a call and see if her team can meet with us next week or, better yet, she would be willing to give us some ideas for free."

Reagan grabbed a handful of Simone's fries. "Is she just a friend, or are you kicking it with her?"

"She's dating my soon-to-be ex-boss."

"You like her, though, right?"

"Why do you say that?"

"You get a goofy look on your face when you talk about her."

"Don't read too much into it. Goofy is my natural expression."

"Uh huh. Is she the reason you're quitting your job? So you don't have to watch her knocking boots with your boss?"

"No."

Reagan leaned forward and grabbed more fries. "Then say her name without smiling."

Simone couldn't even say Kenya's name in her head without wanting to break into a grin.

"See?" Regan pointed an accusatory French fry in her direction. "I knew she was more than a friend. What's so special about her that you'd be willing to ignore every other woman in the world and focus on her?"

Simone was better at writing music than lyrics because she often struggled to put her feelings into words. This time was no different. "I know it probably sounds cheesy, but she puts a song in my heart. The version of your song you like so much? She's the one who inspired it. I came up with the music after I spent the afternoon hanging out with her."

"What would you do if you ever slept with her, write a whole album?"

Simone imagined Kenya underneath her. Reaching for her. Calling her name.

"I don't know, but I'd love to find out."

❖

Simone's text message requesting marketing tips left Kenya uncertain if she should be flattered or amused so she opted for both. She texted Simone back as she watched Mackenzie play tennis against her friend Fernanda, an interior decorator from Milan who had recently set up shop in South Beach and was rapidly building a reputation as the go-to designer in town. Fernanda's looks were stellar, but her tennis game left much to be desired. The score was lopsided in Mackenzie's favor, but judging by the amount of laughs spilling from both players, the score seemed inconsequential.

"Thank you for thinking of me," Kenya typed, "but you are aware I'm in HR not creative, aren't you?"

Simone's response made her smile.

"Dre hasn't put enough money in the promotional budget for me to be able to afford anyone on your creative team so I thought I'd go with the next best thing."

"How do you know you can afford me?" she asked as Mackenzie hit a forehand winner to stretch her lead. "You haven't heard my rates yet."

"So I guess you don't accept food stamps. What if I offered you an endless supply of free drinks instead?"

"Then I'd think you were trying to get me drunk and take advantage of me."

"Little old me? Perish the thought."

Kenya listened to Mackenzie and Fernanda banter in Italian. She couldn't understand a word of their conversation, but it sounded sexy as hell. When Mackenzie had introduced them that morning, she'd said she hadn't known Fernanda very long. They'd met at a party a few weeks ago and discovered they had mutual friends. Now Mackenzie was thinking of hiring her to redecorate her house in order to infuse more of her personality into the place and make it look less like a bachelor pad, a change Kenya would welcome with open arms.

"How can I help?" she wrote.

"Teach me how to get Reagan's name and face in the public eye without resorting to putting up a bunch of flyers no one will pay attention to," Simone replied.

Kenya tried to think of what she would do if she were in Simone's position. Learning one new job was hard enough. From the looks of it, Simone was taking on three or four. Producer, publicist, and A&R rep. Talk about padding a résumé. Simone didn't lack for ambition, that was for sure, but was she taking on more than she could handle?

"Use your connections," she suggested.

"Did you forget who you're talking to? I'm a bartender, not a businesswoman. I don't have any connections."

"Sure you do." Networking, Kenya stressed to each new hire, was a round-the-clock activity. If handled correctly, even a trip to the grocery store could result in an addition to your personal or professional circle. "Think of how many people you come across during the course of a shift. Each is a potential music buyer."

"I never thought about it that way."

"Start. You can also ask Crystal to slip your song into her playlist at Azure or see if you can talk one of the local radio DJs into giving Reagan some air time for an in-studio or call-in interview. If you want to build an audience, help her find a recurring gig at a local performance venue and cross your fingers the crowd will become invested in her success." Kenya was ready to buy in after listening to only one song. Or was it Simone's success she was invested in instead of Reagan's? "That's all the ideas I'm willing to dish out for free. The rest are going to cost you."

"Thanks for the suggestions. Are you in a better mood today? You seemed down last night."

Down wasn't the word for it. Kenya had felt like her personal life was falling apart all around her. Again. Funny how much better everything seemed in the light of day.

"Yesterday was an emotional rollercoaster," she wrote. "I hope to avoid taking a similar trip any time soon."

"Glad to hear everything's okay. Enjoy the rest of your day."

Kenya wasn't ready for the virtual chat to end, even though she couldn't decipher the meaning of most of the emojis Simone had sprinkled into the conversation.

"Are you in a hurry?" she asked. "Don't you want to ask me any questions that aren't marketing-related?"

"I don't want to keep you from Mackenzie."

"You aren't."

"Where is she if not with you?"

Kenya looked up in time to see Mackenzie hustle to reach a drop shot that bounced twice before she could get her racquet on the ball, costing her an opportunity to close out the match. "She's within earshot," she typed as Mackenzie launched into a profanity-laced tirade that proved how seriously she took even what was supposed to be a friendly competition. "Does that count?"

"Just wanted to make sure she wasn't looking over your shoulder. I don't want to get fired before my last day."

Kenya felt a pang of melancholy at the reminder of Simone's impending departure from Azure. And, perhaps, her life. Once Simone started concentrating on her music career, how much time—if any—would she have to devote to anything else?

"Granted, I've only been to Azure a handful of times, but the place won't be the same without you," she wrote. "I'll miss seeing your smiling face when I walk in. And don't get me started on the drinks."

"I'll miss you, too."

Kenya's pang of melancholy bloomed into a full-fledged ache. "You make this sound like good-bye."

"Not when I have nine questions left."

Kenya felt an almost palpable sense of relief when she read the words. She valued the friendship she and Simone had forged. Simone was one of the steadiest influences in her life. She wanted to keep her around.

"Lucky number thirteen," Simone texted. "What are you most grateful for?"

Kenya didn't know how to answer the question. She wouldn't have made it as far as she had in life without the supportive teachers, friends, and family members who had helped her achieve her goals. But how could she possibly single out just one to say she was more grateful for their assistance than the rest?

Mackenzie hit an ace to win her match against Fernanda and jogged to the net to kiss her beaten opponent on both cheeks. Fernanda didn't take the loss too badly, though. She and Mackenzie made a date to go over design ideas, and Fernanda said she would exact her revenge once she started sending in her invoices.

Mackenzie gave Fernanda a playful tap on the butt with her racquet. "Next time, I'll let you win."

"*Ciao*, Kenya," Fernanda said with a sunny smile after she gathered her things. "It was nice meeting you."

"You, too." She waited for Fernanda to leave before she said, "She's the first of your friends who appears to like me instead of tolerating my presence for your benefit."

Her reception on *La Dolce Vita* during the White Party had been rather chilly. None of Mackenzie's friends had made an attempt to get to know her. In fact, the only people who had spoken to her at length were Mackenzie, Celia, and Simone.

"Really? I hadn't noticed. With the amount of money she'll be charging me in the coming months, Fernanda has plenty of reason to smile." Mackenzie gave Kenya a quick kiss and drank a bottle of mineral water in one long swallow. "After I get cleaned up, I have to head to the marina for a while."

"Are you throwing another party today?" Kenya had to head to Orlando soon for her company's annual corporate retreat. She was looking forward to spending a little quality time with Mackenzie before she left town for five days to supervise the various trust exercises, breakout sessions, and group outings executive management had asked her to plan to ensure the team didn't lose either its cohesion or its creative spark.

"No, I have a business meeting with some potential investors. I would invite you to accompany me, but the negotiations are delicate and the sight of you in a bikini would distract me too much. You're welcome to stay here if you like. I should be back in a few hours. Now tell your BFF good-bye and come help me scrub some of the spots I can't quite reach."

"I'll be right there."

"Don't take too long, or I'll start without you."

As she headed toward the house, Mackenzie shed articles of clothing like she was leaving a trail of bread crumbs behind. As Kenya began to follow the path, her cell phone vibrated in her hand, reminding her she hadn't provided an answer to Simone's latest question.

"Did I stump you?" Simone's text read.

"I'm most grateful for second chances," Kenya finally wrote. "And all the people who were willing to give me one."

Unlike hers, Simone's response was immediate. "Before you return the favor, make sure the recipient is deserving."

❖

Simone didn't like working Mondays, Tuesdays, or Wednesdays because the crowds were relatively light and the hours seemed to drag by before closing time. Thursdays were exponentially better. The crowds were larger, and most people were in a good mood because the weekend was in sight. Tonight the vibe in Azure was so festive she was tempted to check the calendar app on her phone to make sure it wasn't a holiday.

"Do you have any idea why we're so slammed?" she asked Amanda as they struggled to keep up with the incoming drink orders.

"Yeah, doofus, it's karaoke night, remember?" Amanda swapped out an empty beer keg for a fresh one and rolled the empty one out of the way. "Every lesbian who thinks she's the next k.d. lang or Melissa Etheridge wants to take a turn on the mic."

"I forgot Mackenzie decided to make karaoke a weekly event instead of a once-a-month thing."

"That's one of the things that can happen when you work two jobs. You end up paying more attention to one than the other, or you wind up sucking at both. Are you sure you want to leave this gig behind?" Amanda indicated the growing crowd. "There are more women in here than even I can handle on my own."

"I'm sure you'll manage somehow."

"I always do," Amanda said with a wink.

In the brief time she had between customers, Simone pulled out her phone and sent Reagan a text. "If you're not busy," she wrote, "get over to Azure. I think I know a way to get you some free publicity."

"See you in ninety minutes," Reagan wrote back. "I need time to put my face on."

"Make it sixty. Your face looks fine the way it is."

"Thanks, boss. See you in an hour."

Simone smiled as she put her phone away. Her smile grew even broader when Reagan showed up fifteen minutes early instead of fashionably late, saving her from having to deliver a lecture about the importance of being on time. A lecture she had received more times than she could count but had only recently decided to heed.

"You rang?" Reagan asked. Her look was casual but attention-getting. She had paired a T-shirt that looked like a '70s-style powder blue tuxedo with knock-off designer jeans and a pair of well-worn Doc Martens. She looked like a million bucks in an outfit that had probably cost less than two hundred dollars.

Simone handed her a thick three-ring binder that contained the hundreds of selections programmed into the karaoke machine's memory banks. "Pick something in your vocal range and put your name on the sign-up sheet."

Reagan wrinkled her nose as she flipped through the laminated pages. "You want me to sing karaoke? I've never even heard of some of the songs in here."

"How about this one?" Simone flipped to a song by Tracy Chapman, a toe-tapping bluesy number that was a complete departure from the singer-songwriter's introspective, folk-oriented early work.

"I can do that one."

"Cool. Now pick one more."

"Why?"

"Because if the first performance goes as well as I think it will, you're going to need to do an encore."

Reagan glanced at the sign-up sheet. "Have you seen how many names there are on this list? It'll be forever before my turn comes around again."

"That's perfect for us. If you're the final performer, you'll be all everyone's talking about on their way home. If your name starts trending on social media, the buzz will only grow from there." Reagan stared at her wordlessly for a long moment. "What?" Simone asked when no comment appeared forthcoming.

"This is really happening, isn't it?"

"Yeah," Simone said, feeling genuine excitement take root within her, "it really is."

She knew it was only a matter of time before some deep-pocketed exec from a major label swooped in to try to steal Reagan from Liberty City Records. Reagan was too talented to stay small-time for long. Until that day came, however, she planned to sit back and enjoy the ride.

❖

"Check this out."

Kenya clicked on one of the links Simone had sent her and angled her computer monitor so Celia could see the screen. The cell phone footage wasn't as sharp or as professionally produced as some videos that had been uploaded to the website by other users, but its raw, unedited quality only added to its authenticity. Its realness.

"Who is she?" Celia asked as a young woman in a powder blue T-shirt put her own spin on a cover of a Tracy Chapman song.

"Reagan Carter. The singer Simone's going to be producing."

"No wonder she's quitting bartending and switching to music. That kid's good."

"Simone uploaded the video last night and it's already had over ten thousand hits."

Celia looked suitably impressed. "That's how Justin Bieber got his start. He developed a following on YouTube, a label signed him, the hits started coming, and now he's worth two hundred million dollars. I just hope Reagan doesn't end up egging someone's house or wearing pants that make her look like she's got a full diaper."

Kenya closed the website after the video ended. "Simone's pretty level-headed. I think she'll keep Reagan on an even keel."

"Are they an item?"

"No. At least I don't think so. I've only heard Simone mention a professional relationship with her, not a personal one." Kenya felt a stab of what felt like jealousy as she considered the idea Simone and Reagan might be lovers. She tamped the emotion down as she shuffled one of the stacks of paperwork on her desk. She had no reason to be jealous. The very idea was absurd. She was involved with Mackenzie, and she and Simone were just friends. Simone was free to date who she wanted. So was she. But Bridget was her friend, too, and she hadn't felt this possessive when Avery had entered Bridget's life. What did that say about her relationship with Simone? What did that say about her? Could she be involved with one woman but have feelings for another? She turned her attention back to work so she wouldn't have to consider the possibility. "Do you have the final head count for next week's retreat?"

Celia consulted her notes. "Yes. Everyone's on board. I called the resort yesterday and confirmed our room reservations. I've also made sure the motivational speaker we wanted still has us on his schedule. Everything's good to go. Since we're allowed to take spouses and children to the after-work events, will you be inviting Mackenzie to join you?"

"I can't see her twiddling her thumbs in our hotel room while she waits for me to finish running my coworkers through their paces. If I were attending the annual HR Professionals' convention in Las Vegas, it might be a different story. The bright lights of Sin City are more her speed than the spinning teacups in the Magic Kingdom. I'd probably be forced to bail on all the morning sessions because she kept me up too late the night before gambling in a casino or exploring the nightlife on the Strip. Besides, she has meetings all next week for a project she's working on so it would be a wasted invitation."

"That's too bad. Juan was hoping for an introduction. Actually, he was hoping to be able to do some deep-sea fishing on her yacht, but first things first."

"Maybe next time. And that takes us to the next item on our agenda." Kenya checked her to-do list. "We've received a request to convert from our current layout to an open office concept. We would keep the conference room for client meetings, but we'd knock down most of the other walls and get rid of the private offices. When it's done well, it makes for a more collaborative work environment."

"And when it isn't, it turns everything into one huge clusterfuck. Wait. Did I say that out loud?" Celia asked with mock innocence.

"I don't come up with the ideas. I just follow through on them." Kenya liked being able to close her door and shut herself off from the world when she was dealing with confidential issues or she simply needed some quiet time. "Because most of the personnel issues we deal with are private, I'll make sure our respective spaces are exempted from any potential renovations."

"Hallelujah. What do you need from me?"

"Team up with the facilities manager, get some contractors in here, and get them to give you some numbers and designs I can take to the management team."

"I can do that. Is there anything else?"

Kenya needed to address the growing debate over a proposed company ban on e-cigarettes, but her ringing cell phone convinced her to table the issue for a later discussion. "That's all for now."

"I'll get started on the items we've discussed and give you an update after lunch."

"Sounds good." Kenya brought her phone to her ear after Celia pulled the door closed with a soft click. "Would it be premature of me to say a star is born?"

"Shh," Simone said. "Don't say it too loud or you might jinx everything."

"I consider myself sufficiently warned."

"You saw the video?"

"I did."

"What did you think?"

"Reagan is as amazing live as she is on record. No wonder you're excited about working with her. Nice marketing, by the way. Whose idea was it for her to sing karaoke?"

"Mine."

"Did you choose the songs, too?" Kenya clicked on the second link and another video began to play, this one featuring Reagan doing a cover of a Bob Marley song. The Marley tune didn't have as many hits as the other video that had been uploaded, but the number was steadily growing.

"I chose the first one. Reagan picked the second."

"Nice job."

Reagan's song choice made Kenya wonder if Celia's question about Simone and Reagan being an item wasn't as far off base as it had initially seemed. Bob Marley was the most popular musician in Jamaican history. He sold millions of records around the world before his untimely death. Was Reagan's decision to sing a song he was known for a testament of her love for his music or for the woman who would be making music with her?

"I didn't call for compliments," Simone said. "Well, I did, but it isn't the only reason I called."

"Let me guess." Kenya muted the sound on her computer. "You have a question to ask me."

"I do, though it isn't one from my list."

"That sounds mysterious."

"You'll probably say no because I'm sure you already have plans, but I figured I'd ask anyway."

"That sounds even more mysterious." Kenya spun her chair around so she could take in the view of downtown Miami outside her office window. "What did you want to ask me?"

"My family's having a get-together Saturday afternoon and I wanted to know if you'd like to come. You wouldn't have to stay long. An hour at most. I thought you could use something to take your mind off the competition."

Kenya got butterflies in her stomach every time she thought about her upcoming performance. She was looking forward to it, but she also couldn't wait for it to be over. She put so much pressure on herself to succeed that the anticipation was often worse than the actual event. "I might be able to spare a few minutes." Even though her schedule was tight, she didn't want to appear rude by turning down Simone's invitation. And whatever Simone had in mind might provide a welcome distraction from Saturday night's big event. "What's the occasion?"

"It's my sister Jayden's birthday. She's turning twenty-nine for the sixth time. Not that anyone's counting, of course."

"I remember when I turned thirty. My friends kept going on and on about it like it was the end of the world. But to me, it was just another birthday. Fifty might give me pause, but thirty didn't scare me."

"I'll let you know when I get there."

"What time does this shindig start?"

"You'll come?"

"You make it sound like so much fun. How could I not?" She hoped it would be better than the last time she broke bread with someone else's family. She still had nightmares about her evening with Mackenzie's parents. Or, to be exact, her after-dinner discussion with Mackenzie's mother that had made the extravagant meal sour in her stomach and had nearly caused her to end her fledgling relationship with Mackenzie.

"I'll text you the time and address. On second thought, I'll pick you up."

"Are you afraid I won't show?"

"No, I'm afraid your BMW wouldn't survive a trip to the 'hood. By the time you were ready to leave the party, all you might have left would be the frame."

The local newspapers were filled with horror stories about unsuspecting tourists wandering into the wrong neighborhoods and getting carjacked or worse. Kenya wondered if she was about to suffer the same fate. "Should I be afraid?"

"Stick with me and you'll be fine. Trust me."

In Kenya's world, trust was easily requested but not so easily given. In the short time they'd known each other, Simone had managed to become a trusted friend. One of the few people Kenya knew without a doubt had only her best interests at heart. Like Bridget, Simone would never lie to her. No matter how much the truth might hurt.

"In that case, I'll see you Saturday."

CHAPTER NINE

Simone placed a can of coconut milk on the counter and watched her mother add it to the simmering goat curry. Her mother stirred the fragrant concoction with a long-handled spoon and took a quick taste. "Better. You can still taste the Scotch bonnet peppers, but they're not as pronounced. We wouldn't want to set your friend's mouth on fire, would we?"

"Do you need anything else?" Simone had run track in high school. By the time she graduated, she had carved out a reputation as one of the fastest runners in Florida. She'd gotten her start running back and forth between her parents' house and the Caribbean grocery store down the street to pick up the various ingredients her mother needed to make her favorite native dishes.

"No, I'm good." Her mother stirred a pot of vinegar, onions, and hot peppers that would reduce to form the sauce for the escovitch fish, one of Jayden's favorite dishes. Along with the goat curry her mother was tending to and the jerk chicken and pork her father had wrapped in pimento leaves that morning and tossed in a backyard barbecue pit filled with hot coals.

"Are you sure?" Simone asked. "You always say you don't need anything, but as soon as I sit down, you suddenly think of something that conveniently slipped your mind during my first five trips to the store."

"Ah, go on with you now." Her mother's thick Jamaican patois provided the perfect complement to the island rhythms blaring from the sound system out back. "You're just afraid I'll make you late to meet up with your lady friend. How long have you been spending time with her, anyway?"

"Kenya's 'spending time,' as you put it, with someone else. She and I are just friends." Simone grabbed some plantain chips from a nearby bowl and shoved a handful in her mouth to prevent her mother from asking any follow-up questions. No such luck.

"How did you meet her?"

"She came into the bar a few weeks ago to attend one of the events we were putting on that night."

"And what does she do for a living?"

"She—"

"Stop talking with your mouth full."

After she swallowed the rest of the plantain chips, Simone pulled a chair from the table and took a seat. She figured she might as well make herself comfortable. Once her mother started asking questions, she could keep going for a while. "She's head of human resources for a marketing firm in town."

"So she makes good money."

"I guess. I've never asked to see her check stub or a copy of her tax returns."

Her mother arched her eyebrows as she stirred the curry, a sure sign she was about to say something Simone might not like. "It's a good thing she's well-off. You'll need someone to take care of you now that you've gone and quit your job."

Simone sighed in frustration. "I don't need anyone to take care of me, Mom. And I didn't quit my job. I changed careers. There's a difference."

Her mother's eyebrows rose even higher. "The difference between getting paid and collecting unemployment?"

Her father's mantra was "idle hands are the devil's workshop." When Simone and her sisters were growing up, their parents had worked three, sometimes four jobs at a time in order to provide for the family. Even though her parents had been retired for several years now, their days were still filled with activity—and her mother's with concern she was living for the present instead of planning for the future. Her future was now. And she meant to take advantage of the opportunity, no matter what anyone else thought about her decision.

"I'll be fine, Mom." She pushed herself out of her seat. "I have to go pick up Kenya. And don't give her the third degree when she gets here."

Her mother began battering and frying red snapper for the escovitch fish. "My house, my rules."

"I've heard that saying more times than I can count."

Her mother wagged a flour-covered finger in her direction. "And it still holds true, so don't you forget it."

"I consider myself warned. I'll be back in a few." Simone gave her mother a kiss on the cheek and drove her bike across town.

The contrast between the neighborhood she had grown up in and the new ones that sprang up every few years never failed to take her breath away. Rich and poor alike called Miami home. The physical divide between them was narrowing all the time, but the metaphorical gap grew wider every day. Simone had managed to carve out a niche for herself in both worlds, though she didn't feel she truly belonged in either. Her dreams were too big for the 'hood, but she didn't have the financial standing to do much more than visit how the other half lived. And not for long, at that.

One day, she thought as she neared the swanky condos in the heart of town, one of these bad boys is going to be mine.

She stowed her motorcycle in the parking garage next to Kenya's building and headed up to Kenya's condo. She took the stairs instead of the elevator so she could burn off her nervous energy. Kenya's visit meant a lot to her, even if it would only last a few hours.

Kenya opened the door wearing a floral print tank top, cream-colored shorts, and canvas tennis shoes. She looked ready for a day at the beach or a vacation in the tropics. Simone wanted to take the tank top's delicate spaghetti straps between her fingers and slowly slide them off Kenya's shoulders. She wanted to run her hands over the newly exposed skin and feel its warmth. She wanted to sample its flavor. Did Kenya taste as good as the coconut-scented lotion she had used or more so? Simone clamped her tongue between her teeth to keep it from wandering off on its own.

Kenya held up a bottle of Jamaican rum. "The owner of my favorite liquor store said this is a good brand. Was he right?"

Simone examined the label. The brand Kenya had chosen was her father's favorite. "My dad loves this stuff. Don't let him see it or he'll add it to his private stash before anyone else has a chance to take a sip."

"What about you?" Kenya asked after they rode the elevator to the ground floor and headed to the parking garage. "What's your favorite whiskey?"

Simone placed the rum in the leather storage pouch strapped to the back of her bike. "I used to prefer vodka."

"Used to?" Kenya pulled on Simone's spare helmet and fastened the chin strap. "What happened? Did your palate change?"

"No, I grew up." Simone tried to explain her newfound sobriety. "I was enjoying myself a bit too much, and I decided to pull back before it became a problem."

"How long ago was this?"

Simone started the bike and raised her voice to be heard over the sound of the engine. "Fairly recently."

"Is that one of the reasons you're giving up bartending? To avoid temptation?"

"Yes." Though not in the way Kenya was thinking. One of the temptations Simone needed to avoid was her, a woman she wanted more than any other but couldn't have.

Kenya cocked her head. "What else don't I know about you?"

"Not much. I'm a bit of an open book."

Simone tried not to tremble with desire when Kenya slipped her arms around her waist and rested her chin on her shoulder. "Then it's a good thing I like to read."

In a perfect world, Kenya would treat Simone's body like a copy of *War and Peace*, taking her time as she read every word. But the only pages Kenya wanted to turn were Mackenzie's. And those were so well-worn they were dog-eared. Perhaps it was time to introduce her to a new story.

"What am I in for?" Kenya asked after Simone parked her bike in one of the few remaining spaces near her parents' house. "I'm a little gun-shy after my most recent family dinner."

Kenya had yet to tell her what went wrong that night, but if she didn't plan on volunteering the information, Simone wasn't going to press her for details. She retrieved the bottle of rum and tucked it under her arm as they walked toward the house. "You won't find any linen tablecloths or sterling silver place settings at this meal. More like paper napkins, plastic forks, and red Solo cups."

Kenya grinned. "Sounds like my kind of party. When I was a kid, my relatives on my mother's side of the family had a family reunion each year on the Fourth of July. My father and grandfather were in charge of the meat. Each year, they would buy a hog and stay up all night barbecuing it and a case of chickens over a pit filled with red-hot coals. My mother and grandmother would stay up to make all the sides. My cousins and I always tried to pull an all-nighter, too, but none of us ever made it past three a.m., no matter how many naps we took to prepare. After we inevitably fell asleep in the living room or the den or wherever we settled for longer than five minutes, we'd wake up the next day to the smell of barbecue, potato salad, baked beans, a huge pan of mac and cheese, and every kind of pie you could imagine. I miss those days."

"Why did they end?"

Kenya shrugged. "The usual reasons, I suppose. The kids grew up and had families of their own, and we slowly lost touch with our old traditions."

"Once people are able to afford the bigger things, they usually forget about the little things."

Simone regarded her cousins playing bid whist on the front porch, her aunts and uncles playing pétanque on the lawn, and her nieces and nephews kicking around a soccer ball in the side yard. She was glad to see her family's traditions had survived. And with Kenya at her side, perhaps she could establish even more.

❖

Simone's sisters, Jayden and Miranda, looked just like their father. Simone, on the other hand, was the spitting image of her mother. They had the same mocha skin, earthy laugh, and mischievous grin. They even sounded alike, though Charlotte Bailey had a much thicker accent than her daughter. The longer they stayed at the cookout, however, the more Simone's roots began to show.

Simone's family was large and welcoming. They made Kenya feel like she was part of their brood instead of a visiting stranger. The contrast between this gathering and the meal she had shared with the Richardsons couldn't be more obvious. Instead of bone china, filet mignon, and perfectly decanted carafes of fine wine, there were paper plates, pit-roasted pork, and bottles of Jamaican rum. The conversation was natural, not stilted. Laughter was plentiful, and so was love.

Mackenzie had invited Kenya to her parents' house. Simone had brought her to her parents' home. Kenya didn't want to leave. The get-together reminded her of her own family gatherings. More food and relatives than you could shake a stick at and a strong-willed matriarch at the helm to keep everything—and everyone—in line.

"I like her, Monie," Charlotte said after she had asked Kenya every question under the sun. Simone certainly came by her love of Q&A honestly, Kenya noted. She had inherited it from her mother. "You should bring her around more often. But she's as skinny as you are. Let me fix you a plate."

"Everything looks and smells wonderful, Mrs. Bailey," Kenya said, "but I need to be able to fit into my dress tonight without letting out the seams."

Not to mention she wanted to save room for the pasta dinner Mackenzie had promised to make her after the charity event ended. She wanted to clean her plate, not push her food around it so she could show Mackenzie how much she appreciated her efforts. How much she appreciated *her*. Aside from rehearsals, they hadn't spent much time together since last weekend. Even though they had just gotten together, it already felt like they were growing apart. With both their work schedules ramping up, things might only get worse from here.

"Nonsense," Charlotte said. "You'll dance better on a full stomach than an empty one. More food means more energy. I'll be right back."

Kenya tried to call Charlotte back, but Simone stopped her with a shake of her head. "Give it up. Once my mother sets her mind to something, no one can convince her to change course. Ask my dad. In forty-two years of marriage, he's never won an argument. Over time, he's learned to give in right away rather than press the issue and risk receiving the silent treatment."

Kenya couldn't imagine someone as vocal as Charlotte ever being silent for long. She could tell the Baileys were a close-knit family. Simone's stories about them only reaffirmed the notion. "Was it hard for you to come out to your family, considering most Jamaicans are opposed to homosexuality?"

"It wasn't easy, but it wasn't as difficult as it could have been. I can't say my parents weren't disappointed by the news, but they didn't threaten to disown me or kick me out of the house.

I got the usual 'What about grandchildren?' speech from my mother, and my dad wanted to know what he had done wrong."

"What did you say?"

"I reminded my mother she already had grandchildren, courtesy of Jayden and Miranda, and I told my dad my being a lesbian had nothing to do with him putting a cricket bat in my hands when I was younger instead of a doll. They were fine after that. Well, my mother's still holding out hope on the grandkids front, but she and my dad aren't as worried about my day-to-day well-being as they would be if we still lived on the island. There, they'd be in constant fear for my safety. Here, things are different. At the end of the day, my father doesn't care who I'm with as long as she's good to me and treats my family with respect."

"And your mother?"

"She wants me to marry someone rich so I won't have to worry about making a living."

"She sounds like my mother."

"How so?"

"When she heard I was dating Mackenzie, her first question wasn't 'How did you meet?' or 'How is it going?' but 'Did she make you sign a prenup?'"

Simone took a sip of the grapefruit soda she'd plucked from a nearby cooler. "Would you sign one if she asked?"

"I don't want her money, and I'm sure she doesn't need mine."

"You didn't answer the question."

"Because we're not there yet. We're sleeping together, not engaged. If we move down that path, I'm sure her lawyers would draw up something and expect me to sign. I would explore my options then."

"This is the first time you've mentioned Mackenzie all day. She used to be your favorite subject. I'm enjoying the respite, but is everything all right with you two?"

Something was definitely off between her and Mackenzie and had been for days, but if Kenya couldn't explain it to herself, how could she possibly explain it to someone else? Fortunately, Charlotte's return spared her from having to try.

"Here you are." Charlotte brandished a sturdy paper plate piled high with fish, pork, chicken, vegetables, and a large dollop of meat stew. "Enjoy."

"Does she really expect me to eat all this?" Kenya asked after Charlotte left to shower affection on one of her four grandchildren.

"I think she plans for us to share. Notice she brought one plate but two forks."

Kenya took a seat in a colorfully striped beach chair. "She wouldn't be trying to play matchmaker, would she?"

Simone sat next to her. "I told her you're seeing someone, but I think it went in one ear and out the other."

"Like I said, she sounds just like my mother. She has selective hearing. She hears what she wants and ignores what she doesn't." Kenya sampled some of the stew and tried not to inhale the rest. The flavors were incredible and the meat was so tender she didn't need teeth to eat it.

"You like the goat curry?" Simone asked.

"Goat?" Kenya paused in mid-chew. "Is that what this is?"

Simone nodded. "Jamaican goat curry is one of my mother's specialties."

Kenya had detected a slight gaminess in the meat, but the unexpected flavor was undercut by the sweetness of the coconut milk in which it had been cooked. "My compliments to the chef," she said, going back for more. "Are there any other surprises on this plate I should know about?"

"The sauce on the fish is a little sour." Simone pinched a piece of fish, peered at it to make sure it didn't contain any bones, and held it out to her. Kenya had the plate in one hand and a bottle of Red Stripe in the other. She didn't want to let go of either. "It's okay," Simone said, bringing her fingers toward Kenya's lips. "I don't have cooties. Take it."

Kenya opened her mouth and allowed Simone to feed her. The intimate act should have made her feel uncomfortable but didn't. In fact, it felt natural. It felt like second nature. It felt... incredible. Her taste buds sang, and her heart picked up the tune.

She told herself to stop staring at Simone's mouth as Simone licked her fingers clean, but she couldn't look away. Had Simone's lips always been so full? So inviting? So downright kissable? Her mouth watered for a taste.

"How was it?" Simone asked.

Kenya finally managed to tear her gaze from Simone's mouth. "Delicious."

"Did you like everything?" Charlotte asked after Kenya and Simone combined to clean the plate.

Kenya felt her cheeks warm. She hoped Charlotte couldn't read her mind. Or her face. The guilt she felt for having lascivious thoughts about Simone was probably etched there. "Everything was wonderful. Thank you."

"I'm glad you enjoyed yourself." Charlotte wrapped an arm around Kenya's and pulled her to her feet. "I know you can't stay long. Before you go, come to the kitchen and fix yourself a plate to take with you. We have more than enough food and I don't want any of it to go to waste. Monie, be a dear and go to the store for me. Even though we have enough food to feed a small army, your father has decided he wants oxtail stew for dinner tomorrow. And wouldn't you know it? I'm out of oxtails. Make sure you pick out some with plenty of meat on them. I don't want to end up with a pot full of bones."

Kenya knew better than to argue. So, apparently, did Simone. "Yes, ma'am," they said in unison.

Kenya allowed herself to be led into the house. In the kitchen, Charlotte handed her a Styrofoam plate and serving spoon and directed her to fill the container with the dishes of her choice.

"Are you and your lady friend serious?" Charlotte asked.

Kenya nearly dropped the serving spoon into what little was left of the goat curry. "Pardon me?"

"If you are serious about her, walk away and don't come back. I don't want you breaking my daughter's heart."

"Mrs. Bailey, Simone and I are just friends."

"I don't think Simone believes that. What's more, I don't think you do, either." Charlotte folded her arms across her chest. "I saw you with her. When you didn't think anyone was watching. You care for her, don't you?"

Kenya set the container on the counter before her shaking hands dropped the contents on the floor. "Of course I do. She's a wonderful person and I feel fortunate to have her in my life. But like I said, she and I are just friends."

"Have you told her that?"

"Repeatedly."

Charlotte's voice was softer than her words. "Then maybe it's time you told yourself."

❖

Simone slipped into the room and found a seat at a circular table in the back just before the lights dimmed. She pulled at the too-tight bow tie knotted around her neck. Between the tuxedo rental, the salary and tips she was missing out on by convincing Amanda to switch shifts with her, and the hundred dollars she'd had to fork over at the door, she was taking a bath tonight in more ways than one. But she had to see Kenya and Mackenzie together. She had to see for herself that their relationship was real and the moment she had shared with Kenya at Jayden's birthday party that afternoon was just that. A moment.

Her heart raced each time she remembered the look in Kenya's eyes when she'd taken the snapper from her. When Kenya's tongue had flicked against her fingertips, setting every nerve ending in her body on fire. When Kenya had stared at her as if she wanted to kiss her breathless. When she'd licked the remaining escovitch sauce from her fingers so she could take a little bit of Kenya into her mouth. So she could taste her on her skin. She had been in a haze ever since, driven to distraction by doubt and desire.

Should she tell Kenya what she had seen in the alley behind Azure that night? If she did, what could she possibly hope to gain except brownie points at the expense of Kenya's broken heart? A hollow victory at best.

She refused the waiter's offer of a glass of champagne, even though she needed something to ease her anxiety. She turned her attention to the dance floor, where the master of ceremonies was reciting the rules.

"Ten couples will be competing tonight," he said. His orange spray tan made him look like a well-dressed jack-o-lantern. The unearthly glow of his too-perfect veneers under the bright lights only added to the impression. "The winners will be determined based on our esteemed judges' scores as well as yours. You should see a set of scorecards on your table. One for each of you. After each team performs, score their routine on a rank of one to ten, ten being the highest and most desirous score. Each scorecard will be counted separately, but feel free to collaborate if you like. My fellow organizers and I want this evening's event to be as interactive and as enjoyable as possible. After all the dancers have performed, representatives from Safe Space will collect the score sheets and tally the results. Then I will have the honor of announcing the winning team. But in the end, everyone at Safe Space is a winner. Thanks to your generous donations, we have not only met our fundraising goal but exceeded it by a whopping fifty percent, insuring Safe Space's doors will remain open to those in need for the foreseeable future."

Simone joined in the spontaneous round of applause. She had learned to be frugal after Mackenzie threatened to fire her. Since then, she had started to save more than she spent instead of the other way around. Her nest egg wasn't as big as she wanted it to be, but it was a start. The fact that her hard-earned money was earmarked for charity had made it easy to part with.

She watched as teams with varying levels of skill took the floor one by one. Or was it two by two? She tried to be as objective as possible with her scoring, despite the various rooting sections chanting and waving handmade signs to sway voters' opinions in their chosen team's favor. Each team had something to offer, but some pairs were clearly more adept than others.

Kenya and Mackenzie were the last team to take the floor. Simone leaned forward after their names were announced. Twin spotlights heralded their entrance. Mackenzie was wearing all black. From her dance shoes to her tight spandex pants to her form-fitting silk shirt. Several women—and some men— swooned when Mackenzie struck her pose, but the sight of her left Simone unmoved. When she saw Kenya all dolled up in a sparkling sequin gown that hugged every curve, however, she felt the earth shake.

The music started, jolting Simone from her reverie. For three and a half minutes, Kenya and Mackenzie moved across the dance floor, acting out a wordless tale of attraction, passion, and seduction. Their movements were flawless. Without, as far as Simone could tell, a single misstep. She, along with the rest of the audience, was mesmerized. The raucous cheering sections that had been so loud all night fell silent.

As Kenya and Mackenzie danced, Simone could see the results of the hours of rehearsals they had endured. She could see something else, too. She could see the familiarity they had with each other's bodies. She could see the ease they felt at being in each other's arms.

She didn't know if Mackenzie was telling the truth when she said her fling with Fernanda was over or if her feelings for Kenya were real, but the kiss she planted on Kenya after their routine ended certainly seemed to have real emotion behind it.

Simone filled out her final scorecard but didn't stick around to see who won. She didn't need to. She had already seen enough.

❖

Kenya's eyes must have been playing tricks on her. Just before the house lights had come up, she could have sworn she had seen Simone sneaking out of the room. As much as she would have liked to get her take on the evening, she knew this wasn't Simone's kind of scene. Black tie and ballroom dancing definitely weren't her thing. She was more a reggae and board shorts kind of girl. Kenya found both equally appealing. Perhaps too appealing. At the cookout that afternoon, Simone had felt like much more than a friend. She had felt like—

"We did it." Mackenzie held the winners' trophy aloft. "We actually did it. We should celebrate."

"That's what we planned to do, isn't it? Over manicotti and a bottle of wine?" Kenya patted her upswept hair to hide the tremor in her hands. Thoughts of Simone had been plaguing her all afternoon. The desire to kiss her today had been so strong. How had she been able to tamp down the urge? A night with Mackenzie would give her a chance to put her day with Simone behind her. She clung to the idea with a hint of desperation. "I've been looking forward to your homemade pasta for days. Having dinner at home will give us a chance to spend some time together before I leave for Orlando on Monday."

"I can cook for you any time. And we'll have plenty of opportunities to spend time together when you return from your little retreat."

Kenya bristled at the slight. The annual retreat was a long-standing part of her company's corporate culture. Mackenzie made it sound like a frivolous outing instead of the important exercise it had always been. The night they met, Mackenzie had said she admired Pierce, Jackson, and Smith's work, but her most recent comment made it seem like the company was large enough to gain her attention but too small to earn her respect. Did Mackenzie feel that way about her, too?

"I don't want to go out tonight," she said. "I want to go to your place, let my hair down, get out of this dress, and kick off these heels. My feet are killing me."

Kenya tried to dig in, but Mackenzie pushed back.

"Don't be such a stick in the mud, Kenya. I'm too wired to sit at home and twiddle my thumbs. Besides, why would I want to make dinner when I can pay someone to do it for me? I can't make any business connections that way."

"What about the connection you're supposed to be making with me?"

"Our connection, as you put it, is just fine. No one else makes you feel like I do and you know it."

That much was true, though Kenya couldn't decide if that was a good thing or a bad one.

Mackenzie took Kenya's hands in hers. "Fernanda and some of her friends are having a late dinner at Azul, followed by a night on the town. They want to know if we'd like to join them. What do you say?"

Kenya didn't want to go barhopping until the wee hours of the morning. She wanted to spend a quiet night at home, sitting and talking with Mackenzie like she had with Simone that afternoon. She and Simone had shared much more than a plate of food today. They had shared an experience. The kind of experience she was supposed to be sharing with Mackenzie. But Mackenzie wanted something else. She wanted glamour, excitement, and pleasure in all its forms. Would she and Mackenzie always want different things, or would they eventually find common ground?

"Dinner sounds lovely," she said diplomatically, "but I've had a long day. My dancing shoes are officially retired for the evening. You can join Fernanda and her friends if you like."

"Are you sure?" Mackenzie asked with a frown that would have seemed sincere if her eyes weren't glittering with excitement. "I could tell Fernanda we'll go out with her some other time."

"I don't want to keep you from doing something you want to do. Have fun with your friends. I'll see you tomorrow."

"You're the best. *Ciao*, darling. Until tomorrow."

Mackenzie seemed all-too-eager to get away. When she kissed Kenya on the cheek, Kenya caught a whiff of perfume that wasn't Mackenzie's usual scent but smelled vaguely familiar.

"Is something wrong?" Bridget asked after she, Avery, Celia, and Juan came over to dish out congratulatory hugs.

"No," Kenya said, trying to convince herself that what she was saying was true, "everything's fine."

CHAPTER TEN

Q uestion 14. What is your most treasured memory?"
Simone typed her text but didn't hit the Send
button. She hadn't seen or heard from Kenya since the dance
competition at the Safe Space charity event last Saturday night.
She had been busy doing double duty polishing the tracks for
Reagan's demo and getting in her final shifts at Azure. Kenya
had been in Orlando all week for something work-related and
wasn't supposed to come home until late Friday afternoon, when
she'd probably be too busy playing catch-up with Mackenzie
to attend her going-away party. Simone wanted to talk to her
before they lost touch, but Kenya might not be checking her
email. And even if she was, she might be too tied up with work
to send a timely response.

Simone sent the text and began the waiting game, the fun
part of not being able to talk face-to-face. Would Kenya get back
to her in a few minutes, within the hour, or never? After spending
time with Kenya Saturday afternoon, she would have thought
the answer would be clear. After seeing Kenya with Mackenzie
Saturday night, however, everything got a whole lot murkier.

God, how she had wanted to kiss Kenya at Jayden's party.
If she had interpreted the signs correctly, Kenya had wanted the
same thing. Then, a few hours later, she had seen Kenya dancing
with Mackenzie. Responding to her touch. Had she misread
what she had seen? What she had felt? Nothing made sense, but

she didn't know where to go to find answers. She couldn't go to Kenya. Kenya had already told her how she felt—told her, in essence, that she was out of her league. But if that was true, why did they keep discovering they had so many things in common?

Simone tried working on a song but couldn't concentrate. She gave up rather than try to force something out of nothing. Reagan deserved her best work, not the unfocused shit she was coming up with today.

She needed to get her act together. Major labels gave their artists and producers nearly a year to complete their albums and get them on the market. Liberty City Records' typical turnaround time was only a few months, which meant she couldn't afford to have too many off days. And today she was definitely off her game.

She started to go out, but she doubted falling into bed with a willing stranger would improve her mood or help her find her missing creative spark. It might even achieve the opposite effect. She didn't need a change of scenery. She needed Kenya. Each moment she spent with her was better than the last. Now those moments might be coming to an end.

Kenya had made her choice. She had chosen to be with Mackenzie. Simone couldn't watch Kenya give her love to someone who didn't deserve her. She needed to walk away. But how was she supposed to break free when all she wanted to do was hold on?

Kenya's response came a little after noon, when she and the other members of her team were most likely taking a lunch break. Simone read the words on the screen knowing she would have less than an hour to reply to the answer to her question and ask one or two more.

"My most treasured memory," Kenya had written, "is hearing Stacy Howard tell me she loved me. I was seventeen and she was the first girl I fell for who reciprocated my feelings. She made me realize I wasn't the only one 'like me.' She made me realize being different didn't mean being alone. You?"

Simone thought for a minute. Most of her favorite memories involved her family. Her childhood hadn't been ideal, but it had definitely been an adventure. One that had helped shape her into the person she was now. She hadn't realized how much she and her family didn't have until they got to America, where everything was available in plentiful supply twenty-four hours a day, three hundred sixty-five days a year. Holidays included. Yet she didn't feel like she had missed out on anything. Quite the opposite, in fact. She felt enriched by the hardships she had endured. She could appreciate how good her present was because she knew how bad her past used to be.

"The one memory I treasure above the rest," she typed, "is the first Christmas my family and I spent in the States. Even though our parents finally had the means to provide my sisters and me with the fancy toys our classmates asked their parents to buy them, they took the time to make us something by hand like they did when we lived in Kingston. My sisters and I were pissed at the time." Simone smiled as she remembered the look on Miranda's face when the Walkman she had asked for turned out to be a Rasta hat crocheted with yarn the colors of the Jamaican flag. The hats were all the rage now but a rarity back then, making Miranda stick out when she was trying so hard to fit in. "It wasn't until I got older that I was able to appreciate my parents' desire to keep our old family traditions alive even though we had moved to a new country."

A few minutes later, Simone's phone beeped, announcing the arrival of Kenya's reply.

"I gathered how important family and tradition are to you from the time we spent at your sister's birthday party. Thank you again for inviting me. When is the next event? I could use another helping of your mother's goat curry."

Simone laughed at the image of a knife-and-fork-wielding smiley Kenya added to the end of her text. She was glad to see Kenya had enjoyed herself on Saturday and wasn't simply being polite when she'd said she had a good time. "Just say when," she wrote in response. "Mom doesn't need an excuse to cook. Just the ingredients and the time to put them together. Shall I pencil you in for next week?"

"LOL. Table for two, please."

The comment reminded Simone of Kenya's response to a question Mackenzie had asked her during the speed dating event. When Kenya had said the one place she wanted to visit was some fancy restaurant in Italy that only served two people at a time. Simone couldn't afford to take her there, but perhaps she could take her someplace even more exclusive. Someplace with room for only one. She could take her into her heart.

"Too late," she said aloud. "She's already there."

❖

Kenya checked the time as she took the last bite of her club sandwich. She had thirty minutes to wrap up lunch and get the afternoon's breakout sessions underway. Plenty of time to try to get Mackenzie on the phone. Something she hadn't been able to do all week. They had been playing phone tag since Monday afternoon. They kept just missing each other somehow. Either Mackenzie was in a meeting or she was. One would leave a message, the other would call back, then the cycle would repeat itself. Kenya felt like she was running on an endless loop. She was tired of exchanging voice mails. She wanted to have an actual conversation with Mackenzie. She needed to hear her voice. She needed to know why she wasn't missing her more than she did.

She excused herself from the table, tossed her lunch container in the recycle bin, and headed to a less-populated area so she could have some privacy.

Her call to Mackenzie went straight to voice mail. Just like all the others. Mackenzie was supposed to be meeting with potential designers and investors for her resort project. Were the meetings going that well or that poorly? Kenya hoped the former was true. She knew how much the project meant to Mackenzie. It represented her chance to further her brand and finally escape her father's sizeable shadow. She would be devastated if she wasn't able to get the project off the ground.

"Hey, babe, it's me," Kenya said, leaving yet another message. "I had a few minutes so I decided to give you a call. I hope everything's going well today. Call me when you get a chance. I want to hear the big news before you draft the press release. I'll be in sessions all afternoon and tonight's Family Night so I don't know when I'll be free, but I'd love to hear from you. If I don't, I'll be home tomorrow night and we can catch up on everything we've missed. I know you can't wait to hear all about my exciting week." She wished she could hit Undo and take the comment back, but it was too late. She had meant it as a joke. She hoped Mackenzie would take it that way. Thanks to stress from work and Mackenzie's desire to go out all the time—as in every night—they were doing enough sniping at each other as it was. The only common ground they were able to find most days was in the bedroom. When, that was, they ended their days in the same room. Kenya wanted them to have at least one conversation on their feet instead of on their backs. "Tomorrow's a half-day, so, depending on traffic, I should be home around four. See you then."

She called Simone next. She decided to reach out to her for two reasons. One, she knew she could count on Simone to be near her phone and, two, she wanted to talk to someone about something other than business for the first time in days.

"What's question fifteen?" she asked after Simone answered on the second ring.

"What's the matter?" Simone said with a laugh. "Are you in a rush to finish the list?"

"No, I've been asking questions all week and I'd almost forgotten what it was like to answer them. Keeping everyone engaged in and entertained by the program is mentally and physically draining. I could use a break."

She could use a break from her life, too, but she didn't see that happening any time soon.

"Then let me help you out. Question fifteen. What is your greatest accomplishment?"

Kenya was proud of some of the programs and policies she had implemented at Pierce, Jackson, and Smith, but she didn't know if she wanted any of them to be included in her obituary, the ultimate listing of a person's accomplishments in work and in life.

"I'm proudest of the fact that everything I've accomplished I've achieved on my own. My success hasn't been based on who I am but what I know."

"You're independent. I like that in a woman."

"What else do you like?"

"About you?"

"No." The question reminded Kenya of the uncomfortable conversation she'd had with Simone's mother a few days prior. When Charlotte Bailey had asked her to walk away from Simone rather than risk breaking her heart. Kenya didn't want to hurt Simone, but she didn't want to be without her, either. The height of selfishness, she knew, but she couldn't force herself to walk away from someone who brought such joy to her life. "What are you looking for in a partner?"

"Why, is there someone you want me to meet?"

It was Kenya's turn to laugh.

"Perish the thought. Setting up my friends is a surefire way to lose one or both of them. I don't want to lose you."

"Or the poor, unfortunate soul who would have to put up with me for at least one night?"

Kenya had a hard time believing Simone wasn't on the market. Not when women were constantly passing along their phone numbers when they gave her their drink orders. Kenya had seen Simone flirt with the women at Azure, but she had never seen her go home with one. In fact, she hadn't seen her with anyone since the night they'd met. Was Simone being discreet with her love life or was she waiting for someone special to come along?

"What about Reagan?" she asked. "Celia thinks you'd make a cute couple." She could picture them together, too, though she wasn't entirely sure she liked the image. Though she had no claims on Simone, she still felt protective of her. Or was it possessive?

"I like her, but not like that. If I weren't working with her and she were a few years older, I could see us going out. But we are and she's not."

"You don't mix business with pleasure?"

"As my father taught me long ago, you don't shit where you eat. I would rather be Reagan's producer than her lover."

Kenya had lost track of all the office affairs she had heard about in passing or the number of sexual harassment complaints she had fielded over the years. She was glad to hear Simone wasn't likely to be involved in one of her own. Or was she glad to hear Simone wasn't likely to be involved with anyone?

"You still haven't told me what you're looking for," she said, returning to the topic at hand.

"I would like to meet someone who knows her own mind and isn't afraid to say what's on it. With a family as loud as mine, I need someone who's able to speak up so she doesn't get drowned out."

"I hope you find what you're looking for."

"Something tells me I won't have to look too hard."

"Have you met someone?"

"You know the answer to that question as well as I do, don't you?"

The big announcement Kenya had prepared herself for had turned out to be an unwelcome return to a recurring theme. "Simone—"

Simone cut her off.

"What are we doing, Kenya? Please tell me because I really want to know. At Jayden's party, I thought we had something special. Then I saw you with Mackenzie that night and—"

"You *were* there. I thought I was seeing things."

"So did I. I had to see you that night. I had to know."

"Know what?"

"If you felt what I did. If you felt something for me. Tell me I didn't imagine it."

"Oh, Simone." Kenya closed her eyes in a vain attempt to escape the truth. "Yes, I felt something for you that day. I would be lying if I said I didn't. But I'm with someone else. Nothing can happen between us."

"And if you weren't with her? What then?"

Kenya suddenly wanted to be anywhere but there. Doing anything but having this conversation. "That's a hypothetical question and I can't answer it."

"Can't or won't? Mackenzie can give you security, but she can't make you happy. Is that all you want? To be secure? Or do you want more?"

"Simone—"

"Talk to me, Kenya. You've never refused to answer one of my questions before. Don't start now. Is being with her what you really want? If it is, tell me now. I need to hear you say it."

Celia waved to get Kenya's attention, then pointed at her watch. It was almost time for the afternoon session to begin. Kenya nodded in acknowledgment.

"I can't do this with you, Simone. Not now."

"Not ever?"

"That's not what I said."

"Will I see you tomorrow night at least?"

Kenya had almost forgotten tomorrow was Simone's last day at Azure. The rest of the staff was throwing a going-away party for her before the evening rush began.

"I don't think that's a good idea."

"I figured you'd say that. If you change your mind, the first round's on me."

"I'll let you know."

Kenya sought Celia out as soon as she ended the call. She felt out of sorts and there was only one thing she could do to make it right.

"Can you cover for me tonight and tomorrow?" she asked.

Celia looked concerned. "Of course I will. What's going on?" She placed a comforting hand on Kenya's back. "Do you need me to call someone?"

"No, I'll be fine." Talking to Simone usually made Kenya feel lighter. Today, she felt like she had the weight of the world on her shoulders. "Call me if you need me."

"Likewise."

Kenya packed her bags, checked out of the hotel, and headed home. She arrived in Miami nearly four hours later. Instead of stopping by her place to unload her car and freshen up, she drove straight to Mackenzie's. She needed to talk to her. About so many things. She needed to take refuge in her arms. She needed to escape the doubt and confusion swirling around her. Inside her.

When she let herself into Mackenzie's house with the spare key Mackenzie had once told her where to find, she saw a note resting on the credenza in the foyer. "Waiting for you," it read. "Come get me."

How had Mackenzie known she was coming home early? Had Celia called to make sure everything was okay and accidentally given Mackenzie the heads-up? No matter. It was water under the bridge now. She ran up the stairs, paused outside Mackenzie's bedroom door long enough to catch her breath, then turned the knob and walked into the room.

Mackenzie was lying face-down on the bed with her head buried between Fernanda's legs. Fernanda raked her French-tipped nails across Mackenzie's shoulders and threw her head back as her keening cries announced an impending orgasm.

Kenya leaned against the doorjamb for support. She felt an unwelcome sense of déjà vu as she watched Mackenzie reach up and knead one of Fernanda's full breasts. As she watched the woman who had professed to love her make love to another woman.

Fernanda arched her back as she came. She said something in Italian and Mackenzie replied in kind. Laughing, Fernanda opened her eyes. She gasped when she saw Kenya standing in the doorway, but she didn't look away or attempt to cover herself. Instead, she smiled, reached out a hand, and said with kiss-swollen lips, "You can join us if you like."

"No, thanks," Kenya said, her voice hoarse from unshed tears. "You seem to be doing just fine on your own."

Mackenzie turned to face her. The expression on her face wasn't one of remorse or chagrin but irritation. "You said you weren't going to be home until tomorrow."

"So this is my fault?" Kenya couldn't believe her ears. Or her eyes. "Is that really all you have to say to me?"

Mackenzie wiped Fernanda's juices off her mouth with the back of her hand. "Darling, please don't be so predictable. You knew who I was when you met me."

"You said you'd changed," Kenya said weakly, "and I believed you."

"I said I *wanted* to change. And you chose to believe me. I didn't force you." Mackenzie reached for a half-empty glass of wine on the bedside table and took a sip. "Obviously, it didn't work out."

"For either of us." Kenya waited for the pain to hit, but all she felt was numb. "This belongs to you. Give it to the next sucker who falls for your lines." She removed the bracelet Mackenzie had given her and threw it with all her might. The bracelet bounced off the wall and landed on the marble floor with a satisfying clatter of scattered diamonds. She turned to leave, but Mackenzie's voice stopped her in her tracks.

"This doesn't have to be the end. We make a beautiful couple, Kenya. All you have to do is agree to look the other way from time to time. If you like, I could do the same for you."

"We've already had this conversation." Kenya turned to face her. Her stomach roiled as Mackenzie played with Fernanda's nipple like it—and the woman attached to it—was nothing more than a toy. Despite Mackenzie's declarations of love, had she, like Fernanda, been just another conquest? A prize to be won? She wanted to be someone's equal, not her accessory. "I can't live like that, Mackenzie. I won't live like that. This may be nothing more than a game to you, but it's my life. And I will live it by my rules, not someone else's."

Mackenzie pursed her lips. "Are you more upset about what you walked in on today, or that Simone knew Fernanda and I were seeing each other and didn't tell you?"

Kenya's heart—what was left of it—sank. Simone knew Mackenzie was two-timing her and hadn't let her know? Impossible. Simone would never keep the truth from her. Not after all the conversations they'd had about honesty and trust. "She wouldn't do that."

"Oh, no? Why don't you ask her? Or are you afraid you'll discover your knight in shining armor is as fallible as the rest of us mere mortals? Let's not kid ourselves. This scene you're acting out right now isn't because of me. You're not hurt because you were right about me all along. You're hurt because you were wrong about Simone. It's not me you've been falling for the past few weeks. It's her. So stop playing the martyr and admit you and I aren't as different as you think we are."

"I never—"

"Be honest, Kenya. How many times did you think of her while you were fucking me?"

"Unlike you, I never brought anyone else into our bed."

"Perhaps not. But who's in your heart? Me or her?"

Kenya winced as Mackenzie's barb found its mark. Was Mackenzie right? Had her feelings for Simone blossomed from friendship into love? If so, it would explain why it wasn't Mackenzie's betrayal that nearly brought her to her knees. It was Simone's.

❖

Simone's phone was ringing, but she didn't want to stop composing long enough to answer it. She jabbed her cell phone's Speaker icon with one hand and kept scribbling the notes to the tune running through her head with the other.

"What's up, Amanda?" she asked after she glanced at the display to see who was calling.

"Kenya just came in looking for you."

That got her attention.

"She's supposed to be in Orlando until tomorrow. What's she doing back in Miami so soon?"

"Beats me. She looked upset, so I gave her your address. I hope that's okay."

"It's fine." Simone put her pencil down and picked up the phone. "Did she say what was wrong?"

"No, but I could make a pretty good guess."

That could mean only one thing. Kenya had found out about Fernanda or whoever Mackenzie had chosen to be her flavor of the week. Now her mind was probably reeling as well as her heart. "Thanks for the heads-up, Amanda. I'll take it from here."

"Take care of her, dude, and let me know how everything turns out."

"Sure thing."

Simone ended the call and hastily straightened her apartment. When she arrived, Kenya would probably be too dazed to pass judgment on how messy or clean the place was, but Simone wanted to make a good impression nevertheless. She shoved her sheet music in a drawer, tossed the empty pizza box in the trash, and sprayed some air freshener to mask the smell of garlic, onions, and pepperoni.

As she waited for Kenya to arrive, she tried to decide how to handle the situation. Should she admit she had suspected what Mackenzie was up to and didn't share her suspicions with her, or, now that the shit had hit the fan, should she play it safe and make sure none of it landed on her?

It didn't feel right keeping Kenya in the dark. It never had. If she had spoken up when she had the chance, none of this might be happening. She needed to come clean, no matter how dirty she might get in the process.

The minutes turned into hours and still no Kenya. Simone tried getting her on the phone, but her call went to voice mail. So did the second. And the third.

"Amanda said you were looking for me," she said, leaving a message. "I'm not sure what's going on, but I'm starting to get a little worried. If I don't hear from you soon, I'm going to come over and beat your door down, so hit me back, okay? You know where to reach me."

Kenya's terse reply came several long minutes later. "I'm not in the mood to talk," she texted.

Simone tried to slow her racing heart as her fumbling fingers tripped over the letters on the touch screen on her phone. "To anyone or just to me?" she wrote.

Kenya's subsequent reply was even more clipped than her first. "Take your pick."

"Tell me what I can do to help."

"Ask me a question."

Simone mentally reviewed the final questions on her list, searching in vain for one that might lighten the mood. So she threw the list aside and went with her gut. "Question sixteen. If you could wake up tomorrow having gained an ability, what would it be?"

"I would channel Cher and turn back time. Next question."

Simone's palms began to sweat. She could feel Kenya's hurt. Her anger. Her pain. She didn't know how to fix any of it—or to adequately explain any part she might have played in causing her distress. Was Kenya unaware she had prior knowledge of Mackenzie's affair? Or, even worse, did she know the whole truth and was trying to fulfill her part of the bargain they had made before she cut her out of her life for good?

"Question seventeen," she wrote. "Who was the last person you hugged?"

"Celia. Next question."

"Question eighteen." Simone felt a mounting sense of dread as she typed the words. "Who was the last person who made you cry?"

"You are. Any more questions?"

"Shit." Simone's entire body went numb. She needed to set things right before the situation spun completely out of control. "Just one," she wrote. "Where are you? I have to see you."

"If you plan to tell me what you started to tell me that day in the Art District, forget it," Kenya texted back. "I already know. What's your excuse for lying to me? I would love to hear it."

Simone hung her head in despair. Everything she had hoped would remain in the dark had finally come to light. Kenya knew. Not just about Fernanda. About her, too. She wanted to blame Mackenzie for ratting her out, but she knew she had no one to blame but herself. She should have stepped up when she had the chance. If she had, Kenya might be thinking more of her right now instead of less.

"I wanted to tell you," she wrote, "but I didn't want to hurt you. What can I do to make it up to you? Tell me what I need to do to make things right."

She hit Send and waited anxiously for Kenya's response. One minute went by, then two. When the reply finally came, she wished it hadn't.

"Simple," Kenya had written. "Forget you ever met me."

Chapter Eleven

I can't do that."

Simone's reply to her demand reminded Kenya of her own response to Mackenzie's request for an open relationship. *I can't live like that*, she had said as she watched Mackenzie bask in the afterglow of her romp with another woman. *I won't live like that.*

Mackenzie had said they could be a beautiful couple, an admission of her preference for style over substance. Who cared if their relationship wasn't working as long as they looked good standing side-by-side in front of the cameras? Was that why Mackenzie had chosen her in the first place? So she could help her pull off the façade of a power couple after her long string of models, actresses, and party girls had failed to give her the respect she so obviously craved?

If Mackenzie had only wanted the semblance of a relationship rather than the real thing, why couldn't she have said so from the beginning? Why had she gone through with the pretense of wooing her when she never intended for them to have the kind of relationship Kenya had told her she wanted? Had the past few weeks been nothing more than a bad joke, or was Mackenzie shallow enough to think her luxurious, jet-setting lifestyle would prove too intoxicating to resist? It nearly had.

Kenya had stayed with her longer than she should have. Longer than she probably would have if Mackenzie had been someone else. Anyone else. But Mackenzie wasn't anyone. She was everything Kenya had ever wanted. Except none of it had been real.

"Give me a chance to explain," Simone's text pleaded.

Kenya powered off her phone without bothering to send a reply. Mackenzie's duplicity wasn't nearly as surprising as Simone's. Mackenzie had a reputation for straying. A reputation her kisses had convinced Kenya to ignore. Simone, on the other hand, had been nothing but honest from the beginning. Or so Kenya had thought. Her instincts had failed her yet again. How could she ever learn to trust someone else if she couldn't trust herself?

Now that her "relationship" with Mackenzie was over, she finally realized what had been missing. Their connection had been on a purely physical level. The sex had been great—mind-blowing, in fact—but that was all there was. The emotional bond that formed the heart of most unions had never developed. Not like the one she had crafted with Simone. Being with Mackenzie had made her toes curl. Being with Simone had made her heart soar. Mackenzie had captured her body. Simone had captured her imagination.

Kenya stood on her balcony and stared down at the harbor. She wrapped her arms around her middle to ease the pain. Two years ago, she had come close to losing everything. Her home, her financial standing, and her emotional well-being. She had thought she had hit rock bottom back then. Today, however, she felt like she had reached a new low. She had fought her way back from the brink before, but she didn't think she could do it again. It was just too hard.

True love couldn't be forced. It had to be found. Kenya's doorbell sounded while she tried to come to terms with the idea that she might never find what she was looking for.

She tried to ignore the ringing, but her visitor was insistent, leaning on the buzzer until it produced one unbroken, discordant noise.

"Okay," she said irritably. "I'm coming." She snatched the door open and slammed it shut as soon as she saw Simone standing on the other side. "No."

"Please, Kenya, you have to let me explain."

"Whatever you're selling, I'm not buying," Kenya said without bothering to open the door. "You've had plenty of time—and chances—to explain. It's too late now. I don't want to hear it. Go home, Simone."

Simone pounded on the door. "Kenya, let me in. It's not what you think."

Kenya opened the door before her neighbors could make a stink about the disturbance. The last thing she needed was a visit from the head of the homeowners' association asking her to keep the noise down. He might jack up the fees even higher than they already were. "How could you possibly know what I'm thinking?"

Simone backed up a step as if Kenya's attack had been physical instead of verbal. "Because I would be thinking the same thing if I were in your shoes."

Simone's eyes pleaded for understanding. For forgiveness. But Kenya wasn't in a forgiving mood.

"You've got ten minutes. Tell me what you came to say, then get out."

Simone stepped around Kenya with the caution of a bomb squad technician approaching a suspected explosive device. "The night I asked you my fifth question," she said hesitantly, "I saw Mackenzie kissing some redhead in the alley behind Azure. I took a picture of them so I could send it to you, but I couldn't go through with it."

Simone held up her phone. Kenya glanced at a picture of Mackenzie kissing Fernanda next to a waiting limousine. The time stamp in the corner of the screen backed up Simone's story.

Kenya turned away, but the image remained with her. "Why didn't you show me that before now?"

Simone put her phone away. "I didn't want you to be blindsided, and I didn't want to end any illusions you might have had about your relationship when you seemed to want it so much. I didn't want to be the one to break your heart."

Kenya thought of all the energy she had put into trying to build a relationship with Mackenzie. Wasted energy she could have conserved if Simone had made one phone call or sent her one text message. "So instead of telling me what half of Miami already seemed to know, you said nothing."

Simone floundered for a moment, obviously at a loss for words. "I was right about you," she eventually said. "When you love someone, they know it. And when you don't—" She briefly lowered her eyes before bringing them back up to meet Kenya's. "When you don't, they know that, too."

Simone had used those exact words to describe Kenya the night they'd met. Kenya didn't want to be reminded of that night. The night her life had changed forever. "You have eight minutes left."

"Why are you pointing fingers at me? I'm not the one who hurt you. Mackenzie is."

"Are you sure about that? When you asked me how I felt about keeping secrets, did you think my answer applied to everyone but you?"

"I didn't want to keep secrets from you. I started to tell you everything the day I took you to the Wynwood Walls, but Mackenzie said she and Fernanda were over and she claimed she was devoted to you. When she offered me a hundred grand to keep my mouth shut, I should have known she was doing it to cover her ass, not to keep you from being hurt."

Simone's eyes widened as if she thought she had said too much. As far as Kenya was concerned, she hadn't said nearly enough.

"She offered you hush money? A hundred thousand dollars. Is that all I'm worth? On second thought, don't tell me." She pushed down the unpleasant image of Simone and Mackenzie tossing figures back and forth until they decided on a final number. "Did you take the money?"

Simone's expression changed from regret to indignation. "Of course not. Did you really think I would?"

Kenya didn't know how to answer the question without hurting Simone's feelings.

"Right now, I don't know what to think. I thought I knew you, but it's obvious I don't. The Simone I thought I knew wouldn't keep something so important from me. She would tell me the truth, not cover it up."

Simone's exasperated sigh sounded like a locomotive letting off steam. "You're not telling me anything I haven't told myself a hundred times over. Do I wish I had told you everything? Yes, I do. If I could do it all over again, would I do things differently? Yes, I would. I screwed up. I admit it. But it is the first and last time I will ever keep anything from you, Kenya, I swear."

"I know. Because it's the first and last time I will give you the chance. I'm done with sweet-talking women telling me I can trust them before proving I can't. By my count, you have three questions left. Let's get them out of the way so we can go our separate ways."

"We don't have to end this way. We don't have to end at all. We can get past this. Just give me another chance. Everyone's entitled to one mistake. Let this be mine."

Kenya held up her hands to keep from postponing the inevitable. She needed to get this over with so she could put this day and everything that had transpired as a result behind her. "Question nineteen?"

Simone opened her mouth to say something but seemed to think better of it. "Fine," she said robotically. "Question nineteen. What's your greatest fear?"

Before today, Kenya hadn't thought twice about revealing her innermost thoughts to Simone. Now the desire to preserve what little self-esteem she had left made her hesitate.

Simone's shoulders slumped as the fight drained out of her. "No matter what you might think of what I did or didn't do, I haven't changed, Kenya. I'm still me."

Kenya wanted to take her at face value, but her emotions were too raw to open herself up to the possibility of getting hurt again.

"My biggest fear," she eventually said, "is being alone. My closest friends are either married or engaged. I want what they have, but I just can't seem to find it." Simone reached for her, but Kenya held her at bay. "Don't." She knuckled away a tear. "Just don't. The last thing I need right now is to have you feeling sorry for me. It just makes everything worse."

"I don't feel sorry for you, Kenya. I—What's the use? You don't want to hear it." Simone abandoned her attempt to give Kenya a much-needed hug and dropped her arms to her sides. "Question twenty. What's the one thing you most regret not having told someone?"

Kenya didn't possess Celia's enviable ability to effortlessly dish out the perfect rejoinder. Most of her witty comebacks didn't occur to her until after it was too late to use them. None of those missed opportunities, however, had attained the rank of lifelong regret. She had been open and honest with Mackenzie from the day they'd met, which meant she had left nothing unsaid. Almost. She could have used a few more expletives on her way out the door. It wouldn't have changed the end result, but she might have felt a hell of a lot better during her drive home.

"I wish I had told Mackenzie to go to hell today instead of holding my tongue. I was trying so hard to retain my dignity that I—"

"Stop." Simone put her hands on Kenya's shoulders and slowly slid them down her arms. Kenya felt every inch of the gradual descent. "Don't give her that kind of power over you. It's over now. She's out of your life. It doesn't matter what she thinks about you or anyone else. She doesn't deserve you. She never did."

Simone took Kenya's hands in hers and squeezed. The gesture was probably supposed to be comforting, but it achieved the opposite effect. Kenya's pulse raced as if she'd taken a shot of adrenaline direct to the heart. She wanted to let go—she wanted to pull away—but she couldn't move.

Simone's eyes bore into hers, asking questions she wasn't prepared to answer. Simone's lips parted and she tilted her head to one side. She leaned toward Kenya as if she meant to kiss her. Kenya's breath caught in a strange mixture of anticipation and dread. It was too soon for this. Too soon. And much too late.

"Last question," Simone said. "Are you ready?"

Kenya nodded, not trusting herself to speak. Not trusting herself to feel the emotions surging through her. Except for one near-slip at Jayden's party, she had been able to hold her attraction to Simone at bay. Why couldn't she do it now? Did she even want to? Because despite everything that had happened, she wanted Simone. More than Mackenzie. More than anyone. More than she had ever allowed herself to admit. But how could she be sure she wasn't channeling the hurt, anger, and embarrassment she was feeling in another direction? She couldn't. Not until she was able to assign meaning to everything she had discovered today.

Simone squeezed her hands again and swallowed so hard Kenya heard her throat click. "I'm going places," she said, her voice trembling with emotion. "Maybe not today and maybe not tomorrow, but someday soon." She paused as if to gather her courage. "Question number twenty-one. Will you come with me?"

The words reverberated around Kenya's head. Simone's question was sincere. Heartfelt. The twenty questions preceding it had varied in degrees of difficulty. On the surface, this one should have been the easiest to answer—a simple "yes" or "no" would do the trick—but it was by far the hardest.

She couldn't rely on her friends. She couldn't rely on her family. For this, she would need to rely on the faulty instincts that had let her down over and over again. This time, she hoped they wouldn't lead her astray.

"I can't," she said, finally finding the strength to pull away. "I just got out of one so-called relationship and I don't want to jump right into another one. It wouldn't be fair to either of us."

"I'm not trying to pressure you into making a decision today. I just wanted to let you know how I feel."

Simone had made her feelings clear from the moment they met. When a simple drink order had turned into something much more complicated. Mackenzie's arrival on the scene had made the situation even more problematic.

Simone and Mackenzie were from two different worlds. Mackenzie had grown up surrounded by money and power. Simone had struggled to make ends meet. Mackenzie was a wildly successful businesswoman, and Simone was still struggling. This time to fulfill her dreams. With Mackenzie, she would have wanted for nothing, but she would never have been secure in the knowledge she was the only woman in Mackenzie's life—or her bed. With Simone, she would lack for creature comforts, but she would know where she stood.

She couldn't go back to Mackenzie after everything that had been done and said. But with all the promises she had made herself about not repeating past mistakes, how could she possibly move forward with Simone?

Mackenzie had spun a web of lies over the past few weeks, but one thing she said today had rung all-too-true. Kenya had fallen for the idea of Mackenzie, but she had developed feelings for the woman standing in front of her now. The woman who had stood by her the whole time. Supporting her. Challenging her. Protecting her. Simone's methods might have been heavy-handed at times, but her heart, it seemed, was in the right place. Now Kenya's heart didn't know where to turn. Mackenzie was everything she had thought she wanted, but Simone was everything she knew she needed. So why couldn't she bring herself to say so?

Simone felt like the answer to every question Kenya had ever asked. She felt like the answer to a prayer. But so had Mackenzie. And look how that had turned out.

"I need to be on my own for a while," she said, unwilling to make yet another mistake. She already had two strikes. First Ellis, then Mackenzie. She didn't want Simone to be the third. She cared for her too much. Even if, at the moment, being in the same room with her hurt like hell. "I need time."

"I understand," Simone said. "Believe me. I do. I know you're hurting right now and I'm not trying to make your pain any worse. I would take it away if I could. I don't want to take advantage of you while you're down, Kenya. I don't want to catch you on the rebound. I'm willing to wait until you have your feet under you. When you do, I'd like to be standing beside you. I hope you want that, too. If you do, you know where to find me."

Simone headed for the door. Kenya watched her go, wondering if she had just let the best thing that had ever happened to her slip through her fingers.

❖

Simone berated herself all the way home. She hadn't gone to Kenya's planning to make a play for her. She had intended to apologize for keeping Mackenzie's indiscretion from her and attempt to make things right between them. Instead, she had made an already bad situation exponentially worse. As a result, she had added to Kenya's confusion rather than clearing it up.

"Stupid, stupid, stupid," she said as she slammed her apartment door behind her and threw her keys across the room.

She sat on the couch and held her head in her hands. She was dying for a drink. She needed to feel the caustic burn of alcohol, cauterizing her pain and taking away the hurt. She grabbed a bottle of vodka from the freezer and poured herself a healthy shot. She raised the glass to her lips but couldn't bring herself to swallow.

Alcohol was a crutch she used to lean on when she needed a confidence boost or she wanted to forget something she couldn't bear to remember. But she didn't want to erase Kenya from her mind. She wanted to safeguard the memories she had made with her as long as she could because she might not have a chance to make more.

She poured the well-chilled vodka down the drain, tossed the empty bottle in the trash, and allowed the memories of the past few weeks to wash over her.

She remembered laying eyes on Kenya for the first time. Flirting with her. Helping her get over her nerves. Seeing her let down her defenses. Then watching her pair up with Mackenzie. She remembered the smile that lit up Kenya's face every time Mackenzie looked in her direction. And the self-doubt that crept in when she didn't think anyone was watching. She remembered laughing with her at Jayden's birthday party. And watching her twirl in Mackenzie's arms a few hours later. And most of all, she remembered the sound of the pain in Kenya's voice when she had asked who was the last person who made her cry and Kenya had said she was.

"What was I thinking?" she asked, kicking herself yet again for not spilling her guts when she had the chance. Now she and Mackenzie were the same in Kenya's eyes. And she didn't know if Kenya would ever be able to forgive either of them.

During her last two shifts at Azure, she felt like she was sleepwalking. She went through the motions—mixing drinks, making small talk, listening to coworkers and customers alike saying how much they would miss her after she left—but it felt like part of a bad dream. It felt like it was happening to someone else. At least she didn't have to spend her last night dealing with Mackenzie, who was conveniently called away "on business" and had asked Jolie to express her appreciation for all the hard work she had put in over the years. Allegedly. Simone figured the good wishes had come from Jolie herself and Mackenzie didn't give a shit one way or the other. Mackenzie was probably only too happy to see her go. In a way, so was she. Even though her future was uncertain, it looked much brighter than her past. As long as she ignored the dark cloud hovering over her relationship with Kenya. Or what was left of it.

During her going-away party, she kept looking at the door, half-hoping Kenya would walk through it. But Kenya never showed. She didn't call or text, either. She just stayed away. Simone hadn't expected anything different, but she wished Kenya had proven her wrong.

Kenya had said she needed to spend some time on her own. Time to think. Time to heal. Simone was willing to give her all the time she needed, but how long was she supposed to wait before she admitted Kenya would never forgive her for not disclosing what Mackenzie was doing behind her back?

Taking refuge in the studio, she poured herself into her music like never before. Reagan complained about a few of the drawn-out recording sessions, but her grumbling lessened when she heard the finished product. It lessened ever more when she saw the galleys for the suggested cover art for her EP. And it disappeared completely the first time a local DJ played her lead single on the radio. Simone's dissatisfaction, however, continued to deepen.

"I gather Kenya broke up with that businesswoman she was seeing," Simone's mother said after Simone sulked her way through a family get-together. "It was all over the papers. I thought that would make you happy. So why are you moping around like your dog just died?"

"I wouldn't be if Mackenzie was the only person Kenya dumped."

"What do you mean?"

"She got rid of me, too."

Her mother dried the soap suds on her hands and turned off the faucet in the kitchen sink. She still insisted on washing dishes by hand despite the presence of the automatic washer Simone and her sisters had pooled their money to buy several years ago. "What happened, Monie? Start from the beginning and go slow."

Simone took a deep breath and told her mother everything that had taken place from the night she had first met Kenya to the day Kenya had tossed her out of her condo. Apparently, for good.

"She needs time," her mother said after she had finished telling the sad, sorry tale.

"I know, and I'm trying to give it to her, but it's hard sitting around waiting for the phone to ring when there's a chance it never will. It's been almost three weeks since I've heard from her. What would you do if you were in her position? Forgive and forget or allow your anger to fester and grow?"

"I can only speak for myself so I won't try to predict how someone else might react. All I know is the old saying is true. Fool me once, shame on you. Fool me twice, shame on me."

Simone raised her bottle of ginger beer in a half-hearted toast. "Here's hoping I won't spend the rest of my life playing the fool."

Her mother dabbed at her eyes with the hem of her apron.

"Why are you crying?" Simone asked, handing her a tissue.

"When your sisters were younger, they used to cry on my shoulder all the time about some boy who had dropped them for someone else or wouldn't give them the time of day to begin with. When you came out to your father and me, I thought I would never be able to sit and talk with you like that. Like *this*." Simone's mother patted her hand. "I'm glad you were able to come to me. I might not understand all the things you do or some of the decisions you make, especially where your career is concerned, but I will always be here for you when you need me."

Now it was Simone's turn to cry. She had always felt like something of a disappointment to her parents. Both her sisters were married with kids and had solid careers. She, on the other hand, was perpetually single and still trying to figure out what she wanted to be when she grew up. Based on what her mother had just said, though, it didn't matter. Because her mother was proud of her no matter what she chose to do for a living or with whom she chose to share her life. She buried her face in her hands and let the tears flow.

"Are those happy tears or sad ones?" her mother asked.

"Both."

"If she loves you," her mother said, "she'll come back. And if she doesn't, you'll find someone who does."

Simone dried her eyes on the sleeve of her T-shirt. "When did you get so smart?"

Her mother smiled wistfully. "This isn't my first rodeo. It's my third. And it's time for you to get back on the horse. Come on."

Simone's mother cranked up the volume on the Rihanna song playing on the radio and pulled Simone to her feet. They danced around the kitchen with reckless abandon. Simone felt lighter with each step. A few minutes later, her sister stuck her head in the room to see what all the noise was about.

"Is this a private party," Miranda asked, "or can anybody join?"

Simone beckoned her inside. Jayden and their father soon joined them. The room quickly filled with laughter and love. Just like the good old days. Simone felt good knowing that no matter how many lovers drifted in and out of her life, the people who had been there for in the beginning would still be there for her in the end.

Chapter Twelve

K enya usually listened to NPR or an audiobook during her drive to work. Today she wasn't in the mood for either. She switched off the recording of Terry McMillan's latest offering and punched in one of her preset radio favorites just in time to hear the last few bars of a song she knew by heart.

"That was 'Miami Dreams,' the lead single from local sensation Reagan Carter's forthcoming *Tales from the City* EP."

Kenya felt a lump form in her throat as she listened to the disc jockey rave about Reagan's song. The track was starting to receive more airplay each day. Kenya felt a personal stake in the song's success. And in Simone's. Simone had said the day they had spent at the Caribbean Festival had provided the inspiration for the song's music.

Each time she heard the familiar strains, Kenya was engulfed by memories of that day. Exploring the colorful murals at Wynwood Walls. Walking through the park. Listening to a variety of bands play while the sights, sounds, and smells of various Caribbean islands floated in the humid Miami air.

That was also the day Simone had started to tell her about Mackenzie's infidelity but had stopped short. When her lie by omission had inserted a wedge between them Kenya hadn't been able—or willing—to remove. She felt as if she had been spinning her wheels for the past few months. Sharing her body with one woman, her soul with another, and being betrayed by both.

Her cell phone rang while she made the slow crawl through downtown traffic. She used the controls on her steering wheel to lower the volume on the radio and pick up the call.

"Have you heard the news?" Bridget asked breathlessly.

"What news?" Bridget's pulse rate didn't rise above seventy unless Avery was modeling a new pair of skimpy lingerie for her or one of the writers on her staff was on the verge of breaking a big story. Kenya prepared to hear about Bridget's latest scoop.

"It looks like you kicked Mackenzie to the curb at just the right time."

After the first few tear-filled days following the dissolution of her relationship with Mackenzie and her friendship with Simone, Kenya had tried not to dwell on either breakup. Bridget's comment forced her to relive what she had almost been able to forget. "What happened?"

"She's being sued for alienation of affection. Apparently, Fernanda has a husband back in Milan. When she asked him for a divorce so she could be with Mackenzie, he went ballistic. If she and Mackenzie can't be faithful to anyone else, how are they supposed to be faithful to each other?"

"Perhaps they have an understanding," Kenya said, thinking of the dubious example Mackenzie's parents had set for her. "The lawsuit won't go anywhere. Alienation of affection was abolished in Florida years ago. Mackenzie's attorneys will convince Fernanda's husband to sign a nondisclosure agreement, pay him to go away, and that will be that."

"Not this time."

Kenya tapped her brakes to avoid rear-ending the Lexus in front of her, the driver of which was too busy inhaling his fast food breakfast to pay attention to the prevailing traffic pattern. "What makes you so sure?"

"Fernanda's husband has a title and even deeper pockets than Mackenzie and her father combined. He says he'll keep fighting until he's taken Mackenzie for every penny she's worth. She's faced scandals before and made it through them relatively unscathed, but both her brand and her wallet are bound to take substantial hits this time around."

Kenya didn't know whether to laugh or cry. Hearing about Mackenzie's misfortune gave her a small measure of satisfaction, but it also saddened her. How had she allowed herself to fall into bed with someone like that? How could she have believed Mackenzie wanted to make a life with her? Love meant nothing to Mackenzie. For her, relationships were nothing more than business deals. A negotiation Kenya never had a chance of winning.

"You're better off without her," Bridget said, almost as if reading her mind.

Kenya blew out a sigh. "I know. It just sucks being back at square one again. I'm tired of starting over. If I have to rebuild my life one more time..." She allowed her voice to trail off, unable to air her innermost thoughts. Her innermost fears.

"Are you all right?" Bridget asked. "I thought you would be turning cartwheels after hearing Mackenzie is finally getting what she deserves."

"If her empire crumbles around her, she's savvy enough to build another one. I want her to know what it's like to have a broken heart. That would be the ultimate revenge."

"No one can break what she doesn't have," Bridget grumbled under her breath.

Kenya smiled at the protective instincts that made Bridget such a good friend. If Bridget and Avery decided to have children, Kenya pitied the kids' prospective dates. Bridget was liable to greet them sitting on the front porch with a shotgun draped across her lap to make sure they didn't get any ideas about taking advantage of her progeny.

"It doesn't matter to me one way or the other," Kenya said. She was surprised to discover she actually meant it. Whatever she once felt for Mackenzie was gone. When she thought of her now, all she felt was regret. Not for the fantasy she thought she had but the reality she had foolishly walked away from. "Mackenzie is out of my life now. Whatever happens in hers has nothing to do with me. But if the case does make it to court, I know which side I'll be rooting for."

"You and me both. Now hang up the phone and get back to work planning my bachelorette party."

"You got it."

Kenya ended the call and continued her morning commute. Her life had been vastly different these past few weeks. No drama, no stress, and no surprises. She went to work, she went home, and that was about it. She had brunch with Bridget and Celia every Saturday morning, she spent her Sunday afternoons preparing for the upcoming workweek, and she spent what little down time she had helping Bridget and Avery plan their upcoming wedding.

Bridget and Avery had hired a wedding planner for the event itself. Kenya's primary tasks as maid of honor were getting Bridget to the venue on time and hosting her bachelorette party the night before the ceremony. She hadn't decided what to do yet to celebrate Bridget's last night of freedom, and she had less than a month to make up her mind since the wedding was scheduled for mid-September. Avery's only demands for Bridget's fond farewell to single life were no strip club visits and no last-minute affairs, two requests Kenya was more than happy to fulfill. She would be even happier if she could think of an activity she, Bridget, Celia, and six of her and Bridget's former sorority sisters would all enjoy.

"A problem for another day," she said, moving the task from her mental to-do list to her wait list.

She turned on her blinker and eased into the turn lane as she neared the exit that would take her to her office. Over the past few weeks, the pain of betrayal had begun to fade and her dark mood grew a little brighter each day. She didn't miss the rollercoaster of emotions she had been on or the constant second-guessing to which she had subjected herself. But she did miss one thing. One person. She missed Simone.

She missed Simone's easy laughter, her nimble mind, her rapt attention, and her tender touch. She missed listening to her rave about her favorite artists and the powerful effect music had on her. She missed hearing Simone's dreams for the future and listening to her stories about the past. She missed everything about her. Yet she continued to stay away. Not because she wanted to. Because she had to.

Her breakup with Ellis had left her life in tatters and her heart in even worse shape. Years later, when she had finally convinced herself she was ready to try and find love again, she had been so worried about not having history repeat itself that she had followed the rules instead of following her heart. Then Mackenzie Richardson had come along.

Mackenzie had been the safe choice. The logical choice. And the wrong choice.

Kenya didn't need someone who could take care of her. She needed someone who cared for her. She didn't want someone who could buy her a gift that cost tens of thousands. She wanted someone who offered her something priceless. Mackenzie could never be that person. But perhaps Simone could.

When she reached her office building, Kenya found an empty parking space, picked up her phone, and did something Simone had spent several weeks doing to her. She asked her a question.

❖

Devonte Shaw, the director Dre had hired to oversee Reagan's first video, had forgotten to get the necessary permits to allow him and his crew to film on the streets of South Beach. He blamed the "oversight" on his assistant, whose primary work qualifications appeared to be how good she looked in a miniskirt and six-inch heels. The answer was pretty damn good, but in

Simone's eyes, her obvious physical attributes didn't make up for her professional shortcomings.

As Reagan lip-synced the words to "Miami Dreams," Simone kept an eye on the street to make sure the cops didn't show up before Devonte and his crew finished filming the scene. If they got caught filming without a permit, everyone present could be subject to arrest and Liberty City Records would be required to fork over a substantial fine. The film in Devonte's cameras would also be confiscated, meaning Dre would lose money twice. Anyone who knew Dre knew there were three things you didn't want to mess with: his family, his food, and his money.

If she was hauled off to jail, who was Simone supposed to call? Most of her friends couldn't afford bail, and her parents would probably leave her behind bars for a night or two in order to teach her some kind of lesson. They still hadn't come to terms with the idea of her new career. Being forced to pay for someone else's ineptitude wouldn't help her convince them that trying her hand at the music business was the right decision. Yet another reason she needed everything to go right today. She had to show her parents she knew what she was doing, even if on most days she was playing it by ear.

"Are we done?" she asked after Devonte directed his lead cameraman to stop filming.

"Almost." Devonte held a light meter in the air, then squinted in the general direction of the setting sun. "We've got time for one more take."

Simone spotted a nearby shopkeeper looking at the assembled group with a scowl as if he thought their presence was the reason for his nonexistent business. "Make it fast," she said after the shopkeeper pulled out his cell phone and disappeared inside his shop. "We've got less than ten minutes before the cops roll up."

"Got it. Let's take it from the top. Girls, you gotta bring it," Devonte said after Reagan and her trio of backup dancers resumed their places. "Give me more energy this time. If you don't look like you're having fun, how do you expect anyone else to?"

"Can't I just stand here and sing?" Reagan asked. "It's hard to remember the dance moves and the lyrics at the same time. I'm not a professional dancer, you know."

Devonte put his hands on his hips as if he wasn't in the mood for excuses. "Neither was Whitney Houston—girlfriend looked as stiff as the Tin Man in some of her early videos—but that never stopped her from being fierce. Fake it until you make it, honey. Ready? Three, two, one. Action!"

Reagan looked to Simone for help, but there wasn't anything Simone could do to ease her growing pains. When she was more established, Reagan would be able to dictate what she would and wouldn't do. Until then, she was at the mercy of the people calling the shots because they knew what worked and what didn't. Simone would have stepped in if Devonte was out of line or if he had asked Reagan to do something demeaning or disrespectful. She remained on the sidelines this time because making herself look silly upon occasion was part of the process Reagan needed to undergo in order to become a better performer.

"You can do it," she said, offering a few claps of encouragement.

Reagan and the rest of the cast ran through their paces again. When the song reached the end once more and Reagan hit her final pose, Simone prayed Devonte had all the footage he needed. She expected the cops to roll up any second so she didn't want him to risk another take.

Devonte peered into the camera, nodded, and waved his arms over his head to get everyone's attention. "That's a wrap."

"Great," Simone said. "Now let's get out of here while the getting's good."

She hustled Devonte and his crew to a nearby van. Once everyone and everything was safely inside, she peeled off a few bills to pay the dancers for their work on the shoot. If Devonte wanted his money, he would have to ask Dre for it. Knowing Dre, though, he wasn't going to dish out even a dime until he had seen and approved the final footage. Smart move considering some of the shortcuts Devonte had taken to this point.

"That was fun," Reagan said excitedly as she bounced on the balls of her feet. Hearing sirens in the distance, Simone hustled her down the street so they could put some distance between them and the scene of the crime. Even though they were trying to maintain a low profile as they dodged the cops, Reagan's face glowed with a sense of accomplishment. "I'm glad you made me do that. What's next?" She didn't give Simone time to answer the question. "I know. Let's go to Azure for a drink."

Simone made a face to show her distaste for the idea. "I haven't set foot in that place since I picked up my last paycheck, but you can go if you want. I have to warn you, though. Amanda says the crowds have really fallen off lately. The numbers increased for a while when Mackenzie's latest scandal first broke, but after the rubberneckers left, the regulars weren't far behind. Most of the bartenders are looking around for other gigs because they heard there might be job cuts coming soon."

"Where do you think Amanda will end up?"

Reagan looked—and sounded—worried. Simone could tell Reagan had a bit of a crush on Amanda and she suspected the feeling might be mutual. Amanda was four years older than Reagan, but Reagan seemed to be the more emotionally mature of the two. If they became a couple, their opposing personalities might end up balancing each other out. A perfect example of yin and yang.

"I don't know what she's going to do," Simone said. "The last time I talked to her, she was kicking around the idea of going into business for herself. A friend wants her to partner with her and buy one of those pedal-powered sightseeing bikes that are popping up all over town."

"The ones that people pay thirty bucks a seat to ride and bike from bar to bar?"

Simone nodded. "Amanda's friend Heidi would be the driver and Amanda would be the tour guide. More like the party host. Since she's always the life of every party she attends, the role would be right up her alley. Her main job wouldn't be to point out the sights but keep the guests excited while they're sweating their asses off. She would also be in charge of establishing and maintaining relationships with the bars in town so the owners would agree to have their places included as stops on the tour, complete with drink specials and priority service for the passengers."

"Are the drinks included in the price of the tickets?"

"No, the tour companies are allowed to provide sodas, snacks, and bottled water, but they aren't licensed to sell alcohol. The passengers aren't required to drink in the bars they visit. Taking a shot or two or three is optional. That way, the tour group keeps its operating costs low and the bars can profit, too. Even if they don't make a sale that day, the guests might come back after the tour is over or recommend the bars to their friends. It's really popular with tourists and people looking for a different or unique way to celebrate a special occasion."

"It sounds like a cool venture. Is Amanda going to do it?"

"She wants to, but she doesn't have the money. She'd have to ask her parents for it and I don't know if they'll pony up." That was why Simone was trying to save as much money as she could. She didn't want to have to ask anyone for anything ever again. She wanted to be able to take care of herself from now on. "Her parents are still holding out hope she'll change her mind and decide to go back to law school. She went for a year before she decided she would rather wear jeans to work than a business suit. Whatever she decides to do, I'm sure she'll land on her feet. She always does."

"I think I will stop by Azure for a while. Amanda could probably use some consoling and I know the perfect way to make her feel better."

"You're just as transparent as she is," Simone said with a laugh. "You two might be perfect for each other."

Reagan grinned. "I'll tell her you said that."

Simone had a feeling Reagan and Amanda would be doing more kissing than talking by the time the night was through. She wished she could say the same, but music was her only love these days. Her real-life prospects were somewhere between slim and none.

"Don't drink too much," she said after Reagan hailed a taxi and climbed in the back. "It's bad for your voice."

Reagan stuck her head out the cab's open window. "You're starting to sound like my mother."

"I'm not *that* much older than you are," Simone said. But as she watched the taxi pull away from the curb, she felt something she had once thought she never would—responsibility.

In the past, responsibility had always been something she would rather shirk than claim. She wanted to have fun, not lead. By example or otherwise. But now she had a career to build and an artist to mentor. Things were different now. And so was she. She only wished Kenya was around to see the changes she had made in her life.

As she listened to a street musician performing a spot-on cover of a Taylor Swift song, her cell phone vibrated in her pocket. She dug it out and looked down to check the display. Kenya's name was printed on the top of the screen and "Are you free for dinner tonight?" was printed on the bottom.

She read the words twice to make sure she understood them—and who they were from. She was pleasantly surprised to see she wasn't mistaken. After all this time, Kenya had indeed reached out to her. And she was inviting her to dinner. Was Kenya planning to let her down easy or to tell her the words she longed to hear?

There's only one way to find out.

She texted her response. "When and where?"

Kenya's reply was immediate. As if she, like Simone, was hovering over her phone, anxiously waiting for the words to appear on the liquid crystal display. "Meet me at my place at seven. I downloaded the new season of *Orange is the New Black* and there are few things sadder than watching a comedy alone."

Simone couldn't stop the grin that creased her face. "Do you need me to bring anything?" she wrote.

Her phone buzzed a few seconds later. "A sense of humor," she read. "I'll provide the rest."

"Dress code?"

"Casual. We can save the black tie for a later date."

Simone clenched her fist, elated Kenya didn't want tonight to be a one-time thing. Even if Kenya didn't have romance on the menu, Simone was eager to partake in the meal.

"See you tonight," she wrote. And she knew she would be able to think of little else all day.

❖

It was said that the way to a man's heart was through his stomach. The path to some women's hearts likely followed the same route, but Kenya suspected Simone was different. For her, the food on the plate was far less important than the conversation held during the meal—and the people sitting at the table on which it was served. Accordingly, Kenya didn't plan on whipping up a five-star meal for dinner. Instead, she stopped at a Cuban café near her condo and picked up a small tray of sliders and a large order of yuca fries after she left the office. The earthy smell of the yuca and the intoxicating combined aromas of the ham, chicken, lamb, and roast pork in the sandwiches permeated her car during her short drive home. Her stomach growled in anticipation, but nerves prevented her from feeling as hungry as she normally would when a meal from Cubanito was in the offing.

She didn't know what tack to take with Simone. Their last conversation had been weighted with emotion. She didn't want to repeat that heavy scene, but the subjects she and Simone needed to discuss were too serious to be taken lightly. How should she greet her? With a hug, a kiss on the cheek, or a simple nod hello?

"Stop thinking so much," she told herself as she parked her car and shut off the engine. "That's what got you in trouble in the first place. Trust yourself. Trust what you're feeling. Don't let ghosts from the past continue to haunt you. If you get hurt again, you get hurt again. But you've got to stop allowing fear to dictate your every move."

Her nerves disappeared almost as quickly as they had arrived. She was finally ready to move on with her life. She was ready to move on with Simone. Wherever the path might lead.

She placed the sandwiches in the oven so they could stay warm, then she took a quick shower, and changed out of her work clothes into a T-shirt and a pair of shorts. She put on enough makeup to be presentable but not enough to make it appear she was trying too hard. She was done acting out of desperation. From now on, she would follow her heart instead of the rules. Even if the rules were ones she had written.

Her doorbell rang a little before seven. She opened the door to find Simone standing in the hall clad in a bright orange jumpsuit and white canvas tennis shoes. A handcuff was fastened around her left wrist, the open end dangling like a charm from a bracelet.

"Remind me to rethink my outfit the next time you have a themed dinner party," Simone said. "I was pulled over twice on my way here. I was told I bear an uncanny resemblance to an escaped con. What do you think?"

Kenya laughed until her sides ached. Leave it to Simone to find the right amount of levity amongst the seriousness. Kenya wrapped her arms around her neck and gave her a hug. "I've missed you."

"I've missed you, too."

Simone put her arms around Kenya and squeezed. Kenya felt her breath go. Not from the pressure of the hug but the feel of Simone's body pressed against hers. Simone's body was firm in all the right places and soft in all the right ones, too. Kenya wanted to explore the flat planes and gentle curves, but she forced herself to let go. This time, unlike with Mackenzie, she wouldn't have her decisions adversely affected by the distraction of sex. This time, no matter where the relationship progressed, she would get it right.

"I'm not too early, am I?" Simone asked. "My dad always says if you're on time, you're late. It isn't a philosophy I typically subscribe to, but tonight I felt like taking it on."

Kenya thought she was prepared for this moment. She had spent her drive home from work mentally drafting a speech explaining why it had taken her so long to reach out. But when Simone tossed one of her infectious smiles in her direction, words failed her.

"I'm sorry about—"

Simone stopped her. "I'm sorry, too, but let's make a deal. From this moment on, let's stop rehashing the past, wipe the slate clean, and start over, okay?"

"Sounds good to me." She ushered Simone inside and closed the door. "I hope you're hungry, and I hope you like Cuban food. I picked up some sandwiches from Cubanito."

"I love that place. And, yes, I'm hungry." Simone shrugged off her costume, revealing the polo shirt and jean shorts she was wearing underneath. "I was at a video shoot all day and was too busy to grab lunch."

Kenya took the food out of the oven and set two plates on the counter. "How did the shoot go?" she asked as she grabbed the ketchup and two bottles of sparkling water from the refrigerator.

Simone began filling her plate. "If the police's response time was a couple minutes faster, the outfit I'm wearing would be real, not a joke."

Simone followed Kenya to the living room, where they settled on the couch. The first episode of the new season of the prison dramedy Kenya had invited Simone over to watch was cued up on the TV screen, but Kenya didn't press Play. Not just yet. She was more interested in Simone's day than the latest antics of Piper, Alex, Red, Big Boo, or the hot new convict all the bloggers were drooling over.

"What happened?"

Simone related the tale of the rogue video shoot and her near-miss with the police. Kenya listened, impressed by Simone's ability to keep her head under such trying circumstances. There was something different about her. A gravity that wasn't there before. It looked good on her.

"While I was trying not to get arrested, did you spend your day in the marketing department of the tourism board?" Simone asked.

"What do you mean?"

Simone indicated the brochures scattered on the coffee table. Each advertised various things to do in Miami. Some for free and others that came at a considerable cost.

"Oh, those. No, I'm not checking out the competition. I'm trying to plan Bridget's bachelorette party and I was looking for some ideas. If Amanda finds funding for her start-up, do you think she and her business partner could have the company up and running by September? If so, that sounds like the perfect venue for Bridget's party. Including her, me, and her six bridesmaids, we would take up eight of the fifteen seats. If I tried hard enough, I could probably find seven other friends who would be willing to join in the fun. Especially if alcohol is involved."

"Heidi has already applied for the business license and designed the company logo. She just needs to get the funding in place so she can pay for the custom-designed bike. I'm not sure how long it takes to build those, but she might be able to ask the vendor to expedite the process."

"Keep me informed, okay? I could go with one of the other companies that are already established, but I would rather support someone I know if possible."

"I'll do that." As Kenya finally started the show, Simone polished off one sandwich and reached for another. "Who are Bridget's bridesmaids, friends or family?"

Kenya fast-forwarded through the opening credits. "Six of our sorority sisters from college. What's with the look?"

"I can see you as a sorority girl, but I have a hard time picturing Bridget as one."

"She had a much different look when we were in college. Back then, she was more Salt-N-Pepa than Grace Jones."

Simone did a double-take. "I'm not saying I don't believe you, but I don't believe you."

"I'll prove it to you."

Kenya pressed Pause again. At this rate, it was going to take them two hours to watch a sixty-minute show. That was fine by her. She was enjoying the return to the old dynamic she used to have with Simone, as well as the start of their new one. Whatever it turned out to be. She dug out a photo album and returned to the couch, where she flipped through the pages until she found the photograph she was looking for. She pointed to a picture of her, Bridget, and several thousand of their nearest and dearest friends rooting for the home team at a Miami Hurricanes football game. Both she and Bridget were wearing 'Canes jerseys, and Bridget was sporting a colorful asymmetrical 'do.

"Do you believe me now?" she asked.

Simone's eyes widened. "Wow. She looks so different. When did she change?"

"Not very long after that picture was taken. During homecoming weekend, she met a girl who said she liked women with short hair. She went directly from the party to the barber shop and has been close-cropped ever since."

"When did she meet Avery?" Simone asked after they finished looking through the rest of the photo album.

"They've been dating for a little over two years and engaged since last November. To be honest, I'm surprised it took that long for Bridget to decide to put a ring on it. She and Avery have been practically living together since their first date."

Simone wiped her mouth and set her empty plate on the coffee table. "Are all these wedding plans giving you any ideas about your own life?"

Kenya set her plate next to Simone's and leaned back on the couch. "No ideas I didn't already have. I would love to walk down the aisle someday, but I'm not going to beat myself up if it doesn't happen."

"What changed? You were doing a pretty good job beating yourself up the night we met."

That night had felt like her last chance to find happiness. She had put so much pressure on herself she had been unable to relax. But that was before she had met Simone. Before Simone had done wonders for her self-esteem by making her feel like the most beautiful woman in the room.

She thought for a moment. When had she learned to take the ebbs and flows in her love life in stride instead of hitting the panic button each time a relationship came to an end?

"I was driving to work this morning when I heard Reagan's song on the radio. I remembered the first time you played it for me. I remembered the excitement—the passion—I heard in your voice when you talked about the changes you had made to the original version of the song and how you planned to approach the rest of the album. I decided while I was sitting in traffic that I didn't want to hear about your life. I wanted to be a part of it."

"You mean you want to—"

"I mean I want to see where this leads. I have feelings for you, but I don't know how deep they go."

Simone took her hand. "Then let's find out together."

❖

Dre pumped his fist in the air as he watched the playback of Devonte's final cut of the video for "Miami Dreams."

"Was I right or was I right?" he asked, spinning around in his chair. He pointed to the monitor. Reagan's image was frozen on the screen. "This girl is the one who's going to put us all on the map. Devonte can be a piece of work sometimes, but he always gets the job done in the end. Cut the checks, Nate." He turned to his nephew/accountant, the college freshman who had talked himself into a job by convincing Dre that running a cash-only business was bad for the bottom line, especially whenever the IRS came sniffing around. "The usual amount for Devonte and a five grand bonus for my friend here for getting this project done on time."

"Thanks, Dre."

"Don't thank me, girl. Just keep doing what you do. Once this video hits the Web, Reagan's CD is going to fly off the shelves."

After Nate handed her a check, Simone made sure her name was spelled right and all the zeroes were in the right place. Then she folded the check in half and tucked it in her back pocket until she could swing by the bank on her way to Kenya's place.

She and Kenya had spent time together every night this week. They watched three episodes of *Orange is the New Black* each night, but they spent so much time talking she would have to watch the episodes again to catch up on everything she had missed. She felt like part of an old married couple and they hadn't even slept together yet. She was used to going out clubbing every night. She hadn't realized just chilling at home could be this much fun. If she had, she might have tried it years ago.

"You know what's next, right?"

Dre's question forced Simone to focus on the present instead of the future. She waited for Dre to answer his own question so she wouldn't disrupt his train of thought. Once he was on a roll, he didn't like to stop.

"MTV, BET, VH1, Fuse." Dre ticked the names off on his thick fingers. "All the music networks are going to pick us up. Next stop top ten, baby. Give me some dap."

Simone reached out and gave him a fist bump.

"I'm starting to get calls from major labels."

"Already?" she asked incredulously. "The EP isn't even out yet."

"They're not calling about Reagan. They're calling about you."

Simone sat up straighter. "Major labels want to work with me?"

"They don't want you to work *with* them. They want you to work *for* them."

"Are you serious?" She imagined the famous artists she would get to work with and the fat checks that were sure to follow.

"Nate." Dre snapped his fingers, and Nate passed him several business cards. "These are the ones I've received so far, but I'm sure there will be more to come. You're hot, girl. I've always known it. Now the rest of the world is catching on, too."

Simone sifted through the cards. She recognized the record labels and A&R reps listed on each. "These guys want me?"

"So do I, but we both know I can't pay you what those brothers can. So it looks like this will be our first and last album together. When you get to the top, don't forget the little people who helped you get there, all right?"

Simone looked at the cards in her hand. "No matter where I go, I'll never forget where I came from."

❖

"Why the change in plans?" Kenya asked as she and Simone walked through the Art District. They were supposed to be at her condo noshing on Indian food while they watched TV, but that was before Simone called a switcheroo and asked if they could visit the Wynwood Walls instead.

"I got some news today, and I wanted to tell you about it here. I wanted to be in the place that inspires me the most with the woman who inspires me the most."

"Then I take it the news was good?"

"That depends on your perspective. When I viewed the final cut of Reagan's video with Dre this afternoon, he told me that—"

Simone stopped mid-sentence when someone called their names. Kenya turned to see Imani Gaithers, the artist she had met during the speed dating event, jogging toward them.

"I thought that was you," Imani said, slightly out of breath from the exertion. Her outsized personality was much larger than her diminutive stature. The top of her head barely reached Kenya's shoulder. She stood on her tiptoes as she gave both of them a kiss on the cheek. "It's good to see you again. What brings you out here tonight? Did you finally decide to take me up on my invitation to check out my gallery slash studio?"

"Is it close?" Kenya asked. "If so, I would love to see your work." She turned to Simone, wondering if what she wanted to say was too important to wait. "Do we have time?"

Simone didn't hesitate. "We have all the time in the world."

Kenya admired Simone's ability to take things as they came. Her schedule was so tightly regimented she had to pencil in time to be spontaneous. She loved how good it felt to be able to do whatever came to mind instead of what was due up next.

"Perfect." Imani linked her arms through theirs. "My gallery is a few blocks from here. I'll show you some works by a few of the artists in my stable as well as some of my works in progress."

Imani's energy was infectious. She bounded down the street as she walked, reminding Kenya of Tigger from Winnie the Pooh. She was wearing the same paint-splattered jeans Kenya remembered from the speed dating event, along with a loose-fitting Jean-Michel Basquiat tank top and a pair of leather tennis shoes that had once been white but were now covered in layers of graffiti rendered in oil paint and permanent ink. Her hair was as much a riot of color as her outfit, her natural hair augmented by red, white, and blue extensions.

"It looks like taking a chance on speed dating worked out well for all of us," she said. "Do you remember Barbara?"

"The legal secretary with a thing for cats?" Simone asked.

"Yes, that's her," Imani said. "We've been seeing each other for a few weeks now. She said you two would end up together. I'll have to let her know she was right."

Kenya started to tell Imani she and Simone hadn't made any official announcements and were still trying to figure things out. But Imani looked so happy Kenya didn't want to burst her bubble so she smiled and played along.

"Here we are."

Imani stopped in front of a gallery filled with contemporary art. The walls and display areas teemed with paintings, sculptures, and assorted installations. Each spoke to Kenya. She would buy the whole place out if she could afford it. Her budget was safe, thankfully, because most of the pieces were already marked Sold. A few prints were available for sale, but the majority of the original works had already been claimed.

"Are all these yours?" she asked.

She drifted toward an updated version of Botticelli's *The Birth of Venus*. Instead of an ivory-complexioned redhead posing demurely on a clam shell while angels circled her, this work featured a cinnamon-skinned '70s-style pin-up with the Afro and ankh pendant to match. The crushed velvet surface and built-in black light on the top of the piece completed the homage. The painting was provocative, sexy, and fun. Everything art should be.

"That one is," Imani said, "as well as the ones along the far wall. The rest were created by my protégés, the students I teach at a local community college when the muse abandons me and I still need to make enough money to pay the rent. I have a show scheduled in a couple of months. It will feature my works as well as a selection of the best student pieces. The event will be held the same weekend as the Art Walk. Every second Saturday, the owners of the surrounding galleries, studios, and showrooms open their doors to the public so the members of the community can see what we do without having to pay through the nose for the privilege. It's a good time. You should come. There's music, food, refreshment, and enough sensory stimulation to fuel a multitude of fantasies. Sort of like Mardi Gras without the floats and the endless supply of Sazeracs."

As she moved up the corporate ladder, Kenya had lost touch with some of the small town facets of Miami that had drawn her to the area in the first place. The Art Walk sounded like the perfect way to rediscover what she had been missing. "I'd love to come."

"Leave me your address and I'll make sure to add you to the mailing list," Imani said. She nodded toward the clerk manning the cash register. "Excuse me, but I think Colin needs my help with a customer. Feel free to look around, and let me know if you have any questions."

"We will. Thanks," Simone said.

"Do you like it?" Kenya asked when she saw Simone staring at the painting that had caught her eye.

"You know who that is, don't you?"

Kenya took a closer look but didn't recognize the model. "No. Should I?"

"Try picturing her in a sweater set and tweed skirt."

Kenya looked again. "Oh, my God," she said as recognition set in. "It's—"

"Barbara the legal secretary. I guess she isn't as uptight as I thought she was. If I'd known she looked like that underneath it all, I might have changed some of my answers to her questions."

"Is that what attracts you to someone? The physical?"

"No. Well, it's not the only thing. Our personalities have to mesh, too. I like to have things in common with someone I'm seeing. Otherwise, we wouldn't have anything to talk about or mutual interests to share. As you could tell from the brief time Barbara and I spent together, we definitely didn't have any mutual interests. What about you? Do you limit yourself to one type of woman, or do you think outside the box?"

Kenya added her name and address to the visitors' log so she could receive an invitation to Imani's upcoming show. "I don't care what a woman looks like as long as she makes me happy."

Simone wrapped her arm around Kenya's waist. "Do I make you happy?"

Kenya didn't have to take time to consider the question before she provided her answer. "Yes, you do. Now what's your big news?"

Outside, Simone leaned against a pop art mural that could have been painted by Roy Lichtenstein. "I'm being recruited."

"By?"

Simone handed her several business cards. "These guys."

Kenya looked through the cards. Each contained the logos of some of the biggest labels in the music industry. "Oh, my God. I'm so happy for you. This is what you've been working for."

"I know, but now that the opportunity has presented itself, I'm not so sure I want to take it."

"Why in the world not?"

"My life is here. My family's here. You're here. I don't want to move to New York, Detroit, or Los Angeles and leave everyone I love behind."

Kenya brandished the cards. "Have you called any of these people yet?"

"No."

"Then how do you know you'd have to relocate? If they're interested in you, it's because they like your sound. If you say you need to stay in the area in order to keep producing that sound, I'm sure they would be willing to work with you."

"And if not?"

"You'll be racking up the frequent flyer miles as you shuttle back and forth between here and whatever studio makes you the best offer."

"But what if I said no? What if I turned down the money and stayed here?"

"What do you mean?"

"I don't have to get rich to make good music. I don't have to have a mansion, a Porsche, or a wristful of bling to bring out the best in an artist. What if I stayed right here and kept on doing what I'm doing? Would that be okay with you?"

Kenya held Simone's face in her hands. "Whatever you decide to do, I will back you up one hundred percent. You don't have to be a millionaire to make me happy. You just have to be you."

Simone drew her into her arms and kissed her. Gently at first, then with a greater sense of urgency. Kenya kissed her back, matching her intensity. She had never been a fan of public displays of affection, but at the moment, she didn't care who was watching or what they might have to say. She only cared about Simone. Kissing her. Tasting her. Falling in love with her.

"What's wrong?" Simone asked after she pulled away.

"Nothing," Kenya said, taking her hand. "Let's go home."

❖

Simone's apartment was closer to the Art District than Kenya's condo so she drove there as fast as the speed limit would allow. After they climbed the stairs, she unlocked her apartment door, closed it behind her, and pressed Kenya against it. She fisted one hand in the soft cotton of Kenya's shirt and slid the other up the nape of her neck. Kenya's brown eyes went dark and her breath hitched.

Kenya pulled Simone to her. Their mouths met in a kiss that seared Simone's skin. She felt as if she had been branded, her body and soul marked Property of Kenya Davis. She let her motorcycle helmet drop to the floor and wrapped her arms around Kenya's waist, drawing her closer.

Kenya's body went boneless and she sighed in her arms. The sigh turned into a moan when Simone placed her hands on her hips and gently squeezed. Simone tasted peppermint on Kenya's tongue. Smelled the ocean on her skin. She wanted more.

"Come with me."

She took Kenya's hand and led her to the bedroom. They had been drawing closer and closer to this moment for days. Now that it had finally arrived, she was tempted to pinch herself. But if this was a dream, she didn't want to wake up anytime soon. If ever.

She put some soft music on—Nina Simone, her namesake—and turned the lights down low.

"In case you're wondering," Kenya said, "the answer to question twenty-one is yes. Wherever you go, I will be by your side."

Simone's vision blurred as tears filled her eyes. She kissed Kenya again. Kenya. The woman she loved. The woman who loved her back. "There'll be plenty of time for that later. Right now, the only place I want you is under me."

Kenya chuckled. The sound, low and sexy, aroused Simone almost as much as the look in Kenya's eyes. Simone saw so much in those coffee-colored depths. Trust. Faith. Desire. Love. Kenya not only wanted her. She believed in her, too. Together, they could achieve all their dreams.

"I love you," she whispered, nearly undone by the force of the emotions flowing through her body. "I love you, and I thought I'd lost you."

Kenya's smile held a hint of sadness. "I thought I'd lost myself years ago. You helped me find myself again."

"How did I do that?"

"One question at a time." The sadness in Kenya's smile disappeared and the light shone through. "I want you to make love to me."

Simone grinned. "I thought you'd never ask."

Kenya was still wearing her work clothes. She had ditched her jacket and heels, but the knee-length skirt and long-sleeved silk blouse remained. Simone unbuttoned the blouse and pushed it off Kenya's shoulders. Kenya's firm, round breasts were encased in a lacy black bra. Simone kissed their gentle swell as she lowered the zipper on Kenya's skirt and let it fall to the floor.

Kenya's underwear matched her bra. Both were entirely too sexy for work.

"Do all corporate bigwigs dress this way?" Simone asked as she traced a finger along the waistband of Kenya's low-slung bikini briefs.

Kenya wrapped her arms around Simone's neck. "I like to keep things interesting."

Simone dipped her head to claim another kiss. "I'm definitely interested."

"So I see."

Simone's nipples had hardened into twin points that pebbled the front of her shirt. She moaned when Kenya ran her thumbs over them.

"Still interested?" Kenya asked.

"You have no idea."

Simone swept Kenya into her arms, carried her to the bed, and gently lay her down. She kicked off her motorcycle boots and reached for her belt, but Kenya stayed her hands.

"Let me."

As Simone straddled her on the bed, Kenya unbuckled her belt. Then Kenya unzipped her jeans and helped her shimmy out of them.

Simone's shirt was next to go. With each article of clothing they shed, Simone felt like they were shedding a barrier that had kept them apart. Mackenzie. Simone's dead-end job and once-uncertain future. Soon, nothing and no one stood between them. Simone had once feared they would never reach this point. Now they were here.

Her hands trembled as she slowly explored the curves of Kenya's body. Kenya's voice did the same when she said, "I can't begin to tell you how good that feels."

"Don't tell me. Show me."

Simone slid her hand through Kenya's wetness and slipped first one, then two fingers inside her. Kenya arched her back and began to move against her. Simone was so entranced by the look of ecstasy on Kenya's face and the unequaled beauty of her body that she almost forgot to match her rhythm.

"Come here," Kenya said.

"What's the matter?"

"Nothing." Kenya reached for her. "I want you to come with me."

Simone covered Kenya's body with hers and groaned deep in her throat when Kenya slipped her leg between hers. She rode Kenya's thigh as Kenya pumped her hips against her fingers.

Kenya's hands were everywhere. Touching her. Teasing her. Taking her higher.

Then she fell. Hard and fast in a giant explosion of light. And Kenya was with her. Under her. Beside her. Inside her. Where she would always be.

Simone drew Kenya into her arms after the last spasm had finally subsided. "How did you know I was the one?"

"Easy." Kenya lay with her head on Simone's chest and a smile on her face. "You asked all the right questions."

EPILOGUE

Five Years Later

Kenya parked her BMW near what had once been one of the hottest nightclubs in South Beach. Azure was long gone now, as was Azul, its sister property across the street. Both had been sold after Mackenzie Richardson, the former owner of both businesses, held what amounted to a fire sale in order to raise cash to pay her astronomical legal bills. After the lawyers for Fernanda's husband were able to force her into paying a huge settlement, representatives for at least a dozen other aggrieved parties attempted to do the same. As a result, Azure and Azul were bought for a song, and Mackenzie's remaining businesses were reorganized in order to distance them from her tarnished reputation—and protect them from the many hands reaching into her pockets. The resort she once hoped would be her legacy never got out of the planning stage after the potential investors she had lined up chose to back someone else.

It was funny how life worked out sometimes, Kenya thought. Mackenzie had been like Teflon for years. No matter how many scandals she found herself a part of, nothing stuck to her. Now, no matter how many charitable donations she made or good works her publicist made sure the press saw her performing, she couldn't get clean.

Everyone's true colors came out in the end. And Mackenzie had certainly showed hers.

Kenya said a silent prayer, grateful she had been fortunate enough to find someone whose colors didn't run. Simone didn't change who she was in order to fit her audience. She was the same no matter what. Kenya loved that about her. Then again, she loved everything else about her, too. From her warm smile and gentle nature to her creative mind and loving heart. Simone was the one she had been looking for all her life. Her head had tried to tell her otherwise. In the end, though, her heart had won out.

She looked over her shoulder when she heard cheers and loud music coming from down the street. A souped-up bicycle was slowly making its way to the last stop on its journey. Heidi Marx was at the wheel. Behind her, twelve tourists pedaled furiously while a grinning Amanda Chun and the three remaining passengers who had scored seats that didn't require any exertion on their parts cheered them on. Kenya stopped to watch them disembark. The passengers picked up their souvenir T-shirts—available for a nominal fee—while the next group waited to take their turn.

Amanda waved to Kenya but indicated she didn't have time to talk. Kenya wasn't surprised. Pedal Power had been in business for four-and-a-half years, and its footprint in what was once a niche market was growing by the day. Amanda and Heidi had graduated from one bike to a fleet of them after positive word-of-mouth from their customers made theirs the go-to outfit for adventurous tourists and residents looking for something new. Their success necessitated the company's move from the tiny rental space it once called home to the impressive complex it had built from the rubble of what had once been Azul. The bikes were stored on the first floor, and the corporate headquarters were housed on the second. Lines for the two-hour tours snaked down the street.

Amanda's girlfriend wasn't doing half-bad either. Reagan's first full-length album had gone platinum, the second had sold twice as many units, and expectations were high for her third release.

Kenya checked her watch. Charlotte served the weekly family meal promptly at seven and she didn't want to be late since whoever showed up last was forced to assume dishwashing duty. She increased her pace as she neared the new home of Liberty City Records. Not so new now. It had been almost three years since the studio moved from its former location in one of Miami's toughest neighborhoods to its new spot in the middle of swanky South Beach.

Azure and its trademark blue doors were gone, but crowds were still lined up outside. This time, instead of waiting to get in, they were waiting to see who would come out. Some of the most recognizable artists in the music business had walked through the gauntlet in the past few years. More were scheduled to arrive. Everyone wanted to work with the hottest producer in the industry.

The security guard out front opened the door for Kenya. She nodded her thanks as she stepped inside. Walking down a hallway laden with certificates, plaques, photos, framed album covers, and the occasional Grammy, she headed to the main recording studio. The red light above the door was on, indicating a session was taking place. Trying not to disturb anyone, she slipped into the back of the room and found a seat next to a magazine reporter who was shadowing Simone for an upcoming article.

Simone sat behind a soundboard. Dre was at her side. In a padded booth, Reagan clutched her headphones while she sang her face off. Kenya loved watching them work. Dre was loud, boisterous, and full of energy. Reagan exuded controlled passion. And Simone was the embodiment of stillness. The calm at the center of the storm.

"That's the one," Simone said calmly after Reagan hit her final note.

"We did it again." Dre gyrated like a football player who had just scored the winning touchdown in the Super Bowl.

He had reason to celebrate. The deal Simone had brokered with the label she had chosen to sign with had not only made her rich but Dre, too. When the label had offered her the chance to have her own imprint, she had made Dre her business partner and taken Liberty City Records along for the ride. Even though their profile had risen significantly, Simone and Dre still continued to mentor and record local artists as well.

For Simone, it was the best of both worlds. Nothing made her happier than stumbling upon undiscovered talent. Taking a lump of coal and turning it into a diamond. Well, that wasn't entirely true. When she had presented her parents with the keys to a new house close to the ocean and far from the 'hood, she had been pretty happy that day, too. So had Kenya, though she had been crying so hard that anyone looking on probably wouldn't have been able to tell.

"Do you have everything you need?" Simone turned to face the reporter. Her face lit up when she saw Kenya had arrived.

Kenya loved that look. It was like Simone was seeing her for the first time. Falling in love with her all over again.

The reporter jotted a few notes and rose from his seat. "Yes, I do," he said, shaking hands with Simone and Dre. "Thanks for giving me a sneak preview of what's sure to be yet another hit. The article should hit the stands in a few months. I'll be in touch."

As Dre conferred with an up-and-coming rapper about one of the tracks on his demo, Reagan came out of the booth and gave Kenya a hug. Kenya hadn't seen her since she had filled in for a flu-stricken Jennifer Hudson at the Academy Awards and her performance had brought the audience to its feet. She looked tired but satisfied. Like she was exactly where she wanted to be. Kenya knew the feeling.

"Easy," Simone said, playfully pulling Reagan away from Kenya. "Save some of that for Amanda."

"You can't blame a girl for trying." Reagan draped a messenger bag over her shoulders and headed out of the studio, a burly bodyguard in tow. A few minutes later, Kenya heard the screams from Reagan's adoring fans as she exited the building and climbed into a waiting limo.

Simone wrapped her arms around Kenya's waist and laced her fingers just above the rise of her hips. "Hello, beautiful," she said, giving her a lingering kiss. "How was your day?"

"Mercifully over. You know how trying creative types can be."

"No," Simone said with a gleeful grin, "I have no idea."

Simone nuzzled the side of her neck and Kenya melted at her touch.

"I could stay here with you like this all day," Kenya said with a sigh, "but we've got to get going or we'll be late."

Simone didn't move. "Tell me something first."

"What?"

"Do you love me?"

Kenya looked deep into Simone's eyes, confident that the emotions she saw expressed in them would only deepen over time. Certain that her eyes reflected the same. "Baby, that's something you will never have to question."

About the Author

Mason Dixon lives, works, and plays somewhere in the South. She and her partner enjoy grilling, traveling, and fighting for control of the remote. *21 Questions* is her third novel. Her previous works include *Charm City* and Lambda Literary Award finalist *Date With Destiny*. As Yolanda Wallace, she has published nine novels—*In Medias Res*, *Rum Spring*, *Lucky Loser*, Lammy Award-winner *Month of Sundays*, *Murphy's Law*, *The War Within, Love's Bounty, Break Point,* and *24/7*. Mason can be reached at authormasondixon@gmail.com.

Books Available from Bold Strokes Books

18 Months by Samantha Boyette. Alissa Reeves has only had two girlfriends and they've both gone missing. Now it's up to her to find out why. (978-1-62639-804-7)

Arrested Hearts by Holly Stratimore. A reckless cop with a secret death wish and a health nut who is afraid to die might be a perfect combination for love. (978-1-62639-809-2)

Capturing Jessica by Jane Hardee. Hyperrealist sculptor Michael tries desperately to conceal the love she holds for best friend, Jess, unaware Jess's feelings for her are changing. (978-1-62639-836-8)

Counting to Zero by AJ Quinn. NSA agent Emma Thorpe and computer hacker Paxton James must learn to trust each other as they work to stop a threat clock that's rapidly counting down to zero. (978-1-62639-783-5)

Courageous Love by KC Richardson. Two women fight a devastating disease, and their own demons, while trying to fall in love. (978-1-62639-797-2)

Pathogen by Jessica L. Webb. Can Dr. Kate Morrison navigate a deadly virus and the threat of bioterrorism, as well as her new relationship with Sergeant Andy Wyles and her own troubled past? (978-1-62639-833-7)

Rainbow Gap by Lee Lynch. Jaudon Vickers and Berry Garland, polar opposites, dream and love in this tale of lesbian lives set in Central Florida against the tapestry of societal change and the Vietnam War. (978-1-62639-799-6)

Steel and Promise by Alexa Black. Lady Nivrai's cruel desires and modified body make most of the galaxy fear her, but courtesan Cailyn Derys soon discovers the real monsters are the ones without the claws. (978-1-62639-805-4)

Swelter by D. Jackson Leigh. Teal Giovanni's mistake shines an unwanted spotlight on a small Texas ranch where August Reese is secluded until she can testify against a powerful drug kingpin. (978-1-62639-795-8)

Without Justice by Carsen Taite. Cade Kelly and Emily Sinclair must battle each other in the pursuit of justice, but can they fight their undeniable attraction outside the walls of the courtroom? (978-1-62639-560-2)

21 Questions by Mason Dixon. To find love, start by asking the right questions. (978-1-62639-724-8)

A Palette for Love by Charlotte Greene. When newly minted Ph.D. Chloé Devereaux returns to New Orleans, she doesn't expect her new job, and her powerful employer—Amelia Winters—to be so appealing. (978-1-62639-758-3)

By the Dark of Her Eyes by Cameron MacElvee. When Brenna Taylor inherits a decrepit property haunted by tormented ghosts, Alejandra Santana must not only restore Brenna's house and property but also save her soul. (978-1-62639-834-4)

Cash Braddock by Ashley Bartlett. Cash Braddock just wants to hang with her cat, fall in love, and deal drugs. What's the problem with that? (978-1-62639-706-4)

Gravity by Juliann Rich. How can Ellie Engebretsen, Olympic ski jumping hopeful with her eye on the gold, soar through the air when all she feels like doing is falling hard for Kate Moreau, her greatest competitor and the girl of her dreams? (978-1-62639-483-4)

Lone Ranger by VK Powell. Reporter Emma Ferguson stirs up a thirty-year-old mystery that threatens Park Ranger Carter West's family and jeopardizes any hope for a relationship between the two women. (978-1-62639-767-5)

Love on Call by Radclyffe. Ex-Army medic Glenn Archer and recent LA transplant Mariana Mateo fight their mutual desire in the face of past losses as they work together in the Rivers Community Hospital ER. (978-1-62639-843-6)

Never Enough by Robyn Nyx. Can two women put aside their pasts to find love before it's too late? (978-1-62639-629-6)

Two Souls by Kathleen Knowles. Can love blossom in the wake of tragedy? (978-1-62639-641-8)

Camp Rewind by Meghan O'Brien. A summer camp for grown-ups becomes the site of an unlikely romance between a shy, introverted divorcee and one of the Internet's most infamous cultural critics—who attends undercover. (978-1-62639-793-4)

Cross Purposes by Gina L. Dartt. In pursuit of a lost Acadian treasure, three women must not only work out the clues, but also the complicated tangle of emotion and attraction developing between them. (978-1-62639-713-2)

Imperfect Truth by C.A. Popovich. Can an imperfect truth stand in the way of love? (978-1-62639-787-3)

Life in Death by M. Ullrich. Sometimes the devastating end is your only chance for a new beginning. (978-1-62639-773-6)

Love on Liberty by MJ Williamz. Hearts collide when politics clash. (978-1-62639-639-5)

Serious Potential by Maggie Cummings. Pro golfer Tracy Allen plans to forget her ex during a visit to Bay West, a lesbian condo community in NYC, but when she meets Dr. Jennifer Betsy, she gets more than she bargained for. (978-1-62639-633-3)

Taste by Kris Bryant. Accomplished chef Taryn has walked away from her promising career in the city's top restaurant to devote her life to her five-year-old daughter and is content until Ki Blake comes along. (978-1-62639-718-7)

The Second Wave by Jean Copeland. Can star-crossed lovers have a second chance after decades apart, or does the love of a lifetime only happen once? (978-1-62639-830-6)

Valley of Fire by Missouri Vaun. Taken captive in a desert outpost after their small aircraft is hijacked, Ava and her captivating passenger discover things about each other and themselves that will change them both forever. (978-1-62639-496-4)

Basic Training of the Heart by Jaycie Morrison. In 1944, socialite Elizabeth Carlton joins the Women's Army Corps to escape family expectations and love's disappointments. Can Sergeant Gale Rains get her through Basic Training with their hearts intact? (978-1-62639-818-4)

Before by KE Payne. When Tally falls in love with her band's new recruit, she has a tough decision to make. What does she want more—Alex or the band? (978-1-62639-677-7)

Believing in Blue by Maggie Morton. Growing up gay in a small town has been hard, but it can't compare to the next challenge Wren—with her new, sky-blue wings—faces: saving two entire worlds. (978-1-62639-691-3)

Coils by Barbara Ann Wright. A modern young woman follows her aunt into the Greek Underworld and makes a pact with Medusa to win her freedom by killing a hero of legend. (978-1-62639-598-5)

Courting the Countess by Jenny Frame. When relationship-phobic Lady Henrietta Knight starts to care about housekeeper Annie Brannigan and her daughter, can she overcome her fears and promise Annie the forever that she demands? (978-1-62639-785-9)

For Money or Love by Heather Blackmore. Jessica Spaulding must choose between ignoring the truth to keep everything she has, and doing the right thing only to lose it all—including the woman she loves. (978-1-62639-756-9)

Hooked by Jaime Maddox. With the help of sexy Detective Mac Calabrese, Dr. Jessica Benson is working hard to overcome her past, but it may not be enough to stop a murderer. (978-1-62639-689-0)

Lands End by Jackie D. Public relations superstar Amy Kline is dealing with a media nightmare, and the last thing she expects is for restaurateur Lena Michaels to change everything, but she will. (978-1-62639-739-2)

Lysistrata Cove by Dena Hankins. Jack and Eve navigate the maelstrom of their darkest desires and find love by transgressing gender, dominance, submission, and the law on the crystal blue Caribbean Sea. (978-1-62639-821-4)

Twisted Screams by Sheri Lewis Wohl. Reluctant psychic Lorna Dutton doesn't want to forgive, but if she doesn't do just that an innocent woman will die. (978-1-62639-647-0)

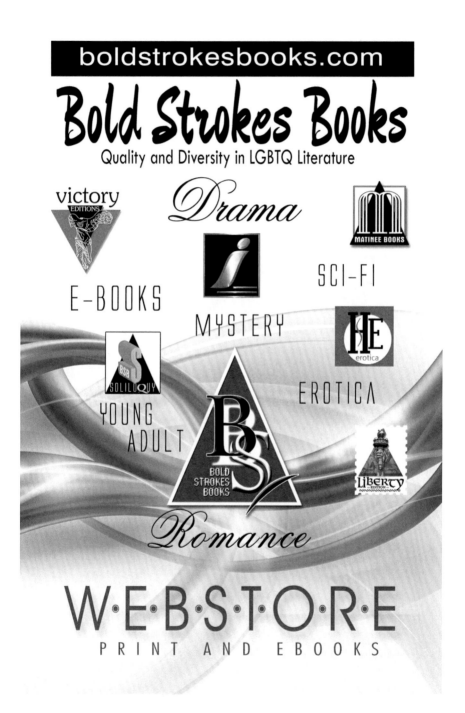